Oliver looked flabbergasted. "Why do you want a divorce now, after all these years?"

"I know, I've left it too long. I should have contacted you much sooner. I would have, if you had given any indication of wishing to marry again, but I was busy, absorbed in my own life, and it was never a priority with me."

"So why has it become a priority for you now?"

"You truly need to ask?" Lily stared at him in astonishment. This conversation was not going as planned. Oliver should be thanking her for being so thoughtful, for taking the time and trouble to come to discuss the matter in person, for having the foresight to realize what he had not.

"You are a marquess," she said. "As a marquess, you now have a title, estates and all the responsibilities that go with them."

"I don't need another lecture on my responsibilities, thank you, and what this has to do with your being here..."

"You'll need an heir, Oliver. To get an heir, you'll need a wife."

"I already have a wife. She's sitting opposite me..."

MARGUERITE KAYE

—

His Runaway
Marchioness Returns

HARLEQUIN
HISTORICAL

ISBN-13: 978-1-335-72378-9

His Runaway Marchioness Returns

Copyright © 2023 by Marguerite Kaye

Recycling programs for this product may not exist in your area.

This is a work of fiction. Names, characters, places and incidents are either the product of the author's imagination or are used fictitiously. Any resemblance to actual persons, living or dead, businesses, companies, events or locales is entirely coincidental.

For questions and comments about the quality of this book, please contact us at CustomerService@Harlequin.com.

Harlequin Enterprises ULC
22 Adelaide St. West, 41st Floor
Toronto, Ontario M5H 4E3, Canada
www.Harlequin.com

Printed in U.S.A.

Marguerite Kaye has written over fifty historical romances featuring feisty heroines and a strong sense of place and time. She is also coauthor with Sarah Ferguson, Duchess of York, of the *Sunday Times* bestseller *Her Heart for a Compass*. Their second book together will be released in 2023. Marguerite lives in Argyll on the west coast of Scotland. When not writing, she loves to read, cook, garden, drink martinis and sew, though rarely at the same time!

Books by Marguerite Kaye

Harlequin Historical

Invitation to a Cornish Christmas
"The Captain's Christmas Proposal"
A Forbidden Liaison with Miss Grant
Regency Christmas Liaisons
"A Most Scandalous Christmas"
His Runaway Marchioness Returns

Revelations of the Carstairs Sisters

The Earl Who Sees Her Beauty
Lady Armstrong's Scandalous Awakening
Under the Mistletoe
"The Lady's Yuletide Wish"

Penniless Brides of Convenience

The Earl's Countess of Convenience
A Wife Worth Investing In
The Truth Behind Their Practical Marriage
The Inconvenient Elmswood Marriage

Visit the Author Profile page
at Harlequin.com for more titles.

Chapter One

Kent, England—November 1876

Lily was about to meet her husband. Hardly a note-worthy event, one would think, were it not for the fact she had not clapped eyes on him since the day she left for France, eight years ago. There had been no contact between them since, but she had spent a great deal of time in the last few weeks imagining how the encounter might play out. Would he have changed? *How* would he have changed? Would he think *her* changed? Not that any of it mattered. They had never really known each other in the first place. Once the knot had been tied they had stuck rigidly to the terms they had agreed upon: a secret ceremony, separate lives. Now it was high time to draw a line under their faux attachment.

Attachment! There had never been any bond between them, unless you counted her poor brother. Anthony had devoted the last days of his life to bringing them together. The marriage he had brokered had served its purpose and soon their relationship, such as it had

been, would be erased from history. This encounter—
re-encounter—would be awkward, but what she hoped
they would both feel would be a sense of relief. She
could never pay the debt of gratitude she owed him,
but at least she could give him the freedom to embrace
the new life which he had lately inherited. And for her
own sake, too, it was time to remedy this most irregular state of affairs.

As the carriage which she had hired in Folkestone
completed the short ascent to the house in Sandgate and
drew to a halt, butterflies fluttered wildly in her stomach. She had no reason to be nervous, she reminded herself sternly. She and her once-husband were nothing to
each other, save former benefactor and dependent. The
fact that he had agreed so promptly when she proposed
this meeting was a clear indication of his own feelings.
It was time to wipe the slate clean, to sever the legal
ties which bound them.

Yet the butterflies grew more insistent as she descended from the carriage and paid the driver. It was
the house evoking those feelings, she decided, not the
man waiting inside. *Abbey Hill.* This had been her home
for three years. She had always loved it, the plain fa-
çade facing on to the road giving no hint of the wonderful unrestricted views at the back, where the garden
tumbled steeply down to the pebble beach and the English Channel. On a clear day, it was possible to see
the French coast.

She had whiled away countless hours watching the
ever-changing vistas when she first lived here: grey skies
meeting stormy seas, pale blue skies segueing into calm
turquoise sea, scudding white clouds and dancing white

horses. When the front windows were open the waves could be heard slapping the pebbles on the shore, a soft murmuring on calm days, a boom and rattle, a crash when it was stormy. In the latter days of their so-called marriage, perched on the window seat in the drawing room, watching the Folkestone ferry plying backwards and forward, she had hatched her escape plan.

It had been winter when she left, never thinking to return. Today, at the end of autumn, the sky was a perfect summer blue. The sea, hidden from view, could still be heard, the wavelets gently stirring the pebbles with a soft shushing sound. The breeze was soft, the sun low in the sky, with only a hint of warmth. Her fingers trembled as she reached for the brass handle on the gate. Watching the carriage drive off, she strove for calm. She was no longer that young, naive woman dependent on a man who had essentially remained a stranger, for the roof over her head, the food on her plate. She had successfully reinvented herself, on her own and on her own terms. Something to be proud of.

The trembling abated. The butterflies ceased their fluttering. Lily tucked a stray wisp of hair back into place and opened the gate. It was time to draw a line firmly under the past.

Oliver put down the invoice with a sigh. He was sitting in the shade on the veranda at the back of the house. He had been trying to work, but his eyes kept wandering from his ledgers and business letters to the sparkling sea, the clear and unexpected blue of the sky, the tantalising glimpses to be had of France when the haze lifted, as it did intermittently. He couldn't concentrate on anything with this confrontation looming. He was dreading it.

Lilian was travelling from Paris, she had informed him. Was that her home now? Their agreement did not permit him to know anything about her life after they parted, not even the name she had assumed, though Iain Sinclair, his man of business, knew how to contact her in an emergency. It had never been necessary. Twice a year, as per their agreement, she wrote to Iain, informing him that she 'remained well' or was 'in good spirits', and Iain paid her allowance and passed on the bland message.

Lilian had been a very young twenty when they married, with little to say for herself. Shy, retiring, biddable, pleasant enough, as far as Oliver could recall, but without any means of supporting herself and therefore easily put upon, which of course was what her brother Anthony had feared. She had needed protecting and Oliver had been duty-bound to promise to do that. He'd kept his word, giving her a place to call her own, saving her from the only alternative fate on offer—marriage to a distant relative, a parson with two motherless children and an expectation that she would add to his brood. Lilian did not need a ready-made family, she needed time to learn how to look after herself, and that was what Oliver had happily given her. He was already wed to his business and had neither the interest nor the time to share his life with anyone else. In that, he remained entirely unchanged.

Those three years of marriage seemed unreal to him now. This house had been closed up when she left. He had almost forgotten that he owned it, until he received her letter. He hadn't recognised her handwriting. It had come as a shock to see her signature. Lilian, she had signed it. No surname. The contents had been even more of a shock. 'It is long past time,' she had written, 'for them to formalise the termination of their arrangement'. Why now? A second marriage, this time to a man of her choice, was the obvious reason. Her request shouldn't have been unexpected. What was more surprising, when he thought about it, was that she hadn't raised the matter before now. He was thirty-four, which made Lilian thirty-one, an age where a woman would be aware that her child-bearing years would soon be behind her. One more reason for him to feel guilty about what he was going to have to do.

On the subject of their divorce the process was clear enough. As far as the law was concerned, his wife had deserted him eight years ago, when she left the marital home. If only the law was equally clear on the subject of his problematic inheritance, he would happily do all in his power to grant Lilian her wish as quickly as possible. Heaven knew, she had asked for little enough when they were married, and nothing at all since she left, but the timing of this request could not have been worse and he was going to have to tell her so. He wished to hell that he didn't have to. If only there was some way to get both cases through the courts at the same time! He really didn't want to have to ask her to postpone her wedding, but he simply couldn't see any other solution.

The sound of a carriage drawing up made him leap to his feet and head indoors, his heart pounding. He had never been one to postpone an unpleasant task. Time to get it over with. Halfway up the stairs, he stopped on the landing where a window gave him a view of the road and the front gate.

A woman was descending from the carriage. She was elegantly dressed in a mint-green silk gown with a darker green ruffle trim and a huge bow over her bustle in the latest fashion. A little hat perched on top of her dark brown hair, a frivolous construction of lace and ribbon that was so impractical it must have cost a fortune. Paris, her toilette screamed, even to his untutored eyes.

Was this really Lilian? She looked far too chic. He didn't recall her hair being so lustrous. But, yes, the slim figure, the graceful carriage were the same. And the eyes—he had forgotten those big hazel eyes that had given her a doe-like appearance all those years ago, but which now looked—what was the word? Sultry—yes, that was it, sultry.

Oliver's image of an older, more faded version of the woman he had married could not have been further from the reality confronting him. The woman holding on to the gate, gazing up at the sky, did not look the *comfortable* sort who had been living quietly in the country, as he'd imagined her. She didn't even look English. She looked exotic, fashionable, extremely self-possessed and, even more disconcertingly, desirable. He cursed under his breath at his own contrariness. Now was not the time to become attracted to the woman who was here to discuss their divorce.

She turned suddenly and he drew hurriedly back from the window. As he ran up the remaining flight of stairs to the drawing room, the doorbell clanged. Oliver sat down, picked up the morning paper to effect nonchalance, set it down again, then jumped, foolishly, in response to the light tap on the door.

'Your visitor, my lord,' the agency servant intoned, stepping aside.

Coming face to face with Oliver was a shock that rendered Lily momentarily speechless. His coal-black hair was no longer cropped short, but worn almost shoulder length, the jaw, which had before been ruthlessly clean-shaven, now sporting a short, neat beard. The dark brown eyes were the same, but there was a fan of lines at the corners, a deep furrow between his brows. The man she had married all those years ago had been classically good-looking, but this incarnation had a much more rugged appeal—and a great deal of it! Under any other circumstances, she'd have been delighted to pursue his acquaintance. Under these circumstances—to say it was unsettling was to put it mildly.

'Oliver.' Lily pulled herself together and gave him her best professional smile. 'How do you do?'

'Hello, Lilian. No need to ask you how you are, you look extremely well.' He took the hand she extended. 'And very different.'

In what way? He was looking at her as if he didn't recognise her, which was hardly surprising for she doubted if he could ever have picked her out from a crowd. Despite the barrier of her glove, his touch was distracting. Lily slipped her hand free. 'I am certainly older and considerably wiser,' she replied brusquely. 'Shall we sit down? We have a great deal to discuss.'

A wistful glance at the window seat informed her that it was bereft of the mound of plump cushions she used to keep there. The room was spotlessly clean and smelled of beeswax, but there were no signs of it having been inhabited: no books or flowers, no letters or papers save today's newspaper, and the furniture was too neatly arranged. She perched on the sofa facing the hearth, where a fire had just been lit, angling herself to sit sideways. The current fashion for bustles, swags and bows showed to much better advantage when one was standing up and required a deal of practice so that sitting down did not crumple and crush one's attire beyond repair.

Oliver took the chair at right angles to her. His taste in clothes had always been muted. Today he wore a plain black suit with a dark blue waistcoat which seemed, to her eyes, more appropriate for winter in the city than a sunny autumn day on the coast. 'I brought an agency in to make the main rooms habitable for a few days,' he said. 'I wasn't sure how long you intended to stay in England.'

'Only as long as it takes to resolve matters,' Lily replied. 'I am anxious to return to Paris as soon as possible. I have taken rooms at the Pavilion Hotel in Folkestone meantime. I must admit, I was surprised when you suggested meeting here. You were never very keen on the seaside.'

'While you had always longed to live by the sea.'

'Did I tell you that?'

'It stuck in my mind, because it was one of the few opinions I managed to extract from you,' Oliver answered. 'It's why I bought this house for you.'

'You *bought* it for me? But I thought—no, I am positive that you told me you already owned it. I'd never have allowed you to purchase a house just to humour me.'

'I know, which is why I omitted to mention it.'

'If I had known—'

'You'd have been mortified,' Oliver interrupted. 'Which is why I made sure you never knew, until now.'

'Then I should very belatedly thank you for being so generous and considerate,' Lily said stiffly.

'I never sought your gratitude. I made a promise to my best friend to look after you.'

'One made under enormous duress.' Lily's toes curled inside her shoes. 'Anthony put you in a dreadful position. When I think back on it, I cringe to think of how unfair it was of him.'

'He was dying, desperate to do what he could to look after you, and I owed him my life.'

'I know the story only too well. You were playing on a frozen pond as boys and the ice cracked and you went under. Anthony jumped in and dragged you to the surface.'

'With no thought for his own safety. If it wasn't for your brother, I would have drowned in the freezing water and, what's more, if he hadn't taken a soaking that day on my behalf, there's a chance he might still be here today. I know,' Oliver said, when she made to interrupt, 'he died of consumption, but *you* know there's a chance that if he hadn't damaged his lungs saving me, he may not have developed consumption in later life.'

'I know that's what made you feel so guilty when he was dying, but I have always felt it was wrong of Anthony to use the sense of gratitude you undoubtedly felt to foist me on to you.'

'What else could he do? You were his only close relative, entirely dependent on him financially, and you
nursed him through his illness. It was perfectly natural
that he should try to look after you as best he could, and
rightly so, in my humble opinion, else you would have
been left quite destitute. Are you telling me that you'd
have preferred the alternative option of marriage to the
widower parson waiting in the wings?'

Even after all these years, the prospect could still
make Lily shudder. 'No, what I would have preferred
would have been that my parents had the foresight to
allow Anthony latitude to bequeath the income from
his trust fund to me. Then I wouldn't have been beholden to anyone and you would not have been forced
to marry me.'

'Anthony didn't force me. The circumstances were
extreme, but the decision we made was still the right
one, wasn't it?' Oliver frowned. 'Do you regret it?'

'I am extremely grateful to you, I owe you a great
deal, but I do regret the fact that it was necessary for
you to rescue me. Unfortunately, I was not at the time
able to rescue myself.'

'We came to an accommodation that worked for both
of us, didn't we?' His frown deepened. 'I never intruded
on your time any more than necessary and you made
no calls on mine. You were happy here, weren't you?'

Happy! Lily looked around her, seeing the pathetic
little ghost of her younger self inhabiting this place,
and quickly banished it. Today was about the future,
not the past. 'You gave me the breathing space to find
out what I wanted to do with my life and I will always
be grateful for that.'

'That's no answer.'

'For heaven's sake! If you must know, I was sick with grief at first, because even though Anthony endured a long, painful death, I still wasn't prepared for it when it came. I was grateful to you, I was *so* grateful that you had spared my brother the burden of worrying about me, and I was grateful that you had spared me the necessity of accepting my cousin's proposal, but that didn't make me happy to accept yours. You were Anthony's best friend, but to me you weren't much more than a stranger and I was beholden to you for the roof over my head.

'Was I happy here? No, of course I wasn't, Oliver. The truth is I resented having to rely on your charity. I didn't want to be your wife but, as you pointed out, I had no choice. I had no idea what I actually wanted to do save the one thing that I had always wanted to do. And I had always assumed that would be impossible.'

Lily stopped and drew a shocked breath. 'I do beg your pardon. We have never quarrelled, let us not start now. I didn't come here to rake over the past. You gave up a great deal for me, not least your single status, and I am very grateful. I can never repay you for what you did for me, but I will do whatever needs to be done now to set you free.'

'Set *me* free?'

'Divorce, Oliver. On the grounds of desertion, which is what we always intended, unless there is a better solution?'

'No, the advice I have is that desertion remains the most appropriate grounds.'

'So you've already consulted a lawyer?'

'As soon as I received your letter. Discreetly, I hasten to add. I was thinking, just before you arrived, that it was actually surprising that it had taken you so long.'

'Your cousin only died six months ago and Mr Sinclair only informed me of that fact about five weeks ago.'

'What has Archie's death to do with your wanting a divorce?'

'What has—why, everything!' Lily was beginning to feel as if they were having two separate conversations. 'Now you are the Marquess of Rashfield...'

'Please! I really don't need reminding and I fail to see why my inheriting the blasted title has anything to do with your being here. I don't need to be set free. I have no wish to marry again, if that's what you're thinking.'

'Not while you are in mourning, perhaps, but...'

'Not ever! Forget about me, Lilian. I take it congratulations are in order?'

'Congratulations?' At last, she realised why they had been talking at such cross purposes. 'Good grief! No, no, no, you have that quite wrong. I'm not in the least bit interested in getting married again.'

'Then why are you here?' Oliver looked equally flabbergasted. 'I mean, why do you want a divorce now, after all these years?'

'I know, I've left it too long. I should have contacted you much sooner. I would have, if you had given any indication of wishing to marry again, but I was busy, absorbed in my own life, and it was never a priority with me.'

'I could say exactly the same thing for myself. Why, then, has it become a priority for you now?'

'You truly need to ask?' Lily stared at him in astonishment. This conversation was not going as planned. By now Oliver should be thanking her for being so thoughtful, for taking the time and trouble to come to discuss the matter in person, for having the foresight to realise what he had not. Clearly, he needed some instruction in the matter.

'You are a marquess,' she said. 'As a marquess you now have a title, estates and all the responsibilities that go with them.'

'I don't need another lecture on my responsibilities, thank you, and what this has to do with your being here…?'

'You'll need an heir, Oliver.'

'I have an heir in the making, my deputy Alan Masterton.'

'I'm not talking about someone to take over the business of your factories, I'm mean a son to inherit your estate.'

'I don't want a son, or a daughter for that matter. I have always loathed the notion of breeding a dynasty, of bringing someone into the world to hand them something they probably have no interest in.'

Was he being deliberately obtuse? Lily tried again. 'As a marquess you'll need an heir. To get an heir, you'll need a wife.'

'I already have a wife. She's sitting opposite me and talking gibberish.'

'Oh, for goodness sake! I am not talking about myself. I mean a wife appropriate to your new station in life. A woman with the correct lineage and education, who knows how to run a stately home and wear a coronet and make conversation with other titled ladies and do whatever else it is marchionesses do. A woman who is suitable to be the mother of your son and heir. A *real* wife, Oliver.'

'I don't want a *real* wife. I never have, which is one of the reasons why I was happy to marry you. I have no time for a wife, never mind a family, and what's more, even if I had the time, I'm not the type who is inclined to share his life with either. I like being my own man. I like making my own decisions.'

'That is something we are in a like mind about, at any rate,' Lily couldn't help say.

'Is it? Then you'll understand what I mean when I say that marriage—I mean a *real* marriage—would be bound to be a compromise,' Oliver said. 'A wife and a family would expect—rightly—to take first call on my time. I'm still growing my business. I cannot imagine a time when I am not devoted to my business.' He jumped up and strode over to the window. 'I have barely slept since I got your letter. I've been dreading your coming here, dreading having to ask you to postpone your wedding on my account, and now you tell me that it's actually my wedding you're planning.'

'I have no interest in getting married and having a family. I cannot think of anything worse.'

'Well, how was I to know that! I thought *you* wanted to settle down and have children. It's what most women want, isn't it?'

'*I*,' Lily snapped, outraged, 'am not most women.'

Her tone made his jaw drop. 'Clearly not.' Oliver dropped on to the window seat and folded his arms. 'What a turn up! You come here thinking you're doing me a favour and it's the last thing I want right now. Are you *sure* you don't want to get married again?'

She drew him a withering look. 'I think I've made my views on that subject crystal clear. I know my own mind, but I'm beginning to wonder if you are in full command of yours.'

'Ha! Understandably, but I assure you I am.' She waited for him to elaborate, but instead he leaned his head back against the window and closed his eyes, giving a huge sigh.

Lily took a breath and clasped her hands tightly together. 'You misunderstood my situation, but you must see that your own situation makes our divorce imperative. Oliver! At least have the decency to listen to me.'

He snapped to attention, looking immediately contrite as he crossed the room to re-join her. 'I'm sorry, I'm simply so relieved not to have to ask you to postpone your wedding. To initiate a divorce at this point in time would be a nightmare for me. Frankly, the timing could not be worse.'

'Why?'

Oliver reached for her hand, but she snatched it away. 'I'm so sorry,' he said again, looking quite crushed. 'I'm not thinking straight. My head—but that's no excuse. I didn't mean to upset you.'

'I'm not upset. I'm confused. If you will explain…'

'I'll try.' He pushed his hair back from his brow and rubbed his eyes with his knuckles. 'In a nutshell. the world thinks I'm not married. More importantly, the trustees of Archie's estates think I'm not married and, while I remain unmarried, they keep control of the estates. For the last six months, I've been trying to overturn the terms of my cousin's will, in order to get control of the estates, but the wheels of the law turn slowly— agonisingly slowly. At the moment I have no idea when the courts will reach a decision. But they will reach a decision eventually and while I'm waiting—well, you can imagine, Lilian, or maybe you can't, but I can— just what an uproar a divorce case would cause if it was initiated now.'

'*Sacré bleu.*'

'You can say that again.'

What would the press make of such a scandal? Lily wondered. A peer of the realm divorcing a woman he had secretly married almost twelve years ago would be bad enough, but if they discovered who the Marquess's wife had become! The English were even quicker to judge than the French. It simply didn't bear thinking of. '*Sacré bleu,*' Lily repeated obligingly, this time with fervour.

Oliver attempted to smile. 'Under any other circumstances, I would have been delighted to renew our acquaintance, but at present...'

'I am as welcome as a spectre at the feast.'

'Oh, no, that is putting it far too strongly. I am very glad we have managed to clear the air. If you can bear to wait another six months, a year at most—'

'But, Oliver,' Lily interrupted impatiently, 'if it is so important that you are married, why did you not tell them that you are married? I am your wife, as far as the law is concerned.'

'I know. It's ironic, isn't it?' He gave her a twisted smile. 'If only I'd produced you earlier. But in the first place I didn't think of myself as married, any more than you did. And secondly, I didn't want to embroil you in a situation not of your making. It's too late now, in any event. There's nothing you can do to help, if that's what you were thinking.'

Lily did not take kindly to being told she was useless. Here was surely an opportunity for her to pay Oliver back properly for all he had done for her. 'There must be something,' she said firmly. 'I'm here now, I would rather not have wasted my journey. If you will explain the situation properly, then I shall put my mind to the problem.'

'I've been putting my mind and the minds of several legal experts to the problem for six months and made very little progress.'

'All men, *sans doubt*. What you need is a different perspective. I can provide you with that. If we can't come up with a solution between us, then I will return to France and grant you your stay of execution, so to speak.' She raised a brow and gave him one of her challenging looks. 'You have nothing to lose and an awful lot to gain.'

Chapter Two

You have nothing to lose and an awful lot to gain.

Oliver watched as Lilian set out the tea things on the table on the veranda, wondering if this really was the same woman he had married. It wasn't so much the way she looked, but the way she moved, the way she spoke, the air of confidence she had, of someone accustomed to being listened to. What it all amounted to was a very attractive someone he would like to get to know better if only the circumstances were different. Who was she?

His wife, that's who she was. He was married to this woman. It seemed impossible. For the first time in months, his interest was piqued by something other than the nightmare that Archie's untimely death had hurtled him into. Happy to be distracted, he let his mind wander. Obviously, Lilian had not been living in a cottage in the countryside with cats for company, as he'd imagined. Where did she call home? Paris, he presumed, but wasn't Paris, like any capital city, an expensive place to live? And those clothes she was wearing looked to his untutored eyes to be what they called *haute couture*.

He had no idea what such a toilette would cost, but he was willing to wager it would take up a significant portion of the meagre allowance he'd had to force her to accept from him.

Which begged the question of how—or where—or from whom she got the money? Work for respectable, middle-class women did not pay well, *that* he knew, and it was horribly limited, too. Could Lilian be a school mistress or governess? The notion was laughable. Why would a governess own such an expensive and elaborate gown? And how did that explain her palpable air of confidence? Lilian spoke to him as an equal. *I am not most women*, she had declared. He couldn't help smiling, recalling her expression, and he couldn't help thinking, looking at her again, that she had spoken the truth. This woman, whoever she was, was not in the common way.

There was one way such a woman could make a considerable living. Shocked, his inclination was to immediately dismiss it as unthinkable. Or was it? He considered it, studying her. The allowance he gave her would not keep her in the style she was evidently accustomed to, but it would not have forced her to earn a living in such a way. Unless she chose to?

He knew nothing of courtesans, but he did know they were lauded and respected in Paris in a way they were not in London. Women who were fêted for their conversation as well as the charm of their company. In bed. His mouth went dry at the thought. Lilian was not a beauty, but she was charismatic—yes, that was the word. Subtly sensual, intelligent and at the same time— remote? No, that wasn't it. Reserved? Better. There were layers to her. Layers that would be extremely rewarding to unwrap. Slowly.

'Milk or lemon?'

Mortified, Oliver stared at her for a moment, uncomprehending until she held up the milk jug. 'Yes, milk, please,' he said, though he rarely drank tea.

She had style, but she wore no jewellery. It wasn't that which made him so sure she was not a courtesan, though, it was her self-possession, her horror of being beholden, her vehement reaction to the reasons for their marriage earlier, which had taken him aback. Even a courtesan of the highest order was reliant on a benefactor. He didn't know Lilian well, but he reckoned she'd wear rags rather than a toilette she hadn't paid for herself. Where, then, did her income derive from?

'So?' Lilian had poured her own tea—with lemon, he noted—and was now giving him one of those *you have all my attention, speak your mind* expressions.

If you want the answer to a question, someone in business had told Oliver a long time ago, follow the money. 'The allowance that Sinclair pays you every six months,' he said.

'What about it?'

Was there an edge to her tone? He wished he knew her better. 'You know I wanted to give you more in the first place.'

She frowned down at her teacup, turning it around on her saucer. 'It was more than sufficient for my needs at the time.'

At the time! 'But it hasn't been increased in eight years. It should have occurred to me...'

'Oliver, I fail to see what this has to do with resolving the tangle you have got yourself into.'

'The tangle, as you call it, is not of my making!' he exclaimed, immediately forgetting all about Lilian's possible sources of income. 'If only Archie had had the sense to put on a pair of shoes, none of this would have happened.'

'He was riding barefoot?'

'He developed blood poisoning from standing on a rusty nail.'

'I thought he fell from his horse.'

'That's the story they put about because it sounds a bit more dignified, but the truth is he was roaring drunk, staggering about the stable yard in his night-gown for reasons known only to himself—do you know, I don't really care why—but that's when he stood on the nail.'

'And died, for want of a pair of slippers. Oh, Oliver!' Lilian struggled to smother her laughter. 'I'm sorry, I'm so very sorry, I'm not mocking your loss. Poor Archie, but the situation is too absurd for words.'

'Unbelievable, isn't it? Archie was my only relative, we were never close—in fact, we were poles part, is the truth—but all the same, I heartily wish he was still here.' Oliver took a sip of tea, his mood darkening. 'I know you wish to help, that you don't want this to have been a wasted journey, but I'm afraid it has been. Basically, I can't get control of Archie's estate unless I'm married.'

'But you are married. To me. Why don't you explain the situation properly? Despite what you think, sometimes two heads really can be better than one, you know.'

And besides, he had nothing to lose. She didn't say it again, but she was right and a little more time in her rather charming and intriguing company was ample compensation. Oliver pushed his half-finished tea to one side.

'It goes back to Archie's grandfather—who was also my grandfather, obviously. He firmly believed that young men were innately irresponsible, unfit to take charge of a large estate unless they were sensibly settled and married. So he nominated a group of his friends who would be responsible for the management of the lands, houses, investments, everything, for as long as his heir remained a bachelor. The clause was carried forward from his will into Archie's father's will, and then into Archie's. It has never been invoked, because both Archie and his father were already married when they inherited.'

'But when you inherited, it was assumed that you were not married,' Lilian said, 'and so the clause was invoked?'

'I thought it was nonsense at first, archaic rubbish that wouldn't hold water in a court of law. But after six months of legal wrangling, I'm no nearer to establishing whether it has any legal status. And in the meantime, the trustees, who are completely unfit, in my humble opinion—'

'Unfit!' Lilian interrupted. 'If they were nominated by your grandfather, I'm surprised any of them are still alive.'

'Of the six he named, there's only one left, but my

far-sighted grandparent allowed their heirs to inherit the responsibility.'

'Even if they themselves weren't married?'

'Ha! That's one of the many ironies of the situation.'

'And another, I presume, is that you *are* married, though as to it making you more responsible— goodness, what nonsense that idea is. Marriage does not alter a person's nature.'

'As witness my cousin. He and his wife, Vanessa, had lived separate lives for years. She was on an extended visit to her sister's when Archie died and she's remained there ever since. I'm beginning to wonder if Archie only married her because he knew about the clause in his father's will.'

'I assume you thought it could be easily broken? At first, when your cousin died, I mean, and that is why you said nothing about being in possession of the required wife? Or at least the proof that she existed.'

'Precisely. You see now that it would look very odd if I suddenly recalled that I had a wife, hidden behind the cushions of the sofa, so to speak, six months later?'

'You think they'd be suspicious and question the truth of it?'

'They'd be bound to and then I'd have to explain the circumstances,' Oliver said. 'Why would I carry on with a long and complicated and very expensive court case, when I already have the requisite wife and have had one for almost twelve years? You and I married for very good reasons, but explaining them to someone else—' He broke off, wincing.

'Yes, it would be embarrassing, to say the least.'

'Then there's my position as one of society's most

eligible bachelors to be considered,' he added, curling his lip. 'For that is what I have become, heaven help me, thanks to that blasted title.'

'*Mon Dieu*, society's most eligible bachelor is not a bachelor at all!' Lilian shuddered. 'What a story that would make in the press, especially if you refused to tell them why you kept me a secret. They would make up the most scurrilous lies.'

'Well, I doubt they'd go that far.'

'Oh, but they would go further, I assure you. The story would run for months. Poor Mr Sinclair would be hounded, for his name is on the certificate as our witness beside my brother's.'

'Sinclair would never talk to the press. Honestly, Lilian, I think you're letting your imagination run away with you. Besides, the only people entitled to see our marriage certificate would be my trustees.'

'Who you can be absolutely certain would not talk to a reporter?'

'Why would they? Even if they did, which I cannot believe they would, it is your real name on that certificate. There is no reason for Lilian Grantham to be linked with whatever name you have assumed for whatever business you go about on the Continent.'

He was fishing and, from the way she raised her eyebrow at him and shrugged, Lilian knew it. 'The scandal could have a very detrimental effect on *your* business,' she retorted.

'You think I haven't played that nightmare scenario out in my head, time after time? A man who has kept his wife secret for almost twelve years! Even my most loyal customers would question whether or not they could trust me again, which is why I cannot suddenly produce you in order to get at Archie's inheritance.'

Oliver groaned, giving way to despair. 'My life has been turned upside down. It's bad enough to be landed with the responsibility of a failing estate and all that goes with it—lands that are so behind the times, you would not believe! But to be unable to put any of it to rights is driving me mad. The trustees won't act, their policy is just to let things totter along without interfering, as Archie did. And every month that passes, Archie's tenants—*my* tenants, heaven help me—are falling further into poverty.

'Land is not worth what it was, unless it's modernised, which has put several of them in arrears with their rents, and I can't prevent the trustees from pursuing them for money they don't have. Every day, I uncover new disasters, new obligations and duties, and I can't do a thing about any of them. I may not know about farming, but I know about modernisation and turning a profit, I understand business. It's infuriating!

'To add insult to injury, now that I'm the Marquess of Rashfield, I have become a public figure. My name is bandied about in the press. I get invitations to join clubs I've never heard of, to dine with people I have never met and never wish to. I'm besieged by tailors wanting to make me coats I don't need and dealers offering me prime horseflesh I'm assured I can't live without. I know I'm in a very privileged position, that's not lost on me, but I wish to *hell* my cousin had not died.'

Oliver swore under his breath, dropping his head on to his hands. 'I'm sorry.'

Lilian reached across the table to touch his arm. 'Do

not apologise. You have—the situation—it's abominable. Would you like me to get you a brandy?'

'No.' He lifted his head, forcing a smile. 'Thank you. I'm truly sorry, this has nothing to do with you.'

'On the contrary. It has everything to do with me. I am your wife.'

'Can't you see that fact only complicates matters? If your existence was discovered…'

Lilian pursed her lips. 'Yes, yes, I do see.'

'The best thing you can do is go back to Paris and get on with your life. I assume you do have some sort of occupation? I mean, you have money—an income— the allowance I pay you…'

'Oh, for goodness sake! As you have pointed out to me at length, you have much more important matters to concern yourself with. I haven't touched the allowance in years, if you must know! It's been sitting in my bank accumulating interest. I have tried to refuse it, but it only sends Mr Sinclair into a flap, so it's easier to take it and pay it into my bank. I now have quite a substantial amount to return to you.'

'I don't want it back!'

'Then give it to a good cause, because I don't want it either.'

He glowered at her, realising there was no point in asking her again why she didn't need it. 'You really don't like to be beholden, do you?'

'No, I do not.' Lilian looked as if she would glower back, then she shook her head, making a visible effort to control her own temper. 'I am trying to help you, but you are making it very difficult.'

'You're wasting your time. The situation is hopeless,

there's nothing to be done. I can live in Archie's houses. I can spend his money—not that I do—but I can't spend my own on putting things right. Effectively, I'm powerless to do anything else except wait for the wheels of the law to grind to a decision.'

'And if it does not find in your favour?'

'I don't even want to think about that.'

'But you must.' Lilian reached across to touch his arm again. '*We* must. Let us both take a moment to regain our equilibrium and turn our minds afresh to the problem.'

Lily pushed back her chair, turning her back on Oliver in order to prevent him telling her once again that she was wasting her time, and wandered over to the edge of the path. Her gaze roamed over the garden, which sloped steeply down, a tumble of rocks and overgrown shrubs all but obscuring the narrow path that led to the gate giving access to the beach.

Hopeless, Oliver said. That in itself was a challenge. She would like to prove him wrong, but more than anything, she would like to find a solution. He was clearly at the end of his tether, and understandably so. A self-made man, with his own business to run and his cousin's business—for that was what it amounted to—in dire need of his expertise! It must be infuriating, to feel so impotent, and to be distracted from his own business at the same time. Infuriating was far too understated a word.

Oh, but how wonderful it would be, if she could come up with a solution and in doing so wipe away the burden of debt she had carried with her for so long. Yet Oliver had had six months and he had come up with nothing, save to try to have the clause proved invalid and, if he could not, then he would be able to do nothing but watch his inheritance fall further and further into disrepair. No wonder that he didn't wish to consider that possibility.

Two minds are better than one, she'd said, but was it true? She turned back to face him. 'Have you made any progress at all with your legal case?'

'Nothing significant,' he said wearily. 'Lawyers love to discuss arcane laws and obscure contracts, but they're less keen to make decisions. One of the biggest obstacles is Sir Everard Hale, the only survivor of the original band of merry men appointed as trustee, and the halest, heartiest ninety-year-old you'll ever meet. If he would step down or take my part it would help immensely, but he has it in his head that he's upholding my grandfather's dying wish, so he won't be budged. Which, incidentally, is a load of boll—balderdash—because my grandfather drowned and his last wish would surely have been to be saved.'

'Or that he had learned to swim.'

Her quip raised a snort of laughter, but it was quickly followed by a groan. 'It's not funny,' Oliver said, coming to join her. 'It's a shame I can't produce you as my wife. Look at you, elegant, chic, a woman with that *je ne sais quoi*! No one would question my reasons for marrying you.'

Look at you, she thought, doing just that for a few indulgent seconds. *Mon Dieu*, talk about *je ne sais quoi*! The astonishing thing was that Oliver seemed to have no idea how attractive he was. Which of course was part of his attraction. That, and the fact that no matter how attractive she found him, he was never going to be her lover, Lily reminded herself. One always desired the unobtainable more.

'My *je ne sais quoi* is quite irrelevant,' she said drily. 'I think we've established that it is too late for you to own up to having a wife. Tell me if—*when* you gain control of the inheritance, what are your plans? If the estate is so rundown, you'll have to spend even more time away from your own business, won't you? And in the future—can one be a part-time marquess?'

'I'm not planning on being any sort of marquess. My plan is to put the lands on a profitable footing and then dispose of all of it. I'm going to let the title lapse, too.'

For the second time in this bizarre conversation, Lily found herself at a loss for words. 'Are you joking?'

'Not in the slightest.'

'Good lord, if those trustees of yours knew that is what you intended to do, they would do everything in their power to prevent you taking control.'

Oliver's lip curled. 'Once I have the law on my side, there's nothing they can do to stop me. If there was another heir in waiting, I might think differently, but relatives are one of the things I lack, now that Archie is dead. I have no desire to become one of the landed gentry. My heart and soul is in my own business.'

'The production of salt. I take it that business is still booming? And your workers' town, New Kilmun, continues to thrive?'

'Yes, to both. I want to expand into canning goods, it's a natural progression, but those plans are on hold until I can divest myself of my inheritance.'

His single-mindedness was impressive, his ideas

truly radical. The extent of her ignorance about the man she had married astounded Lily. As a champion of the underdog in her own way, she couldn't help but admire his aims. 'Will you sell the lands to your tenants? How will they be able to afford them?'

'I'm not sure that I will sell up. I'm contemplating a sort of collective. My instinct is that if everyone involved works together, collaborates for the greater good of the whole estate, they'll fare better. Making that happen, though,' Oliver said ruefully, 'that won't be an easy task. Farmers are notoriously single-minded and resistant to change, but I know from my own business that people are more productive when they are well fed and housed, and even more productive when they have a stake in what they're doing.'

'It's a marvellous idea,' Lily said with real enthusiasm, 'but practically revolutionary.'

'Not really. It's the same principles as I've put in place for New Kilmun.'

'Industry. Factories. It's not the same as England's precious landed estates. Your fellow peers will be appalled.'

Oliver grinned. 'Excellent. I'll be an outcast, which is precisely what I want to be. You approve, I take it?'

'Oh, yes, heartily. No wonder you are frustrated! It's madness to prevent you, who have spent your life improving the lives of all of your employees, make improvements—my goodness, Oliver, it almost makes me want to join ranks with you, just to help get it done.'

'Careful now,' he said, eyeing her with surprise, 'you're beginning to sound like a radical.'

'It's not radical to wish to protect the powerless from

being exploited, or to help people to make a better life for themselves. That's what…' *I do.* Lily bit the words back. 'That's what you do in New Kilmun.'

'I'm a businessman, not a philanthropist.'

'Your success in business owes a great deal to your philanthropy. It seems to me a crime, that a dead man's antiquated notions about marriage and responsibility should be preventing you from putting your ideas into practice. Why are you looking at me like that? As if I have two heads.'

'One head, that I don't recognise,' Oliver replied with a slight smile. 'I feel as if I'm talking to a stranger.'

'The feeling is mutual, I assure you. I really wish I could help you. I can't help but feel there must be a way which would allow me to do so. You need a wife. I am your wife.'

'Sadly, as I've already explained, circumstances make it impossible…'

'I know, I know.' Lily frowned out at the sea. 'In an ideal world, how much time do you think you will need, once you have control of the estate, to make all the changes you want to implement?'

'Sort out Archie's mess, get it on a stable footing, find someone trustworthy to take it forward?' Oliver shrugged. 'Three months? Probably more like six.'

'And this case, how long do you think it could continue before a conclusion is reached?'

Oliver groaned. 'If I knew the answer to that, at least I'd know where I stand, but I haven't a clue. A week, a month, a year, a decade. No idea at all.'

'So our divorce, it could be on hold for a great deal longer than six months?'

'No. Yes.' He clutched at his hair. 'No. I think we have to set a limit. I can't ask you to wait for an indefinite period. Six months, a year at the utmost. If the case isn't resolved by then—oh, God, but it has to be.'

He was deluding himself, Lily thought sadly. The truth was the situation was one he had no control over and, whether he wanted to accept it or not, the possibility that all this waiting could end up being for nothing had to be confronted. She quailed at the idea of being the one to force him to do that. Poor Oliver, a man so accustomed to being in control of every aspect of his life, was in denial.

'This is getting us nowhere.' He forestalled her brusquely. 'Thank you for listening to me, but I'm afraid all it's done for me is confirm that I'm already doing all I can. The law is on my side, I'm sure of it, and I'm sure that sooner rather than later, the decision will be made and we can go ahead with our divorce.'

He was putting on a front and not a very good one. Lily decided against arguing with him, it would only serve to make him more entrenched in his views. Oliver would make the world dance to his tune, that's what he'd always done before, and he refused to accept that he couldn't do it in this instance. 'I'll leave you now,' Lily said, retrieving her gloves from the table, 'but I will come back again tomorrow.'

'Why?'

To put a proposal to him that would resolve the situation was what she wished she could say, but she had no proposal, only a very strong desire to find one. Was there one? The odds were against it, given Oliver's own strenuous attempts, but still…. 'I need some time to think,' she equivocated. 'What you've told me, the impact it has on our divorce…'

'I'm so sorry,' Oliver said, looking immediately wretched.

'Please stop apologising. The situation is not of your making, but I need some time to accustom myself to it. Will you grant me another day?'

'Of course I will. More if you need it, though you'll be wanting to get back to Paris, I expect?'

This was said with an enquiring look that made her smile. Full marks, she thought, for persistence, holding out her hand. 'Until tomorrow, Oliver.' She smiled at him, one of her real smiles. 'Try to get some rest in the meantime.'

Lily would have preferred to walk along the beach to Folkestone, but the ever-shifting pebbles would ruin her sandals and make the two miles more of a slog than a pleasure. Besides, there was always a risk at this time of year that the weather would suddenly turn. Instead, she took the road along Radnor Cliff, where the view of the sea could still be glimpsed in between the houses. It was a route she had walked countless times when Abbey Hill had been her home, familiar despite the years of her absence.

She let her thoughts drift. Nothing had gone as she anticipated today. Her head was spinning. No wonder Oliver was in such a volatile state of mind. 'Infuriating' was how he'd described his situation and she could easily empathise with that, but infuriating is how she found him, too. He was so determined that no one could help him, so determined that there was no other way of looking at his dilemma than his own. He wasn't thinking clearly. He was too close to it to be able to think radically and a radical solution was what was needed.

Yet Oliver himself was a radical thinker. He had made his fortune from finding a way to manufacture high quality salt, using a process that he had designed himself. Lily couldn't begin to understand what that might entail, but it required an innovative mind. Despite that, he hadn't been able to think his way out of his current dilemma. Could it be that there really was no solution, save to wait on the wheels of the law grinding slowly to a conclusion?

But that was not a solution, for there was no guarantee it would find in his favour. The only solution, the only cast-iron guaranteed solution, was for Oliver to marry, which meant that he must first divorce her. Who knew how long that would take, even if he could be persuaded to do such a thing, which was unlikely. Or he must produce the wife he had. Her. Which he could do tomorrow, were it not for all the other issues which made that impossible.

Now her head was going round in circles! *Think, Lily!* There must be a solution. If there was not, she would be left in limbo, too, for she couldn't square it with her conscience to push him for a divorce while he was waiting on his court case to be resolved. For the last eight years, she had put divorce to the back of her mind to concentrate on living her life, but now that she had resolved to finalise it, she didn't want to have to wait indefinitely. To postpone it for a fixed period as Oliver had suggested, yes, that made sense, but it wasn't in his gift to do any such thing.

It had taken Lily a long time, a great deal of pain and setbacks, to gain control of her life, but she had it now and it sat ill with her to relinquish any element of it. She was a marchioness, as things stood. The very notion of that was preposterous. She wanted rid of the title every bit as much as Oliver did. In fact, they wanted precisely the same things. 'So there must be a way for us to achieve them,' she muttered. Oh, but if only she could find it, present it to him! Imagine the relief he would feel and how wonderful it would be for her, too, to be the means to the end. At last, to pay him back for all he had done for her.

She had reached the Leas, the wide promenade on the top of the cliffs which had the best views out over the sea and to France. It was peaceful here, the flower beds neatly laid out though empty now, the few children playing under strict supervision of their nannies. The promenade was preserved for the well-to-do of Folkestone and the guests who could afford to take rooms in the superior hotels there, which Lily could easily have done, but she preferred the buzz of the Pavilion Hotel at the harbour.

She sat down on one of the benches overlooking the old drovers paths which zig-zagged steeply down to the Lower Leas and the beach. What if she could find a solution that would allow Oliver to introduce her as his wife? What would be the implications? Would they have to live together? She wasn't at all sure it would be a good idea to share a roof with him for however long it took. To sleep in the same house, alone, knowing that the man who was legally her husband was also sleeping alone in the same house, only a few rooms away. Or would they be expected to have connecting rooms?

Honestly, Lily! No man was irresistible and there were far more important considerations, such as her business. Perhaps even more to the point, what would Oliver say when she told him what her business was? Would she have to tell him? Would he then consider her unfit to produce as his wife? So many questions, perhaps she ought to forget the whole thing. It wasn't really her problem. She could wait for her divorce. She had waited eight years for it, after all.

Non, non, non. Impossible!

To be secretly Mrs Oliver Turner, that was one thing. To be secretly the Marchioness of Rashfield was quite another. Lady Rashfield! Lily laughed to herself. Preposterous. Yet if she was to assist Oliver, she would have to play the part of Lady Rashfield for—what, a few weeks? A few months? Could she act the part of a wife, married to a man she didn't even know? They had been married for nearly twelve years, but she had no idea how to play a wife. She lived alone, she worked alone with only her assistant, and poor Hélène was for ever complaining that Lily didn't trust her enough and took on far too much herself. They would be bound to argue, for, like her, Oliver was accustomed to living alone, making his own decisions.

She liked the man she had met today, perhaps because they were so alike. She admired his ambitions and empathised with them. He was also *agréable à l'oeil*, as her friend Marie would say. Very agreeable on the eye, in fact. Strange that she had never found him attractive before. Of course, she had been aware that the man saving her from penury was extremely handsome, but the fact that she was entirely dependent upon him for a roof over her head had smothered any other feelings she might have developed. She had been so young, too, and so innocent.

Today, in those first few seconds when she saw him again, she had felt it, that frisson between a man and a woman who find each other attractive. Oliver was one of those men, Lily thought, indulging herself for a moment, who one simply *knew* would be a very satisfying lover. A delicious shiver made her look around guiltily, but the nannies and their charges had gone and the two women passing, walking their pampered dogs, were intent on their own conversation.

It was growing cold. Enough of that, Lily told herself sternly, getting up to continue her walk back to her hotel. She wanted to help him so that she could help herself, not surrender to his charms, no matter what the temptation. A marriage that would enable their divorce. Now there was an irony!

A loud blast of the whistle and a belch of thick smoke announced the arrival of the boat train from London. She wrapped her shawl more tightly around her and stood at the edge of the Leas to watch as it slowed and pulled into the terminus at the harbour where the ferry was already berthed and waiting. Passengers spilled out and porters leapt into action.

She had reserved her rooms at the Pavilion for three nights. The clerk at the reception desk had informed her, in that sotto voce, confidential way that always got her hackles up, that single female guests tended to feel more comfortable eating in their rooms than in the public dining room. Lily never did anything comfortable. She liked the opposite, she found it much more fun. England was so different from France and Paris was very different from both. If she was indeed to play the part of Oliver's wife she had better be prepared for the constraints which would be placed on her liberty here.

If she was to play his wife!

She still had no idea how that might be possible, but it seemed she had already decided that if it was, she would take the part, provided she could be sure it was safe.

Safe? Not a word that sprang to mind when one thought of Oliver. *Eh,* bien, *Lily. You will have to make sure that you play safe.* She would be acting the part of a wife and she would need to remember that. There must be no confusing the drama they would have enact with real life.

An elegant way to put it and reassuring. She checked her watch. There was time to take a look at the Folkestone Theatre, for old times' sake. She wouldn't go in. It was highly unlikely that anyone from those days would still be working backstage, but it was a risk she had better not take. Another issue to add to the list she was compiling, which would have to be resolved. How to ensure that the wife who would help Oliver claim his inheritance would never be connected with the real Lily?

They would need to rewrite their history. Deep in thought, she turned away from the view and began to walk briskly towards the town. She had until tomorrow to come up with a plan that would make all those impossible and contradictory aims achievable.

Chapter Three

The unseasonably warm weather was holding. For the second morning in a row, Oliver sat at the table on the veranda at the back of the house he had come to think of as Lilian's, trying and failing to work. Closing the ledger, he set it aside and wandered over to the edge of the garden and what looked like what had once been a path down to the beach. It was heavily overgrown and full of briars, but he pushed through it, enjoying the soft ruffle of the sea breeze in his hair and the tang of the salty air on his lips.

Ahead, the English Channel sparkled a grey-blue, the haze obscuring any glimpse of France. The path came to an end at a gate which was padlocked and rusty. Beyond, the pebbled beach was almost empty. The metronomic motion of the waves on the shore stirring the pebbles tempted him to climb over, but he resisted at the last moment, unsure of whether he'd be able to get himself back again once he was on the other side.

Making a mental note to find the key and have the hinges oiled, Oliver picked his way back up the steep path to find Lilian waiting. 'Good morning' he said. 'I wasn't expecting you until later.'

'I'm early, I know, but I was anxious to speak to you. However, if I'm interrupting?' She indicated his ledger and letters. 'I can go for a walk on the beach. Is that where you have been?'

'The gate was padlocked and I decided against a feat of derring-do to climb it.'

She was dressed in powder blue today, another of those frothy dresses that was in fashion, festooned with yards of lace, ruffles, tucks and bows, though her toilette was more restrained. While tight lacing and a bustle to exaggerate the figure made some women look, in his humble opinion, both uncomfortable and unstable, Lilian was tall enough and slender enough for the style to suit her. Once again, he felt as if this elegant, self-possessed and extremely attractive woman was a complete stranger. 'Tea?' Oliver asked. 'Or would you rather we went inside?'

'Out here would be lovely and I would much prefer coffee, if that isn't too much trouble?'

'None at all, I prefer it myself—if you give me a moment, I'll go and fetch it,' he said, happy to escape for a moment. He had been overly dramatic yesterday, a stark contrast to his usual demeanour. The situation he was in was extreme, but that was no excuse. Lilian had come back early because she had seen sense, had concluded there was nothing to be done. They would have coffee, and though it would be tempting to while away a few more hours in her company, it would be futile.

Returning to the sitting room which opened on to the veranda, he took the chance to observe her, unnoticed.

She was standing on the edge of the path, looking out to sea, one arm lifted to shade her eyes. Wispy tendrils of hair blew in the breeze at the nape of her neck, and the trailing ribbons in the tiny hat perched on her coiffure fluttered. There was something extremely alluring about the long line of her back in the tight bodice, the gentle curve to the bustle, which tempted him to imagine the curve of her bottom beneath. It was impossible to tell from her gown, but he guessed at long legs, slim ankles.

Her skin had an olive tone to it, not the alabaster white that was deemed beautiful, but the kind of skin that warmed to the kiss of the sun. She didn't powder her face, he'd noticed yesterday. She did tint her lips, though, he'd noticed that yesterday, too. There was a sensuality about her, discreet, subtle, like her perfume, that made him think of making slow, languorous love in the afternoon.

She turned suddenly. 'Coffee won't be long,' Oliver said, embarrassed by his inappropriate thoughts and stepping out on to the veranda. 'Shall we sit down?' He waited until she took her seat before sitting opposite her. 'Yesterday was the first time I've ever sat here. I'm beginning to understand your fascination with the sea.'

'I used to have my morning coffee here every day, even in the winter, if it was dry. I love the sound of the sea, there's something so calming about it. I miss it, when I am in Paris.'

'You don't live in the city all the time, then?'

The agency manservant brought their coffee and she busied herself with pouring, ignoring his question. 'Yes, please,' he replied as she lifted the milk jug.

Lilian took her coffee black. She took a small sip before speaking. 'I have a small house on the coast in a little fishing port called Roscoff, which is more famous for onions.' She took another sip of her coffee, then set her cup down decisively. 'Fascinating as the topic is, I didn't come here to discuss Roscoff onions. Shall we get down to business? I think I may have an answer to your problem. I have a proposal to make.'

Oliver, who had not for a single minute considered such a thing, was so taken aback that he laughed. 'Impossible.'

'I confess, I thought so, too, but where there is a will, as they say. Though you would not admit it, Oliver, your solution, to wait on the law to run its course, is not necessarily going to give you what you want. No,' she said, holding her hand up when he made to speak, 'we went over it all yesterday, there is no point in us discussing it again today. The law does not work to a timetable. If you have a wife, you are in control of the timetable for handover of your estate and for our divorce. And so, logically, the solution must be to find you a wife.'

Oliver gritted his teeth. 'We have been over this, too. I have a wife, but she cannot—you cannot—look, as you've said, I see no point in going over this again.'

'I agree. Let us instead discuss a different wife for you.'

'A different wife! I cannot have a different wife while I am still married to you, unless you're proposing that I become a bigamist.'

'Not at all, though my proposal would require you to marry again.'

'Oh, for heaven's sake!'

Lilian, to his annoyance, smiled. 'If you will listen, all will become clear, I promise you.'

'I don't know how!' Aware that he sounded like a petulant child, Oliver took a deep breath and folded his arms. 'You have my full attention. I won't say another word.'

'Excellent. Very well then. As I said, the only fool-proof solution is for you to marry. You are already married to me…'

She stopped in response to his muffled protest, but he waved her on.

'While you are married to me, you cannot marry someone else in order to secure your inheritance. Yet circumstances make it impossible for you to introduce me as your wife of long standing. Therefore, you must introduce me as your bride. Sorry, did you say something?'

Oliver shook his head, biting his tongue.

'We will tell your trustees that our marriage was a whirlwind romance. That we met in France, where you were taking a holiday to escape the stress of your court case, and it was love at first sight. We were married abroad because you were officially in mourning and we intend to live quietly in the country for the remainder of your mourning period, where you will spend the time learning more about your inheritance. Obviously you won't tell them what you intend to do with that knowledge.

'Then at some point, we will discover that our marriage was a big mistake, that I miss France terribly, that you were in the throes of grief and mistook your feelings. We both acted in haste. And then it will be over.

Voilà.' Lilian sat back, folding her arms and smiling at him expectantly. 'What do you think?'.

'I think,' Oliver replied after a moment's stunned silence, 'that I need a second cup of coffee.'

Lily waited while Oliver refilled both the coffee cups, with enormous difficulty refraining from demanding again, *well, what do you think?* He needed time to digest what she had just thrown at him. Her proposal was outrageous, it came at a cost and with some very real risks, but if it worked, it would give them both what they wanted. Surely he would see that?

He was sipping his coffee, staring over her shoulder, a deep frown marring his brow. The longer the silence went on, she told herself, the more positive the outcome was likely to be. She had finished her coffee and almost come to the end of her resolve before he spoke.

'Is this a serious proposal?' Oliver asked.

'I never make anything else.'

'I can't see how it would work. For a start, we can't simply present the trustees with some fairy tale about a whirlwind romance, they're going to want evidence. Tangible proof, not a fabricated story that we've spun, and we can't produce our actual marriage certificate because the date…'

'I've thought of that. We'll have to get married again. In France.'

Oliver, who had been slumped in his chair, sat up straight. 'Married again! How can we? We're already married, in case you hadn't noticed. Isn't that something of a drawback?' he added witheringly.

'Not necessarily. It's not illegal to marry the same

person twice and in France, the law requires only a simple civil ceremony conducted by a mayor. If you like, we can use Mr Sinclair as our witness again and he can then back up our claim to your trustees. You can trust Mr Sinclair implicitly. Besides, we're not asking him to lie.'

Oliver ran his fingers through his hair. 'Good God! But even if that was possible, the ramifications are unthinkable. We'd have to live together, in the same house. We'd have to act as if we were married in front of people other than just the trustees—staff, tenants, lots of people. Not only married, but in love.' Oliver winced. 'I've never been in love.'

'Nor have I. You needn't look so appalled,' Lily said drily, 'we would only be acting. We'd be sharing a roof, but not a bedroom.'

'I'm pretty sure that sharing a bedroom with you would be a pleasure. That's not the issue.'

'No,' Lily said, willing herself not to blush and refusing to allow herself to be pleased to have her own instincts confirmed, 'it is not an issue because we would certainly not be sharing a room.'

Oliver coloured. 'I didn't mean—I wasn't suggesting any such thing.'

'*Eh bien*, then that is one thing on which we are agreed.'

'Lilian, the question of whether or not we make love is entirely irrelevant.'

'That is what I am saying, because it won't happen.'

'No, because you're going back to France and I am going to wait on my court case coming to a close. What you're suggesting is out of the question. You'd have to remain here in England for—I don't know, months. What about your life in Paris, your business interests whatever they may be? I don't even understand why you have offered to do this?'

She clung to the fact that he was still willing to listen and forced herself to speak patiently. 'I thought I'd made it clear yesterday. Whether you accept it or not, I feel that I owe you a debt of honour, and by helping you I can pay it back. Besides, Oliver, marriage is the only guaranteed solution, you must see that?'

'It will grant me access to my inheritance, but what about our divorce? If we live under the same roof, we'll have to wait for the time period to elapse again after you've gone back to France if we wish to have the marriage dissolved on the grounds of desertion.'

'But at least we would have a time frame. We have no idea how long your court case will take and, more importantly, Oliver, no certainty that it will succeed,' Lily said earnestly. 'You can't ignore the possibility.'

'I really don't want to think about it.'

'Then think about this as an alternative,' she urged. 'Delaying our divorce is a price we would have to agree to pay. I would be less willing to wait if you were not so determined to remain a bachelor and allow your title to lapse. And you should realise that in France, there is no such thing as a divorce, but as long as we eventually divorce in England I cannot see that is an issue.'

'It has to be an issue! If there's no divorce in France and you continue to live in France, and you wish to marry again, even if we are divorced in England, wouldn't that mean you couldn't marry again? In France, I mean.'

'I don't wish to marry again, in any country. We will be divorced, that is what matters. I will have no claim on you and you will have none on me. Besides, you will marry Lilian Grantham, the name I was born with. In France I go by a different name.'

'Which brings me back to the main reason for refusing your very generous offer. Whatever your business is, Lilian, however you earn your living—and judging from your clothes, you are doing well for yourself—I can't ask you to give it up on my behalf.'

Here it was, the opening she had been waiting for. Lily drank the dregs of her cold coffee, steeling herself. She was proud of what she had achieved, she reminded herself, but she was acutely aware that the way she made a living was unorthodox, to say the least. Disreputable, was what far too many people thought. Downright scandalous, she reckoned, was how Oliver's trustees would view it. What mattered, however, was what Oliver thought. Forcing herself to accept that his opinion mattered at all was a difficult pill to swallow.

She reached for the coffee-pot and poured herself the last of the now thick, tarry mixture. A tot of cognac in it would help immeasurably, but asking for that before noon, she thought wryly to herself, would colour Oliver's view of her before she had even begun.

'I have no intention of giving my business up,' Lily said. 'I have worked too long and too hard to contemplate that. I have someone I trust who can stand in for me, keep things ticking over, until I return, provided that I can be contacted by telegram in an emergency. It is not ideal. When one builds something from scratch, it is very difficult to delegate, but it is time I did just that.'

Across the table, Oliver raised a brow, smiling faintly. 'You sound just like me.'

'It struck me yesterday that we are similar in that way.' She was prevaricating. 'Remind me, how long do you think our charade would have to last?' Lily asked, continuing to do so.

'I don't know precisely. I reckon it would take me three months, more likely six, to set the wheels in motion to set up my estate co-operative, collective, for want of a better description, but whether my wife would have to remain for that amount of time—?' Oliver broke off, shaking his head. 'Not that it's relevant, Lilian, because I can't ask you...'

'You haven't asked me!' Lily took a breath. 'Three months is possible. After Christmas is the quiet time in the theatre.' There, she had said it. 'I am a theatrical agent.'

She had expected astonishment. Oliver simply looked at her blankly.

'I negotiate contracts, terms and conditions, with theatre owners and managers, on behalf of my clients.'

'Actors, you mean?'

'Actresses, mostly, though my reputation is now such that I now have several very well-known actors on my books, too.'

'I have to say, if you'd given me a hundred guesses, then I'd never have come up with that. I didn't even know there was such a thing as a theatrical agent.'

Lily smiled thinly. 'As far as I'm aware, I invented the role.'

'Invented! How? Or why? I mean—what made you think— How did you come to dream up such a role?

How did you come to make it work? And to work so well for you?'

'I have always had an interest in the theatre, but I simply don't have the talent to be a successful actress.' There was no need for her to explain how she knew that. Her early experiences were irrelevant and she most certainly wasn't going to tell Oliver the pathetic tale of her starry-eyed and naive failure. 'In Paris I have a friend, an actress, a brilliant actress. But talent, I learned from her experiences, does not necessarily guarantee success.' *Pauvre* Marie, Lily thought. She had talent in abundance, but it was her beauty that had been her downfall.

'You mean,' Oliver asked, oblivious of this bitter memory, 'because there is so much competition?'

'I mean because there are too many men determined to exploit that fact. Theatre owners. Theatre managers. They require personal favours in return for prime roles. Do you see?'

She was relieved to see that he looked appalled. 'That's exploitation.'

'That is precisely what I believe it to be. They, however, believe it is a perk of the job. It is my job to disabuse them of that fact.'

'How on earth do you do that? I mean, if there are actresses queuing up for the best parts, and you tell the man in charge, you can only have so-and-so if you pay her properly and refrain from demanding—what did you call it—"personal favours"? Don't they simply offer the role to someone else?'

'Precisely what happened in the very early days, before my reputation was established. My breakthrough came when I managed to persuade a certain singer to allow me to negotiate on her behalf. She had been touring in America and was extremely popular. There was a great deal of competition between theatres to acquire her services.'

'I don't know what to say,' Oliver said, looking really very rewardingly impressed. 'I'll be honest, I'm struggling to see how you can make a good living out of it, though. Your clients, as you call them, do they pay you a portion of the fees you negotiate for them?'

'It varies.' Lily gazed out at the sea. 'It is very difficult generally to make a decent living in the theatre. Most people, front and backstage, barely scrape by.'

'And despite your efforts,' Oliver said, 'I suspect that too many continue to be the victims of the parasites with power.'

'Unfortunately,' Lily said, eyeing him with surprise.

'It's how the world turns,' Oliver said. 'Those who have take as much as they can from those who don't. Not everyone, but too many.'

'Not you.'

'I told you, Lily, I'm a businessman, not a philanthropist. Having well-fed, well-paid workers gives me a better return.'

'In that sense, we run our business on the same principles. I agree the best terms I can for my clients and my clients in turn do their best in the role in return. Which means the show is more likely to succeed. Which means that my investment in the show will give me a better return. You see, that's where I make most of my money.'

Oliver whistled. 'What a clever idea. You must be very proud of what you've achieved.'

'Thank you.' To her consternation, she was blushing. 'I am.'

'And rightly so, Lilian, which is why you can't possibly hand your business over to someone else on my account.'

'You have handed over your business to a deputy.' Lily eyed him speculatively. 'I will wager that he jumped at the opportunity to prove himself. And I will further wager,' she added when Oliver shrugged sheepishly, 'that he has been waiting for far too long for the opportunity to do so.'

He laughed, holding up his hands. 'True, very true. I am far too guilty of thinking that no one save myself is capable of making a decision. But it's my business,' he added, his expression becoming serious again, 'and I'm forced to put my expansion plans on hold to attend to this other business. It's a damnable position to be in—excuse my language—but that's no reason for me to expect you to do the same.'

'Oliver, listen to me.' Lily leaned forward earnestly. 'The more I think of this admittedly outrageous idea of mine, the more sure I am that we can make it work, and what's more, it's the *only* way. I'm not suggesting it will be easy. I will have to make sacrifices, but I'm willing to make them, and Hélène, I am sure, will be delighted to have the opportunity. My deputy,' she added, in response to his raised brow.

'I won't pretend that I have thought through all the detail of how it would work in practice, I haven't had time, but I am sure that I want to make it work. Not for your sake, but for mine, do you see? It means I will be free of you—of the burden of gratitude and of my husband,' she added with a wry smile. 'To wait for the law to take its course or grasp the opportunity to act now—doesn't that appeal?'

'Of course it does, but there are so many risks, so much we don't know. It's a bloody—blooming madcap idea.'

'Which is why it might just succeed,' Lily said. He was considering it. He was actually taking her offer seriously. Yet she had to caution him. Flattering as it was, that he recognised her ingenuity and her business acumen, he had not yet had time to consider the implications. 'You understand, Oliver, that what I do for a living would not be seen as respectable by your trustees. And that, I think, may be a rather large understatement.'

'What business would it be of theirs? They're not going to think for a moment that a marquess would marry a business woman. The woman I married—who you're suggesting I marry again—is from a poor but respectable family. And in Paris, you are known by another name entirely, so there's no reason why anyone would make the connection.'

'No, but our marriage will have to be announced in the press and the press love nothing more than a scandal. It's a risk.'

'How well known are you in Paris?'

'In my business, well enough. If you mean, am I likely to meet anyone who knows me in English society?' Lily laughed scornfully. 'I don't think so. Would we have to mix with society?'

'Not if I can help it, though I can't say it's something I've thought about. My entire focus has been winning the court case. If I'm to present my wife to the trustees—I've no idea what that will entail.'

Lily caught her breath. 'Are you—do you think it might work?'

'It's so unbelievable that it might.' Oliver left the table to stand at the edge of the veranda. 'I don't know, though, there's a great deal that will need further investigation. What does it take to marry in France? I can set Sinclair on to that one. But how will you and I get on, sharing the same roof?'

'That, I agree, will be an interesting challenge,' Lily said, joining him. 'I warn you, I am very much accustomed to making my own decisions.'

'Ditto,' Oliver retorted. 'You're also very much accustomed to being busy, given what you've told me. Assuming that you're not going to spend your time making lists of linen and plates—according to Archie's housekeeper it is something that is urgently required.'

'Well, why doesn't she do it, if she's the housekeeper?'

Oliver gave a crack of laughter. 'Good answer. Seriously, Lilian…'

'Seriously, Oliver, there must be plenty I can do to help you with your revolutionary plan to rid yourself of your lands and all your tenants.'

'Do you know the first thing about lands and tenants?'

'No, I know a great deal about managing people, negotiating terms, putting the best person in the best role.'

She had clearly surprised him again, but what surprised her was that Oliver, instead of immediately rejecting the idea, looked quite taken by it. 'That will certainly upset the apple cart. What I've seen of Archie's world is that it is traditional and conventional in the extreme.'

'You're going to be upsetting a good many apple carts yourself with your plans.'

'Then the best person to have by my side is a fellow radical.' He laughed. 'Do you know, I think by joining forces, we might make an excellent team.'

'A team?' Lily raised her brows. 'I hope that's not how you will describe us to your trustees, it's hardly romantic.'

'Are we to be romantic?'

'We are to pretend to be in love,' she said. 'With the emphasis on pretending.'

'So we pretend to make love? What does that entail?'

She eyed him deliberately up and down. 'I can't believe you need to be coached in the arts of lovemaking.'

He met her gaze, his mouth hovering on the edge of a smile. 'I'm not in the habit of making love in public.'

Was he flirting with her? 'You need rehearsal in the role?' she said, as much for her own benefit as his. 'Your trustees are English, not French. All you have to do is kiss my hand in front of them and they will be convinced.'

'If they were French, what do you think we'd have to do to persuade them?'

'They are not French,' she retorted, refusing to be drawn.

'What sort of a hand kiss?' Oliver made a flourishing bow, then took her hand, his mouth hovering over her fingertips. 'Like this?'

His smile was teasing. Lily never refused a challenge. 'I think you could afford to be a little more amorous.'

He lifted her hand to his mouth again. She felt the brush of his beard, his warm breath, then his lips pressing a kiss on her fingertips, and all the time his gaze on her face, watching for her reaction. She refused to let him see that he was having any effect on her.

'*I* think,' Oliver said, 'that *you* could be a bit more amorous. After all, we are both supposed to be madly in love.'

Lily simpered, fluttering her lashes, pressing her free hand to her chest. '*Oh, monsieur le marquess.*'

'My love.' He drew her closer. 'There is no need to be so formal.'

There were mere inches between them. He was acting, trying to prove a point, that was all. '*Mon amour.*' Her tone was breathless. He had surprised her, nothing more.

Oliver lifted her hand to his mouth. His beard brushed the fingertips again, then his lips. He kissed her hand again, lingering slightly too long, his eyes still on hers, watching. Her breath caught in her throat. She exaggerated it. He turned her hand over and kissed her palm. She felt the brush of his tongue. He kissed her again, little butterfly kisses from palm to wrist where his mouth lingered, where he would be able to sense her fluttering pulse.

Lily yanked her hand free. 'I think that will be more than a sufficient demonstration for your trustees.'

'For the trustees perhaps, but for myself...'

'Oliver! I know you are teasing, but there is no question of us making love.' Completely flustered, Lily crossed her arms, determined to make her point. 'We will share a roof, but not a bed, you understand?'

'I'm sorry. Truly, Lilian. I didn't mean to upset you. I would never, ever take advantage of you, or of the situation.'

'I am not upset. I would not allow you to take advantage, but I think it is best we are clear on the point from the outset, yes?'

'Yes, of course. I got carried away.'

'It happens,' she said, which was true. 'We will ensure that we do not allow ourselves to get too carried away when we are living together.' Once again, she was aware that she was speaking as much for her own benefit as for his. All he had done was kiss her hand. The kiss had confirmed what her instincts had told her from the moment they met again yesterday, that he would be a very proficient lover, but that was all! Proficient or not, he was out of bounds.

'"When we are living together." You are determined to go through with this, then?'

'If you think it will work?'

'I think it might,' he replied, adding with a smile, 'and I am sure I'm going to enjoy trying.'

Lily held out her hand, returning his smile. 'Then we have a deal.'

Chapter Four

Berkshire, England, January 1877

It had taken a week for Oliver and Lily to agree to the details of their plan, and another seven weeks to put it into practice. The ever-obliging Mr Sinclair suggested they marry in the busy international port of Bordeaux, where they were both required to take up residence for a period before the mayor was permitted to perform the civil ceremony.

Lily had spent most of the time taking the train backwards and forward to Paris to coach a delighted Hélène in her new duties, and the rest of the time carrying out what she could of her work by telegram. Oliver did the same, while it fell to Mr Sinclair to arrange for a notice to be placed in *The Times* and the trustees to be informed of the pending nuptials. Rashfield Manor was being readied to receive the newly-weds, whom Mr Sinclair had accompanied back to England immediately after the ceremony, heading for London while they completed their own journey.

They were alone, it seemed to Lily, for the first time. Only now, as the train began to slow on the approach to the local station nearest Rashfield Manor, did she have time to panic. What had she done? For the next three months, at least, she was going to be living with a man who was still not much more than a stranger, despite the fact that she had now married him twice. What if their deceit was uncovered? What if her real life was uncovered? What if…?

'Lilian? Whatever it is that is worrying you…'

'Nothing! Nothing at all. We have been over and over and over everything, there's nothing for me to fret about. I'm not worried about anything, save the pressing need for a refreshing bath and my dinner.'

'I am sure that Archie's housekeeper will have thought of that and arranged both.'

'Our housekeeper,' Lily corrected him. 'Mrs Bremner. And the butler is Riddell. Mr Sinclair gave me a list of the staff.'

'You're not going to be quizzed on the names of all of the staff, Lilian.'

'It's Lily! You may as well call me Lily, all my friends do, though I know I am to be Lilian here, but I've always hated that name. It seems more fitting for a marchioness, however, so perhaps you'd better not call me Lily when there's anyone else around. Or at all.'

Oliver took her hands, forcing her to meet his eyes. 'We're a partnership, in this together, remember?'

'I know. I remember. However, it's one thing to be making all the arrangements, getting married again, handing over to Hélène and being so certain that I'm doing the right thing. But now that we're here, I've got to actually *do* it. Pull it off. And I do remember we're a team, Oliver, but at the end of the day, I don't know you.' She caught herself, forcing a smile. 'Classic first-night nerves. Or in our case, first day. Don't worry, they always go as soon as I step on stage.'

'Good. I'm experiencing them myself.'

'Then you are doing an excellent job of hiding them.' The train jolted to a halt. The First-Class carriages were at the rear, farthest away from the engine, but the clouds of steam still obscured the view from the window as she glanced out. 'We're here. We're on.'

Oliver opened the carriage door. 'I am afraid we've got a rather bigger audience than I was expecting. Quite the welcoming party. It looks as though we're going to have to put on our act a little earlier than expected.'

He stepped down and, as he turned to assist her, a roar went up. Lily froze on the top step, gazing in shock at the sea of faces on the platform, men, women, children with dogs on leashes, all smiling and shouting and cheering. 'What on earth?'

'These people are here to wish us joy and happiness, *my love*,' Oliver replied pointedly. 'Word of our marriage has travelled fast.' He tugged at her hand.

It was her cue. This was her audience, much larger than she had anticipated, and much more raucous for her debut as the Marchioness of Rashfield, but she was up to the mark. Lily pinned a bright smile to her face. She gave her Marquess a simpering smile and her audience a little wave. 'Either someone has paid these people to put on a convincing show of support,' she whispered in Oliver's ear as she stepped down, 'or they really are pleased to see you.'

'More likely, they're pleased to see the back of the trustees,' he replied, sliding his arm around her waist and, when she instinctively stiffened, whispering, 'you're my blushing bride, remember?'

The embrace was greeted with whoops, whistles and hollers. *'Hip, hip, hooray!'* someone shouted. *'Three cheers for the Marquess and his bride!'*

Lily had never been a leading lady. She had never been centre stage, never had an audience hanging on her every word. She had never been good enough for those roles. This role had been made for her, quite literally. The lines she would speak, every move she made on this stage would be hers. She lifted her hand to flutter over her husband's cheek, turning in his embrace to plant a kiss on his lips. She smiled up at him, quietly satisfied to see the surprise register in his eyes, though he covered it up quickly.

'Mon amour,' Lily said to him.

'My love,' Oliver replied, a wicked glint in his eye that she noticed too late, as he scooped her up into his arms and headed through the parting crowd to the station entrance, where their carriage awaited.

Toilette and equilibrium considerably ruffled, Lily edged farther into the corner of the luxurious coach as the liveried coachman closed the door behind them. 'There was no need for you to go to such extremes,' she said. 'My gown is quite crushed.'

'I reckoned it was the quickest way to get us out of there,' Oliver replied, looking completely unrepentant. 'With my arms full of my wife, I didn't have the time to stop and chat. I was no more expecting that reception than you, you know, Lilian. Lily. I like Lily, it suits you so much better. I thought we both handled it rather well, considering.'

'Mr Sinclair should have warned us.'

'He would have, I'm sure, if he'd known about it. Sinclair is no more used to my being a marquess than I am.' Oliver took off his hat and ran his fingers through his hair. 'I would say thank the stars that's over with, but I reckon we've about fifteen minutes before we face the next ordeal. The staff,' he said, when Lily looked at him blankly. 'After that welcome, I think we have to assume that they'll be lined up on the stairs and waiting for us, waiting to be formally introduced.'

'Oliver, it occurs to me that there's a great deal we haven't discussed about our temporary life together.'

'We've barely discussed it at all. In fact, I think since we agreed to get married again, this might be the longest I've spent alone with you.'

'This will also be our first dinner alone together, without Mr Sinclair for company.'

'He's a sound chap and I don't know what I would do without him, but at the end of the day he's a lawyer and not the most sparkling of company. We will have a butler and at least one footman to help us along if the conversation gets stilted.'

Lily was forced to laugh. 'I'm not worried about running out of conversation. I simply wish we'd had more time to plan.'

'It's a bit late now for regrets. Look,' Oliver said, pointing out of the window, 'we're turning in at the gates.'

'I didn't say I regretted anything.'

'That's a relief.'

'I simply feel unprepared. I hate above all things to be unprepared, it gives such a poor impression.'

Irked with herself and determined to regain her composure, Lily turned her attention to the view from the carriage window. She was a marchioness. She was, albeit temporarily, to be the chatelaine of a country manor and she had no idea at all what that entailed. It was a role, she reminded herself, but she didn't like the feeling that she was going on stage without knowing her lines, especially when her leading man didn't either.

They were in this together. Did that make her feel better? She wasn't sure that it did. She wasn't used to being accountable to someone else. She didn't want him to witness the mistakes she was bound to make. She hated that she had already betrayed her lack of confidence in front of him. She hated to show weakness of any sort to anyone. Then again, he was likely the same, though that would only be a consolation if he made any mistakes. Not that she wanted him to make mistakes.

Lily! Breathe. Breathe. Breathe. Outside, it was a crisp autumn day, yet the drive was unkempt and dark, the trees and shrubs which lined it overgrown and what she could see of the grounds looked similarly neglected. The house was of a classic Palladian design, completely symmetrical with a shallow roof set behind a high balustrade. The central section was divided by four pillars and topped with an ornate pediment carved with a motto she assumed was Latin.

A steep flight of steps led up to the doorway and the overall effect would have been immensely pleasing had it not been for the extremely ugly modern wings which had been added, one on either side, the red brick jarring horribly with the mellow sandstone of the original house, their lack of symmetry a further insult to the original simple beauty of the design.

'It's an eyesore, isn't it?' Oliver said, seeing her expression. 'I think it was Archie's father, my uncle, who added those wings. Archie's contribution is the stable yard which I am told is in the Moorish style.'

'Moorish?'

'He spent some time in Turkey at the end of the Crimean War and took a liking to the architecture. He had plans drawn up for a bath house, but fortunately had not the funds to build it. Here we are and, as I suspected, there they all are. Are you ready, my love?'

Lily would rather stay in the carriage and have it drive her somewhere far away, where she could be on her own, but this had been her idea and she wasn't going to let Oliver or herself down. 'Yes, *mon petit chou.*'

'I'm not sure I want to know, but…'

'My little cabbage,' she said sardonically. 'Though I should tell you, I am not at all fond of cabbage.'

'It is to be hoped we are not faced with it for dinner, then.'

'Will it be formal? Should I wear an evening gown?'

'We are just married and we've been travelling for two days. I don't know about you, but the last thing I want to do is put on evening dress. I shall tell them to put a bottle of champagne on ice and we'll serve ourselves. Then, if you wish, you can sit at the other end of the table and ignore me completely. How does that sound?'

'Perfect. I shall hold you to it.' The carriage stopped

and the door was flung open. Lily pasted on a gracious smile and allowed Oliver to help her down.

Though a fire crackled in the grate, the drawing room was extremely cold if one stood more than a few steps away from the hearth. Oliver pulled the two most comfortable-looking chairs he could find closer to the blaze and set the champagne on a table between them. Archie's wine cellars were extremely well stocked, but given the chilly room there was probably no need to have put the bottle on ice. The curtains on the three tall windows had been drawn, but draughts made them flutter. He pulled one aside to look out at the clear skies studded with stars and allowed himself to wonder what the hell he was doing here.

'The master of all he surveys,' Lily quipped from the doorway.

'I cannot get accustomed to being addressed as "my lord". Every time I hear it, I look over my shoulder. It must have been even stranger for you.'

She shuddered. '"My lady!" It was extremely odd and, no matter how many times I tell myself that it's only a role I'm playing, I doubt I'll ever get used to it. Goodness, but this house is cold. I am very glad to you told me not to put on an evening dress.'

'Come over to the fire.' He watched her as she made her way across the long room. She walked with the grace of a dancer, he mused, and at the same time, there was an air of…authority? No, that wasn't the word. Self-assured, that she most certainly was, and confident. She had that something that drew the attention. *Je ne sais quoi.* That would have to do.

'What is it? You're staring at me.'

'I was admiring your gown.' Not true, but now she was standing next to him, it was an excuse to continue to look at her. 'The style suits you.'

'It is because I am tall and unfashionably slim. The current trend is for more rounded figures, but Monsieur Worth, who designed this and most of my gowns, says—' Lily broke off with a shake of her head. 'You are not interested in fashion and I am more interested in that champagne.'

'Your wish is my command.' Oliver popped the cork and poured the wine, handing her a glass before taking the seat beside her. 'What shall we drink to?'

'To us, would be the conventional answer, since we are supposed to be newly married, but there won't be an us for more than a few months. Shall we drink to that?'

'I'm not toasting our divorce.' Oliver raised his glass. 'To my partner in crime. I barely know you, but I know enough to be confident that I have married a truly extraordinary woman and I am fortunate to have you by my side. Thank you.'

'There is no need to thank me. I am here because I wish to be and there is no need to pay me compliments when we are alone either.' She touched his glass with hers and took a deep draught. 'Your cousin had excellent taste in champagne.'

Chastened, Oliver took a sip, wrinkled his nose and set the glass down.

'You don't like champagne?'

'Not particularly.'

In the uncomfortable silence which followed, Lily finished her drink. She was perched at an angle on the chair that must be extremely uncomfortable, he reckoned, back straight, legs tucked to one side. That gown wouldn't let her sit straight, but even without the bustle, he doubted she would relax. She frustrated him and intrigued him in equal measures. She had played her part impeccably earlier, with not a trace of the panic and trepidation she'd let slip in the carriage. Now they were alone, there was no need for her to act. Feeling churlish, he took another sip of the champagne. 'You must be exhausted. There's no need for us to make polite conversation while we're alone. We'll just sit here, drink our wine, have our dinner and an early night.'

'I'm sorry.' She surprised him by stretching over to touch his hand. 'I'm truly sorry. It has been a long— I was going to say day, but it's been weeks and I'm annoyed—no, I'm furious with myself for being so unprepared. I think tomorrow we should regroup and make a proper plan.'

'That's an excellent idea.' He briefly covered her hand with his own. Her fingers were long and icy cold, the nails carefully buffed and filed. 'Lily suits you much better than Lilian.'

'Lilian was my grandmother's name. I never knew her, but there was a photograph of her I remember, with my mother holding Anthony, looking quite terrifying. Mind you, most people do in those older photographs, for they had to sit still for so long. Anyway, I decided that I wouldn't allow myself to grow into such an awfully stern woman as the woman I was named for, so I called myself Lily and it's how I always think of myself.'

'Anthony always referred to you as Lilian.'

'Yes, he did. I was always Lilian to my family. Anthony was a very conventional kind of brother. I loved him, but I wonder sometimes what would have become of me if he had not died.' She grimaced. 'That's a dreadful thing to say and of course I wish he hadn't died, but if he hadn't, then I wonder, would I have simply dwindled into old age as his housekeeper?'

'He might have married. You might have married.'

Lily tossed back the rest of her wine, shrugging. 'I did marry. I married you. Twice over to boot.'

'And in between the first and the second time, you left Lilian behind and became Lily?'

'Yes, I did. How clever of you to work that out. In Paris, in the theatre world, I am known as La Muguette. My friends know me as Lily. To my bank, and on all my official papers, I am Elizabeth Tyler, which was my mother's maiden name, and is also the name that Mr Sinclair had for me.' She smiled as he poured her another glass of champagne. 'In Bordeaux, I was once again Lilian Grantham, and now I am Lilian, Marchioness of Rashfield.'

'La Moo—Muguette? Is it usual to have two names, in France?'

'It's a nickname, that's all—it is the French word for the flower, lily of the valley. A compliment in a way, because usually only the most famous dancers or singers or actresses have a nickname.' Lily wrinkled her nose. 'Some might say the most infamous.'

'Are you infamous?'

'Not because of my behaviour. I am scrupulously honest in my dealings. In a world where everything is an act, that is unusual. I am respected by all who come in contact with me, even those who wish they did not have to deal with me,' she added, her lip curling. 'But I am a successful woman in what is very much a man's world, a world that everyone who doesn't inhabit it likes to think of as salacious, scandalous, louche. I told you that, Oliver.'

'I'm sorry, it was a misguided joke. I'm not questioning your integrity or your honesty.'

'I should hope not!'

'I'm not! It's a world I know nothing of and I'll admit it, I'm fascinated.'

She eyed him suspiciously. 'You have never said so.'

'When has there been time? Besides, you are so prickly about it, so defensive, and you are already giving me so much, I don't feel I have the right to pry. Not that I'm prying. I'm interested. You are interesting. Good grief, Lily, I'm an industrialist who has lived most of his life in the north of England and who makes salt for a living. Your life couldn't be more of a contrast. When I asked you if you were infamous, what I meant was— Oh, I don't know, I simply wanted to know more.'

'You cannot possibly think yourself boring?'

He laughed shortly. 'My esteemed trustees get a very weary look on their faces when I mention my own business. They look down their noses at my factories.'

'Would they rather do without salt?'

'Ha! I did ask them that. They'd rather I sold the whole lot off. They even went as far as to hint that if I did, they'd condescend to allowing me to invest some of the profit in the lands.'

'How frightfully generous of them. Poor men—first they have a marquess who is tainted by being involved in industry and now, though they don't know it, they are about to get a marchioness who is tainted by association with the theatre.'

'Dirt and decadence,' Oliver said, smiling.

She clapped her hands together. 'Excellent! And when they discover that the only reason we are here is to give it all away and to return to our respective dirt and decadence—oh, Oliver, it is a most excellent plot, is it not?'

'It is a *most* excellent plot,' he agreed, entranced, for there was a gleeful look in her eyes that he hadn't seen before. He took a sip of champagne. 'Do you know, I think I might actually enjoy my part in it.'

'As my lord?'

'As my lord, the industrialist, with my lady, the Parisian theatre agent.'

'You cannot tell them that!'

'No, of course not, but there's no reason why we can't bring a touch of theatre to the roles we have to play. There's nothing in Archie's will that says I must actually step into his rather boring shoes and, though I need a wife, there's nothing that says I must acquire a very boring and conventional wife. Look at you, Lily, you're glamorous, chic, sophisticated, self-possessed...'

'Stop! You are making me blush.'

'You don't like compliments, do you?'

'I prefer to deal in truths.'

'That was the truth.' Oliver took another sip of champagne. 'This isn't bad. I might develop a taste for it.'

Lily, as he had expected, happily changed the subject. 'It is an excellent vintage. I assure you I know from drinking from many inferior bottles. It's an acquired taste, and the cheap version gives one a terrible headache and is to be avoided at all costs, but this,' Lily said, raising her glass to him, 'there is nothing like this for making one feel better when everything feels simply too difficult.'

'Is it working?'

For answer, she shifted on the chair, leaning her head back a little and closing her eyes. 'It would help if I was confident that we were going to have a good dinner.'

He took another sip from his glass. The taste was growing on him. He angled himself to face Lily, whose eyes remained closed. She wore a perfume he couldn't put a name to, not flowers, but citrus and a spice of some sort. 'What would be your perfect meal tonight?'

'If artichokes were in season, or asparagus, that is what I'd have, but this is January, not May. Game, I think. I am very fond of *lapin à la moutarde* or *aux pruneaux*. Or perhaps *pintade aux châtaignes*—ah, but, no, chestnuts are also out of season. For tonight, a rustic *poulet grande-mère* would be most acceptable. What do you think?'

She opened her eyes to find him staring at her, entranced. 'I have no idea what any of them are, but you make them all sound delicious and I would happily listen to you reciting a menu in French, even if it consisted of cabbage, carrots and onions.'

Her eyes crinkled with amusement. 'I am very much afraid that is what we will be served, along with the *rosbif*, which you English are so famed for.'

'You are English.'

'Not when it comes to food. Then I am entirely French.'

'Can you cook?'

'*Naturellement*. In Paris, one of the greatest pleasures is to shop in the markets, and then to cook a meal from the provisions you have bought. I don't do it every day, but at least once a week I make a grand dinner for myself.'

'You always eat alone?'

'Not always. I like to dine out with my friends, but when I am at home—yes, I like to eat alone. Do you find that strange?'

'Not a bit of it, I eat alone most nights.'

'And what do you like to eat?'

Oliver winced. 'You'll think me a heathen, for I like plain food. Not roast beef, which sounds no more appealing in French than in English, but pies, stews and fish.'

'None of those rich French sauces, though?' Lily teased.

'Perhaps you can educate me, make me change my mind.'

'Perhaps we will both be surprised by your cousin's chef. And on cue!' Lily said, as a gong rang somewhere. 'I believe we are being summoned.'

The dining room was even colder than the drawing room, but the food, thanks to the copper chafing dishes in which it was served, was at least piping hot. There was neither guinea fowl nor rabbit, but there was an excellent *blanquette de poulet*, or chicken with mushrooms as Oliver's lugubrious butler described it, and the vegetables were, contrary to Lily's expectations, not boiled to within an inch of their lives. Their conversation had been desultory, confined to the safe subjects of food and the weather despite the fact that, as he had promised, the servants had been banished.

The meal had revived her, the conversation before it had intrigued her, so when Oliver suggested a return to the relative warmth of the drawing room to finish the champagne, Lily was happy to agree. It had been a long day, yet it felt unfinished. She and Oliver were no longer on edge, but the forced intimacy of dinner had emphasised the fact that they still barely knew each other.

'How do you like to spend your evenings?' she asked him, noting without surprise that he chose to drink coffee, for he had barely touched his wine at dinner. 'When you are not forced to make polite conversation with your wife, I mean.'

'I work. Read. Like you, I have friends, though I've not seen any of them lately, for I've been spending most of my time in London, the rest of it here. I've only been home three or four times since Archie died and then only for a couple of days.'

'Home being Cheshire? Near New Kilmun, I think? I am woefully ignorant and it would be embarrassing if I didn't know.'

'You're right. There's so much we haven't thought of,' Oliver agreed ruefully. 'I built a new house about five years ago, not far from New Kilmun, but not in the town itself, which is still expanding. We opened a new processing plant about two years ago and we're moving into canning—or we will be, once I am free from Archie's inheritance.'

'Tell me about your new house.'

'It's not big, it's plain, but warm. I have a steam-heating system in all of the main rooms, so you don't need to huddle up to the fire, as you do here. There's a bathroom, too, with hot water and a shower contraption. I confess,' Oliver said, grinning sheepishly, 'I have a bit of a weak spot for modern conveniences.'

'What about the kitchen? Do you have a gas stove?'

'No, it's coal. Gas-fired ranges are still very unreliable, and coal is what my housekeeper prefers.'

'So you are not entirely self-sufficient, you have a housekeeper?'

'Mrs McNair. She lives in New Kilmun, though she comes in every day, and she has help in a couple of times a week. Her husband is one of my foremen. I like to be comfortable and unlike you, by the sounds of it, I need help. I wouldn't know where to start, if I had to cook dinner for myself.'

'I wouldn't know where to start with a steam-heating system. Or indeed a shower contraption, whatever that is. My apartment is not nearly so well equipped.'

'But it's yours. That's what's important, isn't it, to have somewhere to call your own, where you can shut out the world.'

'Why, yes,' Lily agreed. 'Unlike this place, where you have to invite the world in, in order to live in it. Every day must be like a performance on stage. People like Archie have more in common with my clients than they imagine.'

Oliver smiled. 'That's one way of thinking. I suppose they don't know anything different. I prefer my privacy.'

'You're right.' Lily set down her champagne, which was too flat to drink. 'It is important to have a place to retreat to, to shut out the world. It's why I prefer to dine out with my friends and not to entertain in my apartment.'

'Then we have that in common.'

'Yes, though it's not a trait that's compatible with marriage.'

'It depends on the marriage. From the little I've seen of Archie's world, husbands and wives marry for the sake of the title, to get an heir or two, to continue the line, and they probably know less about each other than we do. When you can afford it, it's easy to live separate lives. When you can't, then it's different.'

'You mean the less well off a person is, the more likely they are to marry for love?'

'Not exactly, but the less well off you are, the more time you're going to have to spend with your spouse, so it's a good idea to marry someone whose company you enjoy. It would be condescending and arrogant of me to generalise about my employees, but they are practical men and women, by and large, and the marriages they make are practical. As to love—lord, I know nothing of that and it's none of my business.'

'What about your parents? Were they an affectionate couple?

'I hardly remember them. My father was the second son. He was given an education and a church living—a genteel one, I believe. My mother was from Stockport, born into a respectable family, but not considered good enough for the Turners. When they married, my grandfather refused to have anything to do with them. They moved north and my father took a living in the town. Under the circumstances,' Oliver said, frowning, 'I suppose it must have been a love match. Whether or not they were happy—I have no memories of them being unhappy, but I was only seven or eight when they were killed in an explosion in a factory.'

'Both of them? How tragic. What on earth were they doing there?'

'Meddling was what I was told by my grandfather, years later. He wouldn't tell me any more than that. I did a bit of digging myself, though. I went back to the rectory where I'd been born and the vicar there directed me to a couple of the survivors who remembered my father very fondly. He regularly protested about conditions. I still have no idea why my mother was with him on that particular day. I don't know how we came to be discussing this, it's not as if my trustees are going to quiz you on my childhood.'

'It's fascinating. I see now why you're driven to look after your workers, why you were so determined to build New Kilmun.'

'I'm not trying to rectify what my father thought was wrong, if that's what you mean. It wasn't only my father who had concerns for the conditions in factories or the low wages. Anyone who takes the time to look around them would see that.'

'Not everyone would do something about it.'

'Something else we have in common, then? Isn't that why you invented La Muguette, because you looked around you and didn't like what you saw and decided to do something about it? What got you into that world, Lily?'

'I told you, I had always been interested in the theatre.'

'Were you on the stage? When you left England, when we agreed to go our own ways, is that what you did?'

It was clear now that he had already guessed. 'That was my ambition, but I didn't have that certain something,' Lily confessed.

'You most certainly had guts.'

She laughed, once again surprised by his reaction. 'Respectable women don't go on the stage, Oliver.'

'Is that what your brother thought?'

'How did you guess?'

'"I've always had an interest in the theatre", that's what you told me. And something about not having the talent to be a good actress. I wondered at the time how you could be so certain. Now I understand what you meant earlier, when you were wondering about what your life would have become if Anthony had lived. Did you discuss it with him?' Oliver grinned. 'I know exactly what you mean, when you say that your brother was the conventional type. He thought my ideas for New Kilmun were pure fantasy.'

'I didn't discuss it. I tried to. That was enough.'

'So you gave up on your dream and became his nurse instead?'

'You make it sound very noble, but it was no such thing. Anthony was my brother and I loved him. It was no sacrifice.'

'You were only twenty when he died. I wonder—but what is the point in asking, what if? Fate intervened and you made the most of it. I would have liked to see you perform on stage.'

Lily laughed. 'Not something a marchioness would expect her marquess to say.'

'But we've agreed, haven't we, that we're going to present the world with a very unconventional couple. Do you know, I'm looking forward to that?' The clock on the mantel chimed, and a few moments later, the bell was echoed by the large grandfather clock that stood in the hallway, and outside, another, deeper tolling.

'It's midnight,' Lily said, counting the chimes and getting to her feet. 'I had no idea it was so late. We should go to bed.' Her words brought a vivid image into her head, of Oliver in her bed, and with it a shiver of desire to make the image real. 'I mean, I should go to bed.' Flushing, she realised too late that she'd made it worse. 'Goodnight, Oliver.'

'Lily.' He touched her arm as she turned away, just enough to stop her. 'We have an agreement. I told you, I would never take advantage of this situation and I am a man of my word.'

'I know that.' Touched, she forgot her embarrassment and turned back to face him. 'One thing I have known for certain about you, from the beginning of our first marriage is that you are an honourable man. I am an excellent judge of character, it is one of my biggest strengths and one of the reasons I am so successful in my particular line of work. I trust you. Besides, I am not the kind of woman who allows herself to be taken advantage of.'

'I meant it,' he said earnestly. 'Whatever your experience is, I'm not the sort of man who would expect—to assume— Dammit, what I'm trying to say is, no matter how much I might want to, I would never— I wouldn't expect you to…'

'I wouldn't ever do anything I don't wish to,' Lily said, touched by his incoherence. 'We're acting, Oliver,' she added, as much for her own sake as his. 'When you throw yourself into a part, sometimes you forget that it's not real.' *No matter how much I might want to.* Was it worse, knowing he struggled, too? It made no difference, she told herself firmly. 'Goodnight, Oliver.'

'Goodnight, Lily.'

She waited, feeling foolish, for him to kiss her, to do exactly what he'd said he would not do, and then, feeling even more foolish, she turned away and made for her bedchamber. It was cold. The sheets were freezing despite the warming pan. Lily shivered, snuggling deeper, telling herself she was destined to lie awake all night, and immediately fell into a deep slumber.

The Times,
18th January 1877

Marriage Announcement

Lately on the Continent, at a private ceremony, the Most Honourable Oliver Alastair Turner, Fifth Marquess of Rashfield, to Lilian Mary Grantham.
The couple will take up residence in their country estate of Rashfield Manor in Berkshire and we understand they have no immediate plans to visit their London town house.

Morning Post,
19th January 1877

A French Twist

The tragically premature death of the Fourth Marquess of R. in May last year, following a riding accident, passed the title and estates to his cousin, Mr O.T., a self-made industrialist.

As we informed our illustrious Readers at the time, the new Lord R. seemed set to become one of society's most eligible bachelors, despite his association with industry, for he combined a personable appearance with both wealth and relative youth, being on the right side of forty years.

Alas, the cream of this year's debutantes were deprived of the opportunity to charm the peer, with the unexpected announcement of his marriage in yesterday's press.

The union, which was formalised in France, was to a Miss L.G., a very English name which we surmise belongs to a very English rose, albeit of obscure origins.

The newly-weds are to take up residence in their country house, Rashfield Manor, where His Lordship will now, thanks to his nuptials, be able to assume control of the estate, which has been held in trust since his cousin's demise.

Fortunately for the traditionalists among us, the county of Berkshire, while rich in heritage and history, has no rivers suited to the industrial process of salt-making from which the new Marquess of R. has made his fortune.

Will this hurried and surprising union result in the speedy production of an heir, as is sometimes the case? It would be most improper for us to speculate. We shall, however, watch with interest, and will not hesitate to bring any developments to our devoted Readers.

Chapter Five

Their first day as man and wife at Rashfield Manor was not auspicious. A telegram from Mr Sinclair had informed Lily and Oliver that the trustees had been given formal notice that they were no longer required. When Mr Sinclair arrived in person shortly before noon, however, it was to express his concern that at least three of the six men were inclined to drag their feet about relinquishing control.

Mention had been made of an extended handover in the light of the new Marquess's lack of experience and though Mr Sinclair was anxious to assure Oliver that he had pointed out there was no such requirement, he was concerned that the will did not specify any clear process for reversion of power either.

A delegation of tenant farmers were the next callers, not half an hour after Mr Sinclair left. They wished to offer their congratulations to the Marquess and his new wife, they claimed, but it quickly became clear that they were on the hunt for information. How quickly would their new landlord take up the reins? When would they have the opportunity to air their many complaints? And what, if anything, would the Marquess do to remedy them?

This Lily learned from Oliver later, for while he was closeted with his tenants, she had been pressed into a tour of the house by Mrs Bremner. When the housekeeper discovered that the new Marchioness wasn't in the least bit interested in inspecting the linen cupboard or interfering with what was clearly the well-established management of the staff, she mellowed considerably. Mrs Bremner had been running Rashfield Manor efficiently and without interference from the previous, almost entirely absent, Lady Rashfield for many years and was more than happy to continue to do this.

Over a cup of very milky, very sweet tea which Lily valiantly drank in Mrs Bremner's living room, she turned the conversation first to the matter of meals, discovering to her delight that the kitchen was presided over by the English widow of a French chef, who would be very pleased to serve what Mrs Bremner referred to shudderingly as more Continental fare and to discuss this directly with her new mistress, provided that Mrs Bremner could continue to specify the menus for the servants' hall. Both ladies now being happy with the devolution of power, Lily asked for another cup of tea, and set about extracting the downstairs inside track regarding who was who and what was what and what should be done about it all.

What Lily and Oliver decided to do was host what they referred to between themselves as their taking-charge party, which would also mark the end of Oliver's official mourning for his cousin. This party would be a public, united statement of intent which would make it clear to everyone that the trustees had been replaced and that the Marquess and Marchioness of Rashfield were now in control.

Tenants, the local gentry, villagers, the six trustees and their families were all invited to this event where, radically, they would all be expected to mingle, dance together, eat together and talk together. 'Letting the world see that the wind of change is finally blowing through draughty Rashfield Manor,' as Oliver sardonically put it.

The date had been set for precisely one week after their arrival, and there had barely been time to draw breath since. Lily had put her theatrical experience to excellent use in organising the various sets for dining, conversation, dancing and respite. Oliver had masterminded the guest list and supplies. Whether or not the whirlwind of activity would prove successful, they would discover in less than an hour, when the first guests were due to arrive.

Having made one last tour of the rooms with Mrs Bremner and Riddell, the butler, in tow, which took an age as the butler moved at glacial speed, Lily was checking her toilette in the mirror in her vast, draughty, bedchamber. She had never had a personal maid and saw no reason to engage one now, having learned all the tricks of the trade backstage in Paris.

Tonight, she had piled her hair very high on her head, allowing a few artful tendrils to fall, but eschewing the fashion for decorating it with feathers, ribbons or flowers. Her gown was one of Monsieur Worth's latest creations, a long princess-style bodice in silk, satin and taffeta, all in shades of gold, tightly laced to show off her narrow waist and to put paid to any speculation about a pregnancy engendered by the vile article in the *Morning Post*, which Oliver had angrily tossed in the fire.

The skirts were straight at the front, making the most of her tall, slender figure, but the back fell in a cascade of ivory lace and gold ruffles and pleats into a train. The neckline was cut into a deep vee at the front and back and the sleeves were elbow-length ivory lace. Gold gloves and slippers completed the toilette. It was chic, very French and very striking, far too ostentatious for the event, and therefore, in Lily's view, perfect. What Oliver would think of it, she wasn't sure. In fact, as she applied a touch of rouge to her cheeks and her lips, she wondered if she had gone too far. She was contemplating ringing the bell to ask for a glass of champagne to be brought to her room when there was a tap on the door.

Oliver held out a glass of champagne. 'May I come in? I thought you might appreciate this.'

'You read my mind. What do you think?' Lily added nervously, for he was staring at her. She took a sip from her glass then set it down. 'Too much?'

'*Sacré bleu.*' Oliver whistled. 'You look absolutely, ravishingly, French!'

'*Merci pour le compliment, monsieur le marquess.*' Lily dropped a shallow curtsy to hide her blushes.

He clutched dramatically at his chest. 'Be still my

beating heart. There won't be a single man at our party who will doubt my reasons for marrying you.'

'Not even your trustees?'

'Former trustees as of tonight, whether they like it or not. Lily, you look utterly exquisite.'

'Monsieur Worth knows how to dress a woman.'

'You know how to wear Monsieur Worth's gown. There's only one thing missing.' Oliver pulled a long glittering strand of gold from his pocket and handed it to her. 'The Turner family jewels, my lady. Most of them are hideous, huge big ugly stones, earrings that would pull your lobes off, but I thought you'd like this. I believe it belonged to my grandmother.'

The necklace was a delicate chain of gold set with diamonds and opals, with a central pendant formed of larger stones set like droplets. 'It's beautiful,' Lily whispered, awed. 'I never wear jewellery, but if I did, I'd have chosen this for myself.' She placed the necklace around her throat, where it sat perfectly in the neckline of her dress. *Parfait*. I can't do the catch…'

'Let me.'

He stood behind her, his fingers warm on the nape of her neck. In the mirror she watched him, his hair smoothed back from his brow, his beard neatly trimmed. 'Done,' he said and in the mirror their eyes met. He smoothed his hands over the exposed skin of her shoulders.

She shivered in response. 'We are rehearsing?'

He hesitated, nodding, then he dipped his head, still watching her reflection, pressing the softest of kisses to her shoulder.

She shivered again. She was acting. He was acting. They had both said so.

He kissed her, tiny kisses along the line of her shoulder to the nape of her neck. 'I think that's enough.'

'Yes,' she said, turning in his arms, meaning yes, it was enough, though it wasn't.

'Yes,' he said, giving a sigh which might be a groan.

They were married. They were meant to be in love. She tilted her face in invitation and their lips met. Briefly. Agonisingly briefly.

'Lily,' he said, her name a whisper. 'Oh, Lily.'

She gave in to temptation, pulling him towards her. He kissed her firmly, the kiss of a man who knew what he was doing, making no attempt to hold her, giving her every chance to push him away. She opened her mouth to him, kissing him back. The kiss of a woman who also knew what he was doing. To prove a point, she told herself. To prove that she could and that it meant nothing. His arms went around her. She put her arms around him. The kiss deepened.

He let her go. She pushed him away. Oliver swore under his breath. Lily cursed herself. 'Enough,' she said, thrown, thinking, *far too much*. 'I think we are ready.'

He nodded. His breathing mimicked hers, fast, ragged, shallow. 'Absolutely, ready, my love,' he said. 'May I say that you look quite ravishing.'

She was not fooled, but nor, she suspected, was he. It didn't matter. What mattered was to continue with the charade. She dropped another little curtsy. *'Merci pour le compliment, encore!'* She allowed her eyes to travel over his figure, allowed her alter ego, his wife, to relish the alluring sight he made in his neatly fitted black evening clothes and to imagine the man beneath. 'My lord! You look extremely—I won't say ravishing, but very handsome.'

'Thank you, my lady.' He gave her a mocking bow. 'Our guests will be arriving any minute.'

'Then you had better wipe your mouth because you have a little of my lip rouge on it.' Lily picked up her glass and drained it. 'A successful dress rehearsal, yes?'

He hesitated only a moment before following her lead. 'Yes. Now it's time to go on stage. Are you ready?'

'Almost.' She dabbed on a little more lip rouge, conscious of him watching her, determined not to let it distract her, and slipped her fan on to her wrist. 'Now.' Lily slipped her hand into his arm. 'What will we do if no one turns up?'

He opened the bedroom door. Voices, laughter, the boom of Riddell's sonorous voice making announcements greeted them. 'I don't think we need to worry about that.'

'We are late for our own party.'

Oliver smiled down at her. 'We're newly-wed and wildly in love. I don't think anyone's going to chide us for it.'

They descended the left-hand side of the staircase from the second to the first floor, pausing on the turn where the two wings joined. Lily checked her train, then turned to him, back straight, head high. Her expression was quite serene, but when she placed her hand on his arm, Oliver could feel her fingers trembling. She gave him a shaky smile. 'I have invested in many plays, but I've never starred in one with so much at stake.'

'While speaking for myself, I am making my debut.'

'And showing an admirable control.'

'Because I have you by my side.' He squeezed her fingers. 'We're in this together, remember?'

He was rewarded with one of Lily's proper smiles. A smile that made her eyes light up, and each time it happened, it gave him a warm glow of satisfaction, for it was a rare sight. 'The curtain's up, let us go forth and conquer.'

Her smile changed as they turned the corner and took the first step on to the landing where the two staircases merged to become the grand staircase. He didn't know how she did it, but she seemed to him to glitter, as if she was under a spotlight, and within a few seconds all eyes were on them. She nipped his arm and Oliver attended to his own smile as he surveyed the huge number of people below in the grand hallway that Lily had transformed into a reception room and ballroom. He could see the trustees standing apart in a huddle. None of them had brought their wives, or, if they had, the women had deserted them.

The gentry were easy to pick out, in a separate group forming centre stage, the men in their black evening clothes, the women more gaudily garbed in silk and feathers. The biggest group, spreading out around the wings of the stage Lily had created, through the big front door which lay open, and out on to the front steps were the people he cared most about here, the ones who had even more at stake than he did. Farmers and their families, dressed in their Sunday best and looking unsurprisingly awkward. But they were here, that was what mattered, and they would report back to those who were not what he was planning to say later.

As they walked together down the rest of the stairs, stopping three from the bottom as she had specified, Oliver caught the haughty, disapproving eye of Sir Everard Hale and, out of the blue, panic gripped him. This was a mistake. He should have divided and conquered. That was what he usually did and it almost always succeeded. There were too many people here, too many different vested interests, too vast a gulf between their lives. The sea of faces swam out of focus before him.

Lily's hand tightened on his arm. He stared at her, frantically trying to recall what he was to say. 'Welcome,' she mouthed, reminding him of his cue.

He cleared his throat. 'Welcome,' he said. 'Ladies and gentlemen.' Take a breath, he remembered. 'My wife and I…'

A muted cheer greeted this phrase, just as Lily had predicted it would. Oliver's panic faded. He smiled down at her gratefully. 'My wife and I would like to welcome you to Rashfield Manor. I never thought I would become a marquess, but thanks to the tragic death of my cousin, that is what I now am. I never believed I would become a husband, but from the moment I met this woman who stands by my side, that is what I wished to be. It was the happiest day of my life when she agreed to marry me. The icing on the wedding cake is that I am now able to take on the full mantle of responsibility that I inherited more than six months ago and to do it with the woman I love by my side.'

Here, Oliver paused to give Lily what she had described as an adoring puppy look, which she returned with what she called her starry-eyed gaze.

'This will be a fresh start,' he continued in a different tone, surveying his audience. 'A new regime.' He looked directly at the cluster of trustees. 'Commencing now,' he said, 'the business of this estate will be run from here, by me.' Consternation on one side of the hall. In the middle, his neighbours were looking uncertainly at each other. In the wings, a definite show of enthusiasm.

'Things will be different,' he said firmly. 'For now, though, my wife and I…' He gazed down into Lily's eyes. Adoring puppy was called for again. She had worked so hard to bring this night about. Without her, he would never have dreamed up an event like this. He abandoned adoring in favour of something more real. Admiration. 'My *lovely* wife and I wish you to enjoy our hospitality. There is food in the dining room. There's a place for conversation in the drawing room. And here, later, I hope you will join us in celebrating our union with a dance.'

He planted an unrehearsed kiss on Lily's lips. He felt the quiver of her response. Feigned? Of course it was! Applause and cheers forced him to release her. He took a bow, holding her hand, while she dropped a curtsy.

'Bravo,' she whispered.

Their performance was exhausting and not all of it went to plan. It proved to be impossible to force the local gentry and Oliver's tenants to mix, so the new Marquess and Marchioness were forced first to do the rounds of the former.

'In France,' she replied, again and again, to the ques-

tion of where they'd met, avoiding being more specific.
'A *coup de foudre*,' she said, placing a hand over her
heart, 'for both of us.'

Oliver, who had been unable to say 'love at first
sight' without grimacing, no matter how much she
coached him, said simply, over and over again, that
she was 'the only one for me and that was that'. Their
English audience, as she suspected, were embarrassed
by the excess of emotion. The few more specific questions about their courtship were countered by a gentle
hand kiss and a besotted smile.

Conversations were quickly turned. Lily lost count of
the number of people she was introduced to, the people
who promised to call on her, to present their daughters
to her, to send her cards for gatherings she would not
attend, to embroil her in good works she had no interest
in. Her failure to take on the role of Lady of the manor
would offend them, but it would be worse and more
dangerous, she had agreed with Oliver, if she made
any attempt to embrace it, to form friendships or alli-
ances that would perforce be abandoned when she quit
the marriage and left the country.

She didn't know these people and they would never
know her, but she hadn't expected to feel guilty about
her deception. Watching Oliver fumbling for an excuse when he was invited to join the local hunt made
her wonder if he was feeling the same. He had been
so intent on securing the future of his tenants, had he
thought about the effect the closure of Rashfield Manor
would have on others, not least the staff?

She was accumulating a very long list of issues to
be discussed with him, but there was no time at pres-

ent, for at last they had cleared the first section of their audience and Mr Sinclair had appeared, ushering them up to the drawing room to face the trustees. Lily had not expected to enjoy the experience of being inspected by the six men as being fit for purpose, but she hadn't anticipated being so riled by their treatment of Oliver.

Their condescending attitude to the new Marquess, whom they addressed as if he were a schoolboy, the smug air of entitlement and arrogance with which they dispensed unwanted and unsolicited advice, brought her temper from a slow simmer to a boil. She need not have worried. Oliver's masterly destruction of the construction of the will, his dissection of the law and, more than anything, the clear authority in his voice brooked no argument.

Though Sir Everard Hale and the two older men stubbornly refused to concede, the three other men shook Oliver's hand and offered him hearty congratulation on his succession and his new bride. His 'very delightful' wife, said one. His 'most beautiful' wife, said the other. His 'quite fascinating' wife, the third said, anxious not to be outdone, begging for a dance later.

'Stupid old fools,' Oliver said, leaving the older men to Mr Sinclair. 'Two of them hadn't ever met Archie.'

'You were very brusque with them,' Lily said.

'Are you worried I'm making enemies? There's nothing they can do. The will was clear on only one thing, that I have to be married, and I am. You were right,' Oliver said, 'it was the only foolproof solution, my clever wife.' He grinned. 'My clever, delightful, beautiful, fascinating wife.'

Lily, who was used to being outshone by her clients,

had found the compliments embarrassing. 'Clearly, the gentlemen need to get out more in society.'

'Oh, I doubt very much they'd meet anyone like you there, my love.'

They were alone in the passageway outside the drawing room. 'Society's loss,' Lily said flippantly.

'My gain. I am extremely fortunate to be able to call you my wife.' Oliver took her gloved hand, lifting it to his lips. 'Lily…'

The sound of the gong made them both jump. 'Supper already,' she said anxiously. 'We're going to have to work very hard to ensure your neighbours don't keep your tenants from joining in. Our cook has made a huge selection of food suitable for every taste, but it is all served in the one room. Do you think it was a mistake?'

'It's too late now. Let's go and see what we can do to persuade people to mix.'

They did not succeed and, as the evening progressed with the various factions refusing steadfastly to mingle, Oliver watched Lily become more and more downhearted. She hid it well. She had the knack of being able to adapt her conversation to her audience, a talent that in his experience was rarer than it should be and one which he reckoned must stand her in good stead in Paris.

She could be standoffish, he'd seen that with those blasted trustees, but she could also set people at ease, finding common ground with almost every woman she spoke to, in conversing about food, kitchens, recipes and markets. He'd had no idea the subject could be so all-consuming, nor that her interest in it was so very French!

When she was less engaged with the topic of conversation she cleverly let the other people talk, throwing in questions when they faltered, and though she never let her eyes drift, he noticed that she had a way of tapping her forefinger against her leg when she was bored. The subjects of babies and dogs had that effect, as did horses, hunting, the weather and any discussion of ailments.

'I shall take my leave of you now, Rashfield.'

Hale and his two cronies appeared at his elbow with a ruthless disregard for the conversation he and Lily had painstakingly struck up with the tenants of one of his best farms. The farmer and his wife immediately withdrew.

'Sir Everard.' Lily made no attempt to hide her annoyance. 'Did not your mother teach you that it was rude to interrupt?'

The old man bristled. 'I beg your pardon!'

'It is not my pardon you should be begging.'

'Sir Everard is leaving, my love,' Oliver said, making no attempt to disguise his relief. 'We don't wish to detain him, do we?'

He waited for Lily to bid the man a polite goodnight. 'Oh,' she said, looking quite downcast, 'but you will miss the dancing, Sir Everard.'

The old man looked pointedly at his stick. 'I don't dance.'

'Gout?' Lily enquired. 'The result of too much claret, perhaps?'

'I don't imbibe.'

'Goodness, you don't dance, you don't drink. What is your particular vice, then, I wonder?'

'If I have a failing, Lady Rashfield, it is that I am overly diligent,' the old man retorted. 'I will bid you goodnight, my lady. And you, Rashfield.'

'*Touché*, Sir Everard,' Lily said, watching him depart. 'I'm not sorry,' she added, turning to Oliver. 'I couldn't resist and you did say that there was nothing he could do.'

'Yes, my love, you were simply following where I led, I see that. I must make a point of setting you a better example.'

'I am not going to rise to that!'

'I didn't think you would.' He smiled down at her as the orchestra struck up. 'Shall we dance?'

'Isn't that a polka?'

'It is. A great leveller of a dance, I hope. Do you know how to perform it?'

'Of course I know how—do you?'

'Oh, I think I'll stumble through. Enthusiasm hides a multitude of technical sins.' The marble floor was bereft of other couples. 'It looks like we'll have to show the way,' Oliver said. 'Tonight's finale. Are you ready?'

Lily hooked her train over her wrist. 'It depends on what you have planned.'

'Make a bow, my love,' he said, twirling her out.

'Oliver!'

She was laughing now, still unsure, but following his cue as she bowed to the audience. They had the attention of everyone in the room, he could see. What the devil did he think he was playing at, making a spectacle of himself like this? It wasn't in the least like him! But it was fun, all the same.

The orchestra were waiting for them, also taking

their lead from him. Oliver took Lily into a hold. He had never danced a polka in a ballroom before and it was not a ballroom version of the dance he led Lily into now. Pulling her closer, he set off on the first circuit of the relatively small space. She followed him easily and gracefully.

'Ready?' he whispered, and without giving her a chance to reply, executed a tight spin, and began on a second, much more flamboyant circuit. She moved fluidly, her lower body tight against his, the line of her back and her arm swaying gracefully. He could smell her perfume, her powder, her soap. Another spin made her gown fly out behind her, all but lifted her feet off the floor, and he felt her breath on his cheek as she gave a little huff of laughter. He forgot where he was.

The floor became crowded. He was dimly aware that they had finally achieved their aim, all of the guests mingling, dancing polkas of hugely varying degrees of competence and flamboyance. When the music came to an end their guests were laughing, clapping, stamping their feet, demanding another. The band struck up again. He would happily have continued to dance with Lily, but as he pulled her into his arms, a man touched his shoulder.

'My dance, I believe?'

The youngest of his former trustees bowed to Oliver's wife. Lily cast him a humorous look. He wasn't jealous. He had no cause to be jealous and no right to feel possessive. Lily wasn't really his wife. All the same, he'd rather not watch her whirling around the floor in another man's arms. He spotted the woman who was their nearest neighbour and made his bow. This time, the polka he danced was rather more sedate.

It was after twelve. The last of their guests had finally left, flatteringly late. Oliver poured Lily a glass of champagne from one of the open bottles sitting in the huge silver bowl full of melted ice. 'You've had nothing to drink all night since the glass I brought to your bedchamber,' he said, handing it to her.

'I've asked Mrs Bremner to send the staff to bed, to leave clearing up until the morning.'

The front door creaked shut and she heard the clunk of the bolts as they were drawn. A few moments later, Riddell appeared. The butler checked that the last of the gaslights were turned down, leaving only the candles burning, then disappeared through the baize door at a stately pace. Oliver poured himself a glass of wine. They clinked glasses. 'To a mostly successful party,' he said.

'Mostly?'

'I only got to dance with my wife once.'

'You didn't ask me again.'

'I couldn't get near you—you were much in demand. Aren't you tired?'

She shook her head. 'I am up there,' she said, indicating the ceiling. 'I need to float gently down to earth.'

'I feel exactly the same. Is it always like that?'

'After a performance, you mean? Sometimes. In the early days, when I didn't know that I wasn't good enough, and the performance went well.'

'I think our performance went very well, don't you?'

'It depends on how you define success,' Lily replied. 'Where did you learn to polka like that?'

'Dance halls in Stockport and Liverpool. I used to go dancing on a Saturday night with some of the lads from my factory, in the early days.'

'Dance halls!' Lily exclaimed. 'You!'

'Yes, even I required some respite from work.'

'Goodness. Did you walk out with any of the young ladies you met there?'

'No, I did not. They were all very respectable young ladies—most of them, at any rate. I was always careful not to give the wrong impression. Even then,' Oliver said, staring into his champagne glass, 'I was the master, you know? It's why I stopped going out with the fellows in the end, too. It got so awkward. One minute you're having a laugh, then someone tells a bawdy joke or makes a remark that might be mistaken for criticism and there's a sudden silence.' He took a sip of his wine and began to meander aimlessly around the room. 'So I stopped going and made new friends. Men who didn't work for me.'

'What about Mr Sinclair?'

'Iain's different. We've been friends for years and, though he does work for me, I'm not his master.'

'Do you miss them, those lads from your younger days?'

'At first I did, but it was a long time ago. They're nearly all married now, family men. We don't have much in common any more, save for the factory and the fact they live in New Kilmun.'

Lily topped up her champagne and sat down on

one of the chairs that lined the makeshift dance floor. 'When I gave up acting and started to represent the women I had been on stage with, it was awkward, too. As their agent, I usually got them much better rates, I saved them from being…from being harassed…but I discovered the more successful I was in negotiating on their behalf, the more they resented me slightly, because I took my cut.'

'A fair share of something they'd never have got on their own.'

'Yes, but they don't all see it that way. When things go wrong, it's easy to blame me because I put them there in the first place. I accept it,' Lily said, 'but at times it makes me—it can be lonely, you know?'

'Especially since your work is unique, from what you've said,' Oliver said, coming to join her. 'At least I have my fellow factory owners to share my woes with.'

She laughed softly. 'I'll wager you don't do that.'

'No, but I could if I needed to.'

'Well, so could I share my woes with my friends, if I wished.'

'But you don't.'

She shrugged. 'I don't know why we are talking about sharing woes. Aside from the fact that you only managed to dance with me once, did you think tonight was a success, Oliver? Seriously.'

'Why would anyone question my reasons for marrying you, after tonight?'

'I annoyed Sir Everard.'

'So did I. You see, even on that front we were united.'

'I think some of your neighbours found me…' Lily shrugged '…not what they expected.'

'What do you think they expected?'

'I don't know. Someone younger for a start, much younger. You know the type, a young lady of *breeding* age. A simpering virgin…'

Oliver burst out laughing. 'We've been married for— what is it, two weeks tomorrow?'

'Today,' Lily said, looking at the clock. 'I did not mean to cast aspersions on your manhood.'

'Thank you!'

'You know what I meant.'

'That the Marquess of Rashfield would be expected to marry a suitable bride.' He screwed up his nose. 'Let me see, one with the correct lineage, who knows how to wear a coronet and make conversation with the other titled ladies. A woman suitable to produce my son and heir. Have I remembered that correctly? And now you tell me that she must also be a simpering virgin, too.'

'No, what I'm telling you is that several of the ladies here tonight thought so.'

'I'll wager none of the gentlemen did, though.'

'None of those gentlemen would ever have perceived me to be a suitable bride.'

'More fool them, then! What does it matter what any of them thought anyway, Lily? You asked me, did I think this night has been a success? Seriously, I think it was a triumph. We've done what we set out to do, paraded ourselves in front of the country set, my tenants *and* the trustees, as loving newly-weds. We achieved all of that in one night! I couldn't have played my part with a different woman by my side. Your *suitable* woman would have bored me to tears. You, on the other hand— do you know, I rather like being married to you.'

'You mean, temporarily.'

'I mean temporarily. Simpering virgins are not for me.'

'That's as well, for I am neither simpering nor a virgin.'

The former was obvious, the latter he had worked out for himself, though he was not prepared for her to be so blunt. 'Neither am I,' he said, to buy time to work out his response.

'You are a man.'

That look she gave him, not ashamed but definitely defiant. Was he shocked? No, he was envious. Oliver finished his champagne and set the glass down on the floor. 'I'm thirty-four, you are thirty-one, of course we've both had lovers,' he said. 'It's not as if we're married—well, only to each other, and that didn't count, we agreed from the start it would be in name only.'

'I never took a lover when I was living under your roof.'

When? he wondered and with a pang of regret wished, pointlessly, that it had been him. No, that wasn't right. What he wished was that he could be her lover now. What he wished was that she hadn't been so insistent on making that impossible. 'I think it would be a good idea if we agreed that neither of us will take a lover while we're living under this roof,' he said.

'I would not dream of...'

'It was a joke!' Oliver said hastily, cursing his own ineptness.

'Not a very good one.'

'No.' He wanted to make love with her. Every instinct told him they would be good together. He had no idea why he was so certain, though the kiss they'd shared tonight had been proof. He'd never felt like this before, he was absolutely certain, and almost as certain that she felt it, too. Yet she was set against it. Rehearsing, that's what she'd called their kiss.

Perhaps she was right. The situation was complex enough. Oliver stretched his legs out, muffling a yawn. 'It's late. Your former lovers are none of my business, any more than mine are of yours. I don't even know how we got on to the subject.'

'Suitable wives.'

'Oh, yes, suitable wives.' He reached for her hand. 'Thank you, most eminently suitable wife, for making tonight such a success. You were the best leading lady this man could ever want.'

'I couldn't have asked for a better leading man.'

Acting. Role-playing. Was she fooling herself? He didn't care. He got up, pulling her with him. 'Indulge me, then, in a second dance. After such a performance, I feel an encore is called for.'

'There's no music.'

He pulled her into a close hold, one arm around her waist. 'We don't need music.'

Lily rested her head on his shoulder and slid her free arm around his neck. They began to move, slowly, around the dance floor. 'Are you sure this is an encore and nothing else?'

Holding her like this, he was sure of nothing save that he didn't want it to end. 'I made a promise,' he said. 'It is an encore, providing you don't wish it to be anything else.'

If he had not been holding her so closely, he wouldn't

have felt her stumble. It was reassuring, knowing she found the situation so confusing, but it would be easier if she didn't. And if she didn't, he wouldn't be finding it confusing. 'Forget it,' Oliver said. 'Let's stop trying to give it a name and enjoy the dance.'

She sighed. He thought she was going to let him go, but she nestled closer. He tightened his hold on her and they continued to dance, moving slowly, saying nothing more. Her fingers crept round his neck to curl into his hair. He slid his hand down from her waist, following the line of her bodice, to rest on her hip. Still they danced, their bodies as close as their clothing allowed.

If she stopped dancing he would let her go. He didn't want to stop dancing, so he stopped thinking. Her hand drifted down from his neck, tracing the line of his spine through his evening coat, sliding it under the tails, to rest on his buttocks. He stopped dancing. She lifted her head from his shoulder and met his gaze. Lids heavy. No question of what she wanted, but he had to ask all the same. 'Lily?'

'Lily,' he'd said and she knew it was a question, she knew she should refuse him, but she couldn't.

'*Encore*, Oliver,' she said. Again, it meant. Another kiss, she meant. But if he took it for the end of their performance, she didn't care.

The kiss was like their dance, slow and languorous. A kiss that could go on for ever. That could be the beginning of the night, or the end. She stroked his face, enjoying the bristle of his beard on her palm, the softness of his mouth on hers, then the touch of his tongue. Her tight bodice became constricting as her nipples hardened. Their hands unclasped. Their kiss deepened. She slid her hand up inside his coat, smoothing over the silk of his waistcoat, feeling his muscles tense in response. Her clothing thwarted him, her bustle, the layers of lace and ruffles. He abandoned the attempt, smoothing his hands over her arms, her back.

He broke the kiss, but only to kiss her neck, tilting her back just a fraction to kiss her collarbone, her shoulder, then down, fluttering, rousing kisses along the line of her gown, licking into the deep vee and the valley between her breasts. His breath was warm on her skin. More kisses along the neckline, back up to her shoulder, her collarbone, her neck, and then their mouths met again. Less restrained, but not unleashed. Deep kisses that made her belly clench, set up a clamouring for more inside her.

Encore. Did she want more? The question crept its way into her foggy brain at the same time as their kisses drifted to a close. Unquestionably. Would it be a good idea? Unquestionably not. Did he think so, too?

He let her go. It was up to her. She forced herself to step back. It was the right thing to do, even though it was what she least wanted. *'Bravo,'* she forced herself to say.

His smile was twisted. *'Bravo,'* he replied sardonically. 'Go to bed. I'll check the gas and snuff the candles.'

Lily nodded. They understood one another. Tomorrow, she would be glad of that. 'Goodnight, my lord,' she said, picking up her skirts and making for the staircase.

Chapter Six

Rashfield Manor—two weeks later

Lily poured herself a cup of coffee and buttered a warm bread roll. Across from her, Oliver was flicking through his correspondence. A fat package addressed to her in Mr Sinclair's hand lay unopened by her plate, letters, notes and contracts which Hélène sent to be checked and authorised, though the truth was, her very able deputy had already made all the decisions and was merely being courteous. There were arrangements for Hélène to telegraph Mr Sinclair if there was anything urgent. The facility had so far not been used.

It was more than two weeks since their taking-charge party, and Oliver had set about taking charge with gusto, spending a great deal of each day visiting his farms. He had thrown himself into a study of the lands he had inherited, intent on understanding the complex relationship between the different farms and produce, how they worked, as well as the economics of their successes and failures.

With the help of Mrs Bremner's nephew, Lily had built a model of the estate which sat on a table in the study. Like a stage set for a new production, it could be reshaped and reconfigured depending on Oliver's latest thinking—and he had already done a great deal of reshaping and reconfiguring work on it. Six months of waiting to take control of his inheritance had produced a vast number of pent-up ideas which he was keen to try out.

Lily's role was to talk to people, farmer's wives and their children, villagers, shopkeepers, anyone who had an opinion on how the estate should be run, what the problems were and who the problems were. It was fascinating work and she thoroughly enjoyed it, for it was precisely the kind of work she did every day, though in a very different milieu. She would never be a countrywoman, farming would never hold a fascination for her in the way the theatre did, but she was pleased to discover that her instincts had been right. She was proving useful.

'You haven't opened your post.' Oliver pushed his own correspondence to one side. 'Do you miss the theatre?'

'I've not had much time to think about it.'

'You've been an invaluable help here. You know that, don't you?'

'I am very good at getting people to talk,' she replied, picking up her coffee cup to disguise her blush.

'And at finding out what their hidden talents are. I'm going to have a chat with the miller, Jamie Edgehill, today as you suggested. Sound him out about the plan, see what he thinks. He'd be a good champion to have on our side. I had no idea that being the lead bellringer held so much sway locally.'

'The fact that he's married to the local midwife helps,' Lily said drily.

'I know, never underestimate the women,' Oliver teased. '*Do* you miss the theatre world?'

'Not yet. I like to be busy and this is a very new challenge. Hélène seems to be relishing the responsibility just a little bit too much for my liking. I'm worried that when I go back to Paris, I'll find she has set up on her own. It's silly of me, because I'm delighted that my business is in safe hands, but...'

'You don't like the feeling that someone else can manage it as well as you?'

She laughed sheepishly.

'I feel the same. I keep expecting a telegram from my man at New Kilmun telling me he needs me to hotfoot it there, but it hasn't come yet. However, at least we've got things underway here.'

Lily took a sip of coffee. 'We are not proving very popular with our more genteel neighbours.'

Oliver shrugged. 'That was never the intention. We made it clear at our party that things here were going to change. They can accept it or not, I don't see what difference it makes. If I get this right, we'll have a group of tenant farmers who collectively control a far bigger mass of land than all of them put together. All that power, in the hands of the "great unwashed",' he said, his lip curling. 'They'll be up in arms.'

'Exactly what you don't want to happen.'

'I didn't mean literally.'

'Even so, but if we can avoid estranging them, so much the better.'

'What do you suggest?' He smiled wickedly. 'Put on some form of entertainment, a play perhaps, for them?'

'Oh, perfect! Do be serious, Oliver.'

Oliver got up. 'I'm fed up being serious. It's a lovely morning, for once. Look, it's actually stopped raining. Shall we take a walk in the garden?'

'Don't you have work to do?'

'Always. And so do you,' he said, nodding at her unopened packet. 'But we can afford an hour to ourselves. We've talked about nothing but Rashfield Manor and Rashfield estates for two weeks. We've forgotten that we're supposed to be the newly wedded Lord and Lady of the manor, wildly in love.'

'We won't have an audience, unless you count the gardeners.'

He held out his hand and she took it, letting him pull her to her feet. 'We had fun, the night of the party, didn't we?'

'I don't see...'

'I've been worried that I—that you thought we'd taken it too far,' Oliver blurted out. 'Our act. The encore afterwards. That after all I said, all I promised, you thought I'd taken advantage.'

She stared at him, completely bewildered. 'How? Why?'

'You've been so businesslike, even when we're alone.'

'So have you!'

'Because I thought—' He broke off, smiling ruefully. 'I kept thinking about what you said. "Goodnight, my lord".'

'It seemed wise,' Lily said limply, after a moment. 'It happens all the time in the theatre. Leading actors and actresses, they get carried away with their roles. Being in a play together, it's a highly emotional experience, but it's not real emotion and it's easy to forget that.'

'So you were reminding me.'

'Both of us. I was reminding both of us.'

'And that's why you've been so brusque.'

'Businesslike, you said. I thought it was what you wanted.'

'And when we've been out on the farms together...'

'Acting wildly in love would simply have embarrassed those people. You know that, Oliver. Besides, that tale—it was only for your trustees. To prevent any awkward questions. We've done that, haven't we?'

'Hale is still querying my intentions, directly and through Sinclair, but the rest have gone very silent. Perhaps we should hold a dinner party for our neighbours?'

'Why would we do that?'

'Practice.' Oliver gave her a look, the one she had named 'adoring puppy'. 'You never know when we might be required to perform again, my lady.'

She had refused to allow herself to fret over his sticking to the rules of their engagement. She had refused to allow herself to wish that she had not been so strict. It would have been too easy to cast caution to the winds that night and to allow their kisses to lead to lovemaking. She remembered telling herself at the time that she would be glad she had not and she had been glad. Most of the time, she had been glad.

Some of the time—lying in bed at night, some of the time—she had allowed herself to imagine making love with Oliver. It was a futile exercise, making her ache with longing, and the depth of the ache serving to emphasise the rightness of her decision not to! She did not recall ever feeling like this about any other man. She desired. Desire was sated. The love affair came to an end. Was it because she was so set on refusing to sate her desire for Oliver that it burned so determinedly? She'd thought that before, that it was natural to long more for what one could not have. If she gave in, just once, would it restore her perspective?

The idea was dizzyingly attractive. Besides, Oliver was right, they might indeed be required to act again and they were out of practice. She smiled saucily at him. 'What kind of practice are you imagining? A stolen kiss in the walled garden, perhaps?'

For answer, he swept her theatrically into his arms. 'Or the breakfast parlour.'

He was acting, Lily told herself, as she put her arms around his neck. And so was she. 'Riddell might come in at any moment. You don't want to give him an apoplexy.'

'Definitely not. We wouldn't even know he was having one for about twenty minutes!' Oliver brushed his cheek against hers. 'You smell delicious.'

His beard tickled. 'You smell of lemon.'

'Soap.' He nibbled the lobe of her ear and she shivered. 'Lily?'

'Mmm…?'

'Do you really think that Riddell is of an apoplectic nature?'

She smoothed her hand over his cheek, then curled her fingers into his hair, pulling him towards her. 'I've never once seen him flustered.'

'That's reassuring,' Oliver murmured, his lips inches from hers. 'Oh, Lily.'

Oh, Oliver, she thought, as their lips met, because she wasn't acting and she wasn't at all sure that he was either. But he knew exactly how to kiss, exactly how she liked to be kissed, and it was only a kiss. No one had ever got it so right before. If she didn't kiss him now, she might never kiss him again and she'd have missed out on the kiss of a lifetime.

Lips. Tongue. And hands. Feathering over the nape of her neck. Feathering down her arms, then wrapping around her waist. Letting her make her own mind up about moving towards him, pressing herself closer like this, and then that sigh he gave. Or she gave. Her hands sliding under his coat. The slippery silk of his waistcoat. The taut slope of his buttocks. Breathe. His eyes dark with desire. The way he looked at her. Mouths again. More kisses.

A click of the door handle. Startled, they turned around in time to see it slowly close. Flushed, dishevelled, both of them. 'I think that was a pretty successful rehearsal,' Lily said, in an attempt to bring herself back down to earth.

Oliver drew her a straight look. 'I wasn't acting.'

She was too shaken to risk being so honest. She wished he had lied. 'When one is immersed in the role,' Lily said, 'that's how it feels. As if it's not acting.'

'I wasn't acting. I find you extremely attractive. I don't know because I've never kissed an actress before, but I didn't think you were acting either.'

She turned away to pick up her coffee cup, but it was

empty. She set it down. 'I wasn't,' she confessed, unable to lie.

'I stand by what I said from the start. I would never take advantage of the situation, but if you wish—' Oliver broke off.

Lily looked round. 'If I wish what?'

'Nothing. I'm not thinking straight. Forget it. I have some telegrams to send and you have your post to attend to. I'll have some fresh coffee sent up. I'll be in my office.'

The door closed behind him.

If you wish…

Lily sat down at the breakfast table and pulled the packet of correspondence towards her. *If you wish us to be lovers?* If she had met Oliver in Paris, she would have taken him as a lover. She could not recall ever feeling so strongly attracted to a man. Her last lover had been over a year ago now. A wine merchant. She never took a lover connected with the theatre.

Would it be a mistake to take Oliver as her lover? Everyone assumed they were lovers—or at least that as man and wife they made love! If Oliver's kisses were the perfect kisses, would he be the perfect lover? The shiver that went through her made it clear what her body thought of that question. If they became lovers, it would add authenticity to their claim to be married.

Honestly, Lily? Now who is getting carried away with her role?

She had never felt like this before. That in itself should be a warning to keep him at arm's length. Oliver was different. She didn't know why and she didn't want to find out why because different would mean something more lasting and Lily didn't want lasting.

'His Lordship suggested that a fresh pot of coffee would be amenable, my lady.'

Lily jumped. 'Oh, Riddell. Thank you. I didn't hear you come in.'

'No, my lady,' the butler replied solemnly.

Was that a knowing look he drew her as he picked up the empty coffee-pot? She decided it was safer to tell herself that she had imagined it. 'Thank you, Riddell.'

The door closed, leaving her alone once more. She didn't want to need someone else. She had her own life. She didn't want to share it with anyone. But oh, oh, oh, she didn't want to miss out on the promise of that kiss. Just once…

Non! She was thinking like an idiot and she was not an idiot. Time to get back to the real world. Lily broke the seal on the packet of letters. All of them were in Hélène's hand. Mr Sinclair had enclosed a compliments slip.

I regretfully draw this to your attention.

Attached to it was a newspaper clipping.

Morning Post,
9th February 1877

A Very Convenient Marriage

When the marriage of the Fifth Marquess of R. to an unknown lady was announced last month, there was much speculation as to the reasons for the hasty nature of the alliance. Those of a generous nature thought the new peer anxious not to make the mistake of his predecessor and to secure the succession.

A guest at the party given by the newly-wed couple has, however, informed us that Lady R.'s figure is unfashionably and unnaturally slender. A female of more mature years than any of the genteel guests were expecting, the Marchioness has a penchant for ostentatious gowns and seems to be equally ostentatious in her emotions.

Though Lady R. was born in England, by nature, we fear, she is thoroughly French. The lady's politics are also unrepentantly French—of the Revolutionary kind.

The gentry of Berkshire who attended the party were astounded to discover that the invitation had been extended to Lord R.'s tenants and that all classes of guests were expected to dine in the same room, from the same plates, and eat the same food.

Readers, there must now be some serious reservations about this insurgent Marchioness. Though the Marquess of R. was born into a noble family, he was bred not to the aristocracy but to industry. His predecessor, knowing that such a man would require a great deal of indoctrination and support, had the excellent sense to appoint a group of six wise men, trustees who would ensure that the customs and traditions of his estate and lands would continue unsullied.

Marriage has put an end to that support, dragging up the anchor that the trustees provided and setting this new, untutored peer adrift on uncharted seas. An English Rose—a young lady raised properly—would have provided the ballast he needed. The same cannot be said of the siren Marchioness he has acquired.

It is a well-established fact within the cognoscenti that the most senior of the trustees, Sir E. H., had strong reservations about the industrialist's ability to manage landed gentry estates. Now we have to question his judgement in his choice of wife.

Who is this mysterious woman? Must suspicions be aroused by her lack of family and history? Is she fit, Dear Reader, for the elevated position marriage has given her? Was Lord R. duped into marrying her? Or is it possible that there is an even more dastardly reason for this very unconventional alliance? A convenient match driven not by passion but by profit?

Is this the reason why the couple are so determined to remain in the country and eschew the pleasures of the ton? *Our country source tells us that since her appearance at the party, Lady R. has become something of a recluse.*

We have posed a great number of questions about this misalliance. Only Lord and Lady R. know the answers. For now.

Chapter Seven

'Oliver!' Lily burst into the study. 'Oliver, something dreadful has happened.'

'What on earth?' He jumped up from his desk. 'An accident?'

'No, no, nothing like that. Here.' She waved the newspaper clipping at him. 'Mr Sinclair sent it. He knows you don't read the *Morning Post*.'

'No sane person would, for very good reasons. Chock-full of gossip, tittle-tattle, society news and lurid advertisements. I much prefer *The Times*. Why would Sinclair imagine…?'

'Here.' She handed him the clipping. 'Read it.'

'It's from last week. You look very pale.'

'So will you, when you've read that.' Lily closed the door, leaning against it, breathing hard. 'Oh, God. Just read it, Oliver.'

He cast her a worried look, but returned to his desk and began to read. She watched the emotions flit across his face. Anger. Disgust. Disbelief. She'd felt them all when she read it. Her knees were shaking. Frowning deeply, Oliver was reading the piece again. She thought she might be sick. What had Mr Sinclair thought when he read it? How many of their neighbours took the *Morning Post*? It was only a matter of time before word spread across the county to everyone, readers and illiterate alike. She tottered over to the chair in front of the desk and sank on to it, crushing her bustle.

Oliver set the clipping carefully down on the blotter. 'I have never in my life read such outrageous, vile, scurrilous balderdash!' He stopped, took a breath. One of his hands was curled into a fist. 'How bloody dare they!'

Lily sat mute, her hands clasped tightly together to stop herself from shaking. She was sickened and disgusted, but there was a bit of her that was thinking, *I knew this would happen.*

'The press don't like it when women refuse to fit the role they've defined for them.' Her lip curled. 'The weaker sex, refusing to be weak. They hate it.'

'You can say that again. "Insurgent Marchioness." "Revolutionary". Not fit for the "elevated position" society has given her,' Oliver read through gritted teeth.

'I told you that everyone would expect you to marry a simpering virgin. An "English Rose".'

'And I told you that is the very last sort of woman I'd ever marry,' Oliver said furiously, screwing the clipping up in his fist. 'They make me sound like I haven't a mind of my own. A dupe!' He swore viciously under his breath.

'I'm so sorry.'

'What the hell have you got to be sorry about? This isn't your fault. This marriage may have been your idea, but I committed to it. We're in this together—how many times do I have to tell you that?'

'They're not going to give up now. They're going to dig and dig until they find more dirt.'

'They aren't going to find any! We are legally married. There's nothing to connect you with your life in Paris.' Oliver swore again, getting to his feet to pour her a tot of brandy. 'Here,' he said, his tone considerably gentler. 'I'm sorry I shouted at you. This isn't your fault.'

Lily took the glass and had a small sip. It was good cognac, but she didn't need false courage. 'You're right,' she said, setting the glass down on the desk. 'It's not my fault, but it's done now and the consequences could be fatal for you.'

'I can't see how.' He returned to his seat behind the desk and unfurled the clipping, reading it again with his mouth curled in disdain. 'An industrialist, who has built his business from scratch and who has the audacity to refuse to exploit his workers must be a revolutionary! So a living wage, decent housing, schools and medical care are what the readers of the *Morning Post* think revolutionary!' He screwed the clipping up again and threw it in the direction of the fire. 'As for my being fit to look after my cousin's estate! They want to come and look for themselves at the state of some of those farms.'

'They'd probably think that leaking roofs and communal privies are exactly what your tenants deserve,' Lily said.

'Ha! You've got a point there. I should leave the farmhouses to rot and forget all about the steam-threshing machine I was thinking of buying. Let them carry on doing everything by hand, pulling their children out of school when they need more help. In fact, now I think about it, why are you encouraging them to put their children into school in the first place? Let them remain ignorant. It's what my trustees would do. Oh, if only I had not cut myself free from the—what was it?—"ballast" they provided,' Oliver said bitterly.

'You don't think that one of them may have been behind this article?'

'Hale, speak to the press? No, I'm pretty sure he regards journalists as even lower down the evolutionary ladder than industrialists. Whoever it was will learn soon enough that they are mistaken, if they imagine it will hold us back. Sewage like that only serves to make me more determined. Don't tell me you feel differently?'

'Of course not!'

'Could we speak to a journalist, do you think? Put our side of the story?'

'Oliver! No! *Non, non, non! Mon Dieu*, that would be the very worst thing to do.'

'I don't see why not. It would allow me to put the record straight about a few things.'

'But it wouldn't. Look how they have twisted the truth. Made implications. Taken the worst or most salacious meaning from the situation. You think they would do any differently with your own words? The truth does not sell newspapers. What sells newspapers is gossip, innuendo, scandal, self-righteous indignation. They want to vilify us because we are breaking the rules.'

'What rules?'

'Their rules. Women are the weaker sex. We are sad, frail little creatures with feathers for brains. Those of us who set ourselves up against men, who succeed in the world of men, we must be revolutionaries, sirens, or harlots. And you,' Lily exclaimed, 'you are a rough, uneducated man of the industrial North! How dare you come to the heart of England and try to change established ways that have been in place for generations? They are not interested in the truth, they're not interested in change, they are only interested in selling newspapers.'

She came to an abrupt halt, her chest heaving, and took a sip of her cognac. 'Do not speak to the press,' she said in a calmer tone. 'It would be a huge mistake.'

'A mistake you made in the past?' Oliver asked her in a gentler tone.

She nodded.

He got up, pulled another chair beside hers and sat down. 'I'd like to understand. You're right, I've no experience with this sort of thing. I've had detractors who have tried their best to stop me doing what I do because it makes them look bad, or because it forces them to change their ways when they start to lose their workers to more compassionate employers.' He took her hand, covering it with his own. 'Will you tell me what happened? Or would you rather not?'

It was mortifying. She would much rather not talk about it, but Oliver needed to understand what he was facing. Lily reached for the cognac glass with her free hand, then changed her mind. 'You remember I told you that my breakthrough as a theatrical agent came when one of the theatre's darlings asked me to negotiate on her behalf?'

He nodded.

'Her name was Hortense. What I didn't tell you was

that the theatre owner in the case was also the man who seduced my friend, Marie. She had his child, a little girl, who is my goddaughter. He did not— He won't even own her,' Lily said tightly. 'Marie is an actress. "The child could be any man's", according to him. So you see, when I had the opportunity to negotiate for the star every theatre manager in Paris was desperate to claim, my motives were—they were not of the purest.'

'Revenge? But why didn't you have your singer, Hortense, perform in another theatre? Wouldn't that have been a better form of revenge?'

'I thought of it,' Lily said, nodding, lost in the memory. 'But his was the best theatre for her career and it was a real coup for this man to have her. So instead I made him pay very, very dearly for the privilege and it meant that I could give my percentage to Marie.'

'Meaning that he paid for his child, even though he didn't know it?'

'Oh, but he did know it because I told him. That was my mistake, I think. That was what made him turn to the press. There is a newspaper in France called *Le Petit Parisien*. It is very like the *Morning Post*— advertisements and scandal.' Lily shuddered. 'The story was of his triumph in securing La Snédèr—that was Hortense's stage name. According to the newspaper, I tried to force her to perform at the Café des Ambassadeurs, one of the venues in Paris called *cafés concerts*. They are infamous places, where women perform for the pleasure of men who— No, I won't say any more, but the Prince of Wales was a regular visitor there at one time.'

'But what they published was a lie!'

'It didn't matter. I tried to correct what was written, but what the newspaper published was a—a history of my short career as an actress. I will not tell you what they said, how they described me, the men they claimed— No.' Lily gave in to the temptation of the cognac and took a sip. 'It could have been curtains, as they say, for me, but Hortense, she stood up for me in the press and behind the scenes. She was at the peak of her popularity. I was very lucky and will be for ever grateful to her. In the end, I lost a little business, but I gained a great deal more.'

'But what you couldn't do was correct the slur on your name?'

'It never pays, Oliver, that's what I'm trying to say. And also—also, if you attack them, they will simply attack us back.'

'By uncovering your real identity? I don't see how anyone could possibly make the link between my wife and La Muguette.'

'I don't see how it is possible, but...'

'There you are then, stop fretting about it. In the highly unlikely event of a link being made, is there anything that you've done that you're ashamed of?'

'No!'

Oliver got up to retrieve the clipping from the floor, folding it out on the blotter of his desk, frowning. 'There's another way to respond. We could brazen it out. Show we have nothing to be ashamed of. Take the fight to them.'

'How would we do that?'

'Go to London. Open up the town house. Stop giv-

ing the impression we're lurking here with something
to hide.'

'What on earth would we do there?'

'Introduce society to the new Marquess and Marchioness of Rashfield. Go to parties. The theatre, Lily.
Maybe even the opera.'

'What would be the point? We'll be shunned, after
that article.'

'Oh, I don't think so. Every day, Sinclair refuses
a stack of invitations on our behalf. We have novelty
value already and now,' he said sardonically, 'we have
notoriety. I don't think we'll be shunned. I think we'll
be sought out. We'll have the town house opened up.
We'll throw our own party to celebrate our nuptials.
Take centre stage in the metropolis, Lily. You've conquered Paris, now do you think you can help us conquer London?'

'You're not serious?' she said, but there was a glint
in Oliver's eye, a man going into battle and relishing
the challenge, that she couldn't help but to respond to.
Besides, he was right—the combination of novelty and
notoriety was intoxicating to most people, she knew
that from her own world. 'Do you think we can do it?'

'The question is, do you think it will work? You
have experience of the press that I don't. How will this
rag react? Is there any way we can influence what they
write?'

'We could offer them an exclusive. It might not work,
but it could be worth the risk. "The newly-wed Marquess and Marchioness of Rashfield are proud to introduce some French *ooh, là-là* to London society,"' Lily
said, warming to the idea, '"and prove to the world just

how deeply in love they are.'" Her smile faded. 'Alternatively, perhaps it's time to consider my leaving?'

'No! Absolutely not. How will it look to the world if you simply disappear so soon? It will look as if that journalist was right, that our marriage was one of convenience. You can't go now. Unless—has all this stirred up your worries about your own business? Do you want to go back to Paris, Lily?'

'No!' Her vehemence took her aback, making her add, 'I won't be hounded out of town.'

'Good, because I don't want you to go. The more I think about it, the more I like the idea of beating these newspaper men at their own game. We'll show them that our marriage is real and, when the time comes, we'll also show them that an industrialist and his insurgent Marchioness are a damned—dashed—sight more revolutionary than they would ever have guessed. What do you think, my lady? Will you join me in confounding everyone?'

'Oliver…'

'My lord,' he corrected her, pulling her to her feet.

'My lord,' she said, noting the timely reminder but unable to resist his smile. 'It's a risk. There are no guarantees that we'll be able to persuade the *Morning Post* to tell our story to our advantage.'

'If we don't, they're going to carry on telling it their way, until some other new scandal comes along, aren't they?'

'Probably.'

'So we're not going to simply roll over and let them away with that, are we? What would La Muguette do?'

'She would fight fire with fire.'

'We could fight fire with passion.'

He made no attempt to pull her into his arms. 'A passion for justice,' she said, turning his words to a more acceptable meaning because she wanted to stay and to fight. What he was suggesting was so appealing. To show the world, to flout convention, to play the press at its own game and to triumph, how could such an ambition not sing to her heart?

And all of it in the name of what was right for Oliver and for the people here at Rashfield. To give power to the powerless, to snub their noses at convention—oh, how could she help but be inflamed by such an idea? To fight fire with passion. Her passion for helping the powerless. Her passion for proving herself. And the passion they were starting to feel for each other? No, that was the one thing that was not real. A weapon merely with which to fight. And on those terms she could surrender.

'Allons-y,' Lily said. 'Let's do it.'

Let's do it, she'd said and Oliver threw his arms around her. A jubilant gesture, a celebration of their decision to fight, that's all he meant it to be. He smiled at her. 'Let's do it,' he said, and she smiled back at him, and it was so difficult to think straight when she smiled at him like that. It seemed only right, it seemed only natural, it seemed inevitable, for their lips to meet. And when their lips met, when she kissed him, Oliver forgot to think. Her kisses were the perfect kisses, though he'd never before thought other kisses less than perfect.

When Lily kissed him, he thought he would be happy to go on kissing her for ever. The way she slid her hands under his coat. The way she sighed when he kissed her neck, when his hands cupped her breasts over her gown. Pleasure and frustration excruciatingly intertwined. The combination of slenderness and litheness in her figure was the perfect combination.

He murmured her name as she pressed herself closer, curling her fingers into his hair. Their lips met again and their kisses deepened. They were in his office, he reminded himself. This was not the place. Not the time. Her gown seemed to cover every inch of her and he had no idea how to go about unlacing her. He shouldn't even be thinking about unlacing her, but now he had allowed the notion to enter his mind...

He dragged his mouth from hers. 'Lily.' Her mouth was smudged from the rouge she wore and his rough kisses. Her eyes were huge. Her cheeks were flushed. She looked utterly delectable. 'We can't. Not here. I mean, we can't,' he said again, because that's what he should be thinking, but what he was really thinking was, *we can, we can, we can.*

She shook her head. He had no idea what that meant. Was she agreeing with him or disagreeing? 'It's not even midday,' he said, somewhat preposterously.

Lily sank on to the chair. 'I don't know what you mean by that, Oliver. It's too early?'

The absurdity of the situation made him want to laugh. He shook his head, sitting down beside her. 'I don't know what I mean. I'm not thinking straight.'

'You're right, this is not the time.' She said something in French under her breath. He thought he caught the word 'never'. 'This is wrong! We cannot— I cannot— We need to think straight. If we really do mean to take London and the *Morning Post* by storm, we're going to have to be clear-headed about it. We cannot indulge ourselves in celebrating when we have not even begun.'

She drew him a look with this last sentence, daring him to contradict her. Why was she so determined to dress up her desire as something else? Why was he finding it so easy, at the most critical moments, to succumb to desire? Good questions and far too distracting to pursue. '*Eh bien,* as you would say, we'll fight fire with passion, but make sure the passion is under control.'

His attempt at a joke fell flat. Lily fell to studying her nails, which meant that she was thinking over what to say. She was usually careful with her words, a habit, he presumed, acquired from her line of work. He had developed the same trait. *Always think before you speak* had stood him in good stead over the years, but he was suddenly impatient with her determined efforts to nullify his feelings and to deny her own. He wanted to know what she was truly thinking, not what she was planning on telling him.

'Lily!'

She looked up, her brows raised in enquiry.

'I don't know what the hell is going on between us, but I need to know if it's the same for you.' This wasn't at all what he'd planned to say, but it was exactly what he did need to know. 'This thing, whatever it is,' Oliver said, making a vague gesture, 'between us. I don't know about you, but I've never felt such—' He broke off, at a loss. This was what happened when you spoke without thinking!

'I've never wanted any woman the way I want you. No, that's not what I mean, that makes it sound like lust, and it's not. I mean—I need to know if it's only me that feels this…' He swore under his breath. He didn't have the words for this conversation.

'I feel that it would be right between us,' he finished lamely. 'That's what I feel and I need to know if it's only me, if it's some sort of wish-fulfilment, because if it is then it's better you tell me and I'll keep my hands to myself.' Which made him sound like some lecherous uncouth youth, but if he said any more, he'd only make it worse, and he was already blushing. Blushing, in the name of God!

Lily had resumed her intense study of her fingernails, but he thought he could see a faint trace of colour in her cheeks to match his own. 'You're not imagining it,' she said finally. 'I find you— We seem to be—well matched?' She winced. 'Well suited?' She gave him a wry smile. 'I am no more used to discussing such things than you are. I've never felt so— Frankly, I find myself thinking, wondering about, imagining and it is proving a distraction. That's something I've never experienced before. Though I have never before shared a roof with a lover either.'

'Nor have I!' He clutched at this straw. 'You think it could be that? Proximity?'

'I have no idea. Perhaps. Or our roles. You remember what I said to you about the immediacy of being on stage?'

He wanted to accept what she was saying, but he knew it wasn't true and, now he had opened this painful conversation, he was determined to bring it to some sort of conclusion. 'I don't feel as if we're acting. It feels different between us. More real.'

'But this isn't real,' Lily said, pouncing on his words.

'We're in a situation of our own making, but it's only temporary.'

Could that be it? Not acting, but an escape from reality? Oliver wanted to clutch at his hair and thump his head on the desk, but even that extreme measure wouldn't help him understand. Did he need to put a name to it, to understand it? It would be over soon—wasn't that the salient point? 'When will you need to be back in Paris, to help with casting for the new season?'

'March, April at the latest,' Lily replied, after a moment's thought. 'Why?'

'An end date,' Oliver replied, 'that's what we need. We'll make sure that your role as the Marchioness of Rashfield is over by then.' April was weeks away. More than sufficient time for him to put his plans into action, he told himself, to explain away the mild panicked feeling welling up inside him. Lily had her life, he had his. 'You'll go back to Paris in the spring. I'll go back to Cheshire and New Kilmun, and in three years we'll qualify for a divorce on the grounds of desertion.'

'And in the meantime, you will be the Marquess of Rashfield. I am your loving bride, the Marchioness,' Lily said with an odd smile. 'Yes?'

Nothing was as it seemed. Nothing was real. It was a reassuring explanation and what's more it made sense. Neither of them had ever been in a situation like this. Oliver resolutely put aside the flicker of doubt that told him she was wrong. He couldn't trust his instincts on this. None the less, 'Is that what you honestly think?' he found himself asking.

'Yes, I—' She broke off, shaking her head. 'Honestly? If I had met you in Paris, if we had never met before, then I believe that this…' she waved her hand, imitating his own vague gesture '…we would have been attracted to each other. Would we have acted on that attraction? It's unlikely that the circumstances would have been conducive. But here, we have too many opportunities for indulging ourselves.'

Lily got to her feet. 'The morning is nearly gone. If we're going to continue with our work here and introduce ourselves to London society, we've got a great deal to do, don't you think?'

In other words, the discussion was over. 'I think the best thing would be for me to send a telegram to Sinclair,' he said, 'ask him to pay us a visit.'

'An excellent idea. And I'll go and deal with the rest of my correspondence.'

She left without a backwards glance. Nothing had been resolved between them, save that they had agreed there was nothing to be resolved. All this emotion, he thought grimly, and it wasn't even noon yet. Oliver dropped on to his chair behind the desk and picked up his pen. He might as well follow her example and deal with his own letters.

Chapter Eight

London—three days later

Rashfield House in Mayfair had not been used since Archie had died. 'And from what I can gather,' Oliver said, as he and Lily got into a hackney at Waterloo Station, 'he rarely entertained. I sent a telegram to Mrs Murray, the housekeeper, to let her know we were coming. She's Mrs Bremner's sister, as it happens, and has been looking after the place with a skeleton staff since Archie died. What's wrong, Lily?'

'I think we may have overstretched ourselves. No staff. A house that's been closed up for months. And we don't actually know anyone in town.'

'Are you giving up before we've even started? It's not like you to be defeatist.'

He expected her to smile, tilt her chin at him and rise to the challenge. Instead, Lily shrugged. 'Choose your battles, Oliver. It might be safer for us to ignore that horrible piece in the *Morning Post*.'

'In the hope that some other scandal will take precedence? Or that they'll dig the dirt on someone else? You know that Hale has already been in touch? He told Sinclair that he's going to send a man to Bordeaux to "verify the validity" of our marriage.'

Her eyes flashed. 'Let him! That's precisely why we went to such trouble to ensure that our marriage was perfectly legitimate. For goodness sake, you'd think the man had a vested interest in depriving you of that blasted estate. What would happen if you never married? Would it be in the hands of Sir Everard Hale and his five musketeers until you die?'

'I'd like to think that the law would have ground out a decision before then.'

'But what if that decision goes against you? Oliver, who is your heir?'

'I don't know. There's talk of a third cousin in America. I have no intentions of dying any time soon. Let Hale do his worst, he'll learn soon enough it will only make me more determined to have things my way.'

'And holding a party here in London is a vital part of that?'

'This will only work if we are of one mind. If you have changed your mind, then we won't do it.'

'But you think that would be akin to rolling over and playing dead, don't you?'

She understood him pretty well. 'I've never been one for playing safe,' Oliver said. 'When I put wages up at my very first factory, I was told that I'd get lazy workers. When I introduced steam-heated pans into the salt-making process, I was told that the salt would be tainted and no one would buy it.

'When I built New Kilmun, I was told that people

would never move there, that they'd prefer to live in the city. My plans for the canning factory—my board are telling me that I'll poison the nation and bankrupt us all. If someone tells me that I can't do something, it makes me determined to prove them wrong. I know that's not necessarily a positive trait...'

'It's one we share, though.' Lily bit her lower lip. 'There's so much at stake.'

'The plans we are starting to put in place are not at risk. Whether Hale accepts it or not, we are legally married. The future of the Rashfield estate is not at stake. How quickly and smoothly we can make that happen is what's at stake here. And for me, just as importantly,' Oliver said, 'so is my own reputation. That article has reached New Kilmun. I had a letter from my own deputy, asking if I'd seen it. I understand, Lily, that it would be a mistake to get into an overt battle with the paper, but I cannot let it lie.' The carriage rumbled to a halt. 'If you're having second thoughts about our plan of attack, then we'll think of something else, but I am not going to simply roll over and do nothing.'

Lily smiled at him. 'Onwards, then. Let's go and take a look at the battleground.'

While Oliver paid the driver, Lily stood at the foot of a shallow flight of stairs. The door was painted glossy black. The windows of the narrow, three-storey building were shuttered. Three days ago, in the immediate aftermath of reading the newspaper article, Oliver's idea had seemed like an excellent one. Since then, she'd had ample time for second thoughts. Hosting a party for the county set and their tenants had been, in comparison to this, a simple task, made considerably easier by the combination of Mrs Bremner and Riddell, and the fact that Rashfield Manor was already fully equipped with staff.

This town house was closed up. The people that Oliver intended to woo were not only strangers, but strangers without a vested interest in their success. Oliver had already refused countless of their invitations. He had fleetingly been society's most eligible bachelor, then had the bad taste to marry Lily, whose lineage was nothing more than shabbily genteel, whose family was as non-existent as his own and whose more recent history...

Lily! For what seemed like the thousandth time since she had read the *Morning Post* article, she told herself it wasn't a risk. If she and Oliver were to present themselves to society as he wished, then she had more than enough to worry about without adding that on to her list. Such as a ball to which no one came.

The hackney rumbled off. The front door was opened by a middle-aged woman dressed in grey. Lily fixed a smile to her face and mounted the steps holding out her hand. 'Mrs Murray? How do you do? I am Lady Rashfield. It's a pleasure to meet you, I've heard nothing but praise from your sister, Mrs Bremner, who has been a godsend to me and who sends her best wishes.'

The housekeeper, who had dropped into a curtsy, held out her hand in surprise. 'My lady. How do you do. And my lord,' she added. 'It is a pleasure to see you here. On behalf of the household, such as it is, I would like to extend our congratulations on your nuptials. There's a fire lit in the drawing room, if you wish tea to be served?'

'Thank you,' Lily said, stepping inside. 'Perhaps later. We'd like to take a look around first.'

'Most of the rooms are still under covers, my lady. His Lordship—His late Lordship—didn't use them much. Bachelor parties, that's all he held here, so there was no need—if I'd known in advance, my lady…'

'Please, Mrs Murray, don't fret.'

'But the dust, your lovely gown…'

'This old thing,' Lily said, thankful that she was not wearing one of Monsieur Worth's creations, but had instead dressed for practical purposes in a dark blue wool coat and dress trimmed with black braid. 'You should know, Mrs Murray, that my husband and I are thinking of holding a ball here in London to celebrate our recent nuptials.'

'That would be wonderful, my lady. As I said, there's been nothing but bachelor parties here for years. Not that His late Lordship was a bachelor, of course, but my lady rarely came to town and—and— Oh, it would be wonderful to see the house used as it was intended. But it will take a great deal of preparation. We will need to hire staff. When are you intending the event to take place?'

'Two weeks from now, Mrs Murray,' Oliver said. 'I know it's very short notice, but…'

'Short notice!' The housekeeper put her hand over her heart. 'My lord, it's impossible.'

'Nothing is impossible if you set your mind to it, especially if there is money to be thrown at the problem.

We'll draft in your sister and Riddell to help with the arrangements. Now,' he said, taking Lily's arm, 'lead on.'

'I think Mrs Murray may well be right—I'm not at all sure that it is possible in the timescale,' Lily said to Oliver two hours later. They were in the ballroom alone together. 'There's simply too much to be done, even with Mrs Bremner's and Riddell's assistance.'

'Don't underestimate Riddell. He may deliver glasses of sherry that have turned into port by the time they make it to the dining room, but he is a master of his craft.'

Lily couldn't help but smile. 'I know, but even if it could be achieved, don't you think that it's far too much expense to go to, for something that might ultimately fail? Why would anyone choose to come to our ball when there will be countless other entertainments on offer the same night? They've never met me, you told me yourself back in Sandgate that you had made a point of turning down every invitation…'

'I was in mourning for my cousin. That's over now. I'm married and I want to introduce my wife to the world.'

'It won't be enough in and of itself. We will need to come up with some way of making our ball stand out, make it something new and fresh that will also appeal to the readers of the *Morning Post*.'

'In that case, we'd be better hosting a circus than a ball.'

'Oliver, be serious! I don't know how you can take this so lightly. One cannot present the *ton* with a troupe of tumblers and a talking donkey. Next thing you'll be proposing we serve them fried fish and porter.'

He grinned. 'Isn't that exactly the kind of party that an ill-bred industrialist and his insurgent Marchioness would host? And just look at this room. You said yourself that the sound is very good and that dais, which I presume is intended for the orchestra, would make an excellent stage.'

'Oh, perfect. And we'll have a dance-hall orchestra play a polka—that should get high society rushing to our door.'

'Wait! I think we might be on to something. No, listen to me for a moment,' Oliver said, 'I'm serious. You remember how everyone joined in the polka at Rashfield Manor? Even our standoffish neighbours enjoyed letting their hair down a little. What if we give the great and the good of society a flavour of the popular entertainments that everyone else enjoys without them having to mingle with the dreaded "great unwashed"?'

'What do you mean?'

'Exactly what you said—or something like. Make our ball a performance in every way. We could have singers, magicians, acrobats—you know the kind of thing, surely, better than I do?'

'But I don't. I don't know anything about the music-hall scene in London, which is where we'd have to find that kind of act. I wouldn't know where to start.'

There was at last a smile trembling on her lips that was recognisably her real smile. Lily had put on an excellent show, as ever, as the housekeeper showed them round, but he knew her very well now. He took her hands in his, leading her over to one of the windows where the shutters had been thrown back to give a view on to a terrace with steps down to an enclosed garden at the rear of the house. 'Why are you so daunted by this? You've been on stage in front of theatre audiences full of hundreds of strangers—is what we're discussing so very different?'

'I told you, I was never a leading lady.'

'You've been my leading lady for weeks now and you've already got one hugely successful ball to your credit.'

'It's not the same.' Lily got up and walked the length of the ballroom to the dais. 'We can't simply go to any old theatre in London, then go backstage and try to hire the acts.'

'We won't go to any old theatre.' He got up to join her, encouraged. 'We'll go to the best. I'll find out which one.'

'How?'

He tapped his nose, smiling and hoping to hell that Sinclair would be able to guide him. 'Leave it with me.'

'What about our train back to Rashfield Manor?'

'We'll stay here tonight instead. I'll have Mrs Murray make up two rooms, unless you'd rather stay at a hotel?'

'That would look very odd, if it was discovered. Actually, it will look very odd if we are discovered at a variety theatre.'

'Highly unlikely, I think. Besides, no one knows us, yet. What else?'

'You're serious.'

'I am. The more I think about it, the more I like the idea. Come on, admit that you're tempted.'

'A little.' She thought about it, then smiled, more broadly this time. 'A lot. But as to hiring acts…'

'That's your milieu. What is wrong with going backstage after the performance to offer an act a good fee for a one-night-only private performance? Is it illegal?'

'No, not at all. If the variety theatre in London is anything like Paris, then the performers will be struggling to earn a living, unless they are that rare thing, a star.'

'All the more reason for us to offer some respite, don't you think?'

'That's one way of looking at it.'

'Admit it, it's an excellent plan.'

'It has merit, but it would still be a mistake to try to engage anyone backstage after a performance. You've never been backstage, have you? It's chaos, Oliver. People getting changed, taking off their greasepaint, discussing the performances, arguing about who made what mistake or missed what cue—my goodness, the accusations! There's props everywhere and costumes—most theatres are cramped, and most performers share dressing rooms. There's dressers and friends and lovers all jostling for space, and of course admirers jostling for access.

'The performers are exhausted or depressed or occasionally floating on their success. They want food and drink or sleep or love or all four, they don't want to discuss another engagement with a complete stranger, especially if they are already spoken for. Some of them may not even be there, because they've gone on to another theatre. And then the theatre manager is bound to be wandering about, protecting his interests.'

'Good grief! You make it sound like Bedlam.'

Lily smiled. 'It is. When the performances have gone badly or the audience has been unappreciative, it's hell, too, but on a good night, it can be— There's no place like it.'

'Was it hard, giving up the stage?'

Her smile faded. 'It was what I had dreamed of from when I was little. You know what that's like.'

'I'm sorry, that was a really stupid question.'

'At least I tried. It was difficult, you know, giving up on my dream because I'd had it so long, but I simply wasn't good enough and, to be honest, even if I'd been better I wouldn't have made it. There are some things that are not worth sacrificing, even for your dream.'

He couldn't begin to imagine what she had endured. She had wrapped her arms around herself, a comforting, defensive gesture that made him curse his own insensitivity, but knew better than to try to touch her or to offer comfort.

'Don't pity me, Oliver,' Lily said, misreading his expression. 'I have found another way to live my dream. I still have all the excitement of being in the theatre.'

'I wasn't pitying you, I was thinking how odd it was, that while I was obsessively building my own dream, the woman I was married to was plotting and planning hers and I had no idea.'

'You never asked. And as to plotting and planning, when I was living in your house in Sandgate—well, I certainly had plenty of time to plot and plan, but I wouldn't have done anything that could have compromised your name. Such as going on stage,' she added, when he looked confused. 'So I remained backstage, until I went to France and changed my name.'

'Backstage?'

'The theatre in Folkestone.' Lily unfolded her arms. 'You look surprised.'

'I never thought—guessed—imagined—what did you do?'

'Whatever was needed. Prompts. Rehearsals. Helping with costumes and stage sets. Running errands. Looking after dogs and children. Fetching food. Mopping up tears. Moral support.' She smiled reminiscently. 'I was a Jill of all trades.'

'But never actually on the stage?'

'Oh, I was never off the stage, but never in front of an audience. I was starry-eyed, naive, but I was a hard worker, too.'

'So your decision to go to France, was that for a part?'

'In a chorus. I went with one of the regular actresses at Folkestone who had a proper role. We— Oh, but that's ancient history, Oliver.'

'It's fascinating.'

'No, it's not. It's sad and sordid in places and I don't wish to talk about it.'

'All that time I was focused on building my dream, you were fighting for yours in a very different way.'

'We were never part of each other's lives. That was our deal, and if we hadn't had that deal, I wouldn't be the woman I am today. Your allowance, in the early days in Paris, is what helped me and my friend to survive. You see now why I am here? Why I want to pay you back?'

'You really are a—a remarkable woman.'

She coloured faintly, turning to look out the window.

'We have both of us worked hard to make our lives our own. Now we have to work together to ensure that we can return to these lives, and if that means putting on a variety show in front of society…' she turned back to face him '…then that's what we'll do.'

'Look at this place. You could work your magic, transform it, bring the music hall to Mayfair. Our party, or whatever we call it on the invitation, will stand out from every other ball and soirée and musical evening on offer. Then, imagine what a story it will make for the *Morning Post* to tell. The subversive couple, hosting a revolutionary entertainment. And lastly, it will mean we're doing things on our own terms. That means a great deal to me and I know it does to you, too. We'll be the Marquess and Marchioness of Rashfield on our own terms. Do you see? Lily, what have I said to upset you?'

'I'm not upset.' She dabbed at her eyes, trying to smile. 'I'm touched. Impressed. I feel humbled.'

'I'm the one that feels humbled.' He lifted her hand to his mouth, pressing a kiss to her fingertips. 'You are the most unusual woman I've ever met.'

'I'll take that as a compliment.'

'It's not a compliment, it's the truth. I couldn't have asked for a better wife.'

'Temporary wife.'

He kissed her hand again. 'One of the many reasons why you are the best.'

She dropped a mock curtsy. 'Thank you, my lord. Now, if we are to go to the theatre tonight, had you not better establish which one? In the meantime, I shall seek out Mrs Murray and break the news that we are spending the night here.'

* * *

Though the newly renamed Canterbury Theatre of Varieties was located in Lambeth, it was one of London's more respectable variety theatres, unlike the more popular Oxford Theatre in Westminster which had lately gained a reputation in the press for being frequented by 'loose women'.

The Canterbury was also one of the largest music halls in the city, recently refurbished and enlarged to accommodate an audience of up to two thousand people. It was luxuriously fitted out, with chandeliers to supplement the gaslights and a glass roof that could be opened up to let out the constant fug of cigar smoke. Customers sat at small tables, paying sixpence for the downstairs seats and ninepence for the more expensive seats in the balcony, where the bar was also located.

Lily and Oliver were shown up the grand staircase to their table with an excellent view of the stage, which was a simple platform with a painted backdrop set on the lower floor with a grand piano and a harmonium, neither currently in use. Her 'milieu', Oliver had called this earlier, and he was right. As soon as they stepped through the doors and into the foyer, her heart beat with excitement.

As they sat down, they were assaulted by noise from all sides: people calling out to each other from one side of the balcony to the other, across the hall downstairs. Two tables of young men, clerks of some sort, were singing in a round. There was a constant stream of new arrivals greeting their friends before moving to their own table and in front of the stage more groups of men talking, eyeing the room and gazing up at the balcony.

The doormen had been thorough in their vetting. Everyone that Lily could see was respectably clad, the men in plain black or grey suits, a few in their working clothes and boots. The women, too, were in grey and black and brown dresses and jackets, hats and gloves. Lily motioned to Oliver to keep his own hat on as they sat down at their table.

The night was too young for the air to be polluted by cigar smoke, but it was rich with the scent of cheap perfume, spilt beer, spirits, wet wool and flannel from the damp London fog and under it all the acrid smell of unwashed bodies. Lily breathed it in deeply. How she had missed this!

The Canterbury had its own unique ambiance—every theatre did. The drinks, the food and no doubt the acts to come would be very different from Paris. But the badinage, the bonhomie, the sense of anticipation, the high spirits of people desperate to escape the drudgery of their everyday world to spend a few magical hours in this palace of dreams, where someone else cooked, someone else cleaned up and all that was to be done was enjoy oneself with gusto! That was the same atmosphere in every theatre of her acquaintance.

A serving maid appeared, demanding their pleasure. Having no notion of what was served here, Lily shrugged, a gesture that went unnoticed for the young woman had eyes only for Oliver. When he asked her what she recommended, the maid happily embarked on a colourful and detailed recital of the fare, needing little encouragement to explain the local delicacies. Lily leaned across the table to put her hand on his coat sleeve. 'Will you choose for me, darling? You know what I like.'

The order was quickly taken after that. 'You know I have eyes only for you, *darling*,' Oliver teased.

'I was merely trying to speed things up, else the show would have started before we were served our drinks.'

'That's a pity. I rather liked you playing the possessive wife, though there was no need. I am yours, my love, and only yours.'

He was smiling at her, teasing, flirtatious. He had hold of her gloved hand over the table and out of sight, his thumb was circling her palm. Circling her palm, that's all he was doing, yet she felt as if he was touching her intimately. Under the table, she moved her foot to rest against his. A tiny intake of breath was the only indication that he had noticed. 'Lovely Lily,' he said. 'That should be a song, don't you think?'

'Ah, but you said I was not lovely.'

'I said you were not beautiful. Beauty is something to be admired from afar. Loveliness…' Oliver slid his foot between hers. Their legs brushed. 'Loveliness is something to be enjoyed close up. Though perhaps Luscious Lily would suit you better.'

She shuffled forward on her chair so that their legs brushed. 'Like a peach?'

'Not exotic enough.' He leaned closer. 'Have you any idea how much I want to kiss you?'

'*Oui.*' She smiled at him, throwing herself into her role, running the tip of her tongue along her upper lip.

'Lily…'

'Your drinks, sir. A beer and a sherry cobbler. And your pies.'

Lily jumped, but Oliver looked wholly unembarrassed, putting a coin on the tray. 'Thank you.'

The maid pocketed the coin. 'You don't need to worry about them pies. I made sure you got the proper beef.'

'Proper beef?' Lily eyed the steaming pastry dubiously. 'It smells good enough.'

Oliver took a small bite. 'Tastes good, too.' He grinned, picking up his beer. 'Here's to us, my lady.'

She clinked her glass against his tankard. 'To peerage on our own terms. Cheers, my lord.'

By the time the chairman, as the master of ceremonies was known, in this case a flamboyant individual who went by the name of Leopold Lovejoy, took to the stage to announce the first act at length, the audience had grown restless and raucous. Though Lily had drunk the sherry cobbler, she had refused another drink and merely nibbled on the pie crust, leaving the meat despite the waitress's assertion of its authenticity. Her cheeks were flushed, her eyes sparkled as she looked around her, a smile playing on her lips. She felt totally at home here and she was savouring every moment of it.

The chairman urged the audience to indulge in the impressively imbibeable intoxicating liquor on offer and then, with a drum roll, he held up his arm, his gavel raised. 'Ladies and Gentlemen, may I present for your delectation and delight, a Continental operatic accolade. A delectably delicious diva. I give you the one and only Miss Annie Adams.' He slammed his gavel on his dais as the audience roared their approval.

The delectably delicious diva turned out to be a statuesque woman dressed in a scarlet satin and net gown.

She launched into a performance of operatic arias that made both her chins and her impressive bosom quiver. Oliver was not in the least musical and had never attended the opera, but he could appreciate she had an excellent voice.

'Mezzo-soprano,' Lily whispered, 'though there's nothing remotely Continental about her. I've certainly never come across her, but I think she would be an excellent opening act, yes?' She smiled 'To lull our guests into a false sense of security, you know?'

'Just another musical soirée kind of thing?'

Lily nodded. *'Exactement.'*

Exactement. When she spoke French—and she spoke it more often when she was excited or angry—he found it absurdly arousing. As the chairman returned for another loquacious announcement, Lily leaned forward to study him and Oliver watched her, entranced. Lord and Lady Rashfield were going to bring the music hall to Mayfair. He wanted to laugh, it was such a preposterous, aptly appealing idea—lord, he was beginning to sound like the chairman.

He and Lily were going to preside over something that Mayfair had never seen and the *Morning Post* was going to herald the event to the world in appropriately extravagant terms. He was going to make sure of that. And Lily—this wonderful woman who was his wife—lord, he really had been infected by the chairman's alliteration—Lovely Lily was going to aid and abet him.

A short ballet followed the diva, the men in the audience, as instructed by the chairman, duly titillated by the tantalising troupe of young ladies in tights. Lily's only comment was that the dancer second from the left was out of time with the rest. A siffleur was next to be introduced, who turned out, to Oliver's disappointment, to be a whistler who imitated bird calls. The audience responded with cat calls, which saw the premature departure of the unfortunate man.

He was replaced by an aged ventriloquist with a dummy dressed in a boy's jacket and shorts whom the audience tolerated, but which Lily did not. 'A talking dog would have had more novelty value. Scruffy schoolboys, real or dummies, may amuse their doting parents, but no one else.' The conjuror who came next, however, had Lily's full attention and Oliver's, too, as she pointed out, in a whisper, the sleight of hand behind each trick.

'He will do, I think,' she said as a dove flew from an apparently empty hat towards the glass ceiling of the theatre.

In the next act, a man in white robes put a long stick or cane in his mouth. His assistant, a buxom woman in a tightly laced, low-cut dress that seemed to Oliver to be made entirely of feathers and sequins, placed several heavy objects on the stick: first a book, then what appeared to be a marble pin dish—'Papier mâché,' Lily hissed—and finally a candlestick. With a flourish, the assistant lit the candle. The cane had not wavered. Oliver raised a questioning brow at Lily, but for once she was at a loss and simply shrugged.

The chairman, Leopold Lovejoy, performed a song called 'The Rat Catcher's Daughter' with which the audience seemed very familiar. A heroine who drowned in the Thames, a hero who cut his donkey's throat and then his own to prove his love for her, did not seem

to Oliver the stuff of comedy, but the audience loved
every stanza.

The final act of the eveting was another singer, announced as the Lambeth Lark. She was heavily made
up, her features accentuated with greasepaint, bright red
lips and cheeks, lashes so long they looked as if they
might tangle. Her emerald gown, however, though it
hugged her figure so tightly Oliver thought it must im-
pede her breathing, was demure, cut high at the neck,
the sleeves ending at the elbows. She wore matching
green gloves, but no hat. The audience greeted her with
whistles and jeers. The Lambeth Lark began to sing.

'I was a good little girl, till I met you,' she trilled.
'You set my head in a whirl, my poor heart, too.'

Lily smiled over at him as the woman began to pace
the stage, looking saucily out at her audience. He took
her hand across the table and she tucked her foot against
his. 'I think this might be our final act.'

'When I was young and innocent,' the singer continued, 'you stole into my heart. You taught me things I
now repent, whenever we're apart.'

'We wouldn't dare.'

'No?'

The song continued in the same vein for several
verses, saucy innuendo that was not actually vulgar.
The woman gave a bow. The orchestra struck up the
refrain again, but instead of singing another verse, she
began, very slowly, to pull her glove off her hand with
her teeth. In the auditorium downstairs, men got to their
feet, waving their hands, stomping their feet. When the
glove was thrown into the audience, there was a mad

scramble. Tossing of hats. Cheers. A bow. And the show was over.

'*Eh bien, mon amour,*' Lily said, getting to her feet. 'I think we have seen enough to construct our own performance. If,' she added, with a challenging look, 'you have not changed your mind?'

'After what I've seen tonight, I'm even more determined. Do you think we'll be able to persuade any of these people to perform for us? Not the whistler,' Oliver added hastily.

'Most definitely not the whistler. I don't know, I don't see why not. It would be better if we had a discussion with Mrs Murray tomorrow to first ascertain whether we'll have a stage for our performers.'

'You're right. But if we can?'

'Then we'll do it. There is a strong possibility that we will be ostracised. We will certainly be the talk of the town.' Lily put her hand on his arm. 'But that is what we're aiming for, yes? The madcap Marquess and Marchioness of Rashfield putting on a comic show for the world.'

Chapter Nine

At some point in the Canterbury's history, a railway viaduct had been built which forced the theatre's entrance to become a tunnel running underneath it. As the crowd surged towards the exit at the end of the performance, Oliver and Lily held back until the crush had subsided, emerging into a dark and very cold February night. The rain had stopped, which was fortunate as they were forced to walk to Waterloo Station before they could find a hackney for hire to take them back to Mayfair.

'I told Mrs Murray that we'd be perfectly happy with coffee and bread for breakfast tomorrow morning,' Lily said, looking out at the inky dark of the London streets, where the gaslights marked their progress. 'We can take it in the little parlour on the ground floor that looks out over the garden. The dining room is vast and the parlour was much more easily set up for two, but I'm not sure I convinced her. It seems your cousin liked to eat even his solitary breakfast in a formal setting.'

'And to have enough food to feed an army served

to him, if you remember the first breakfast we had at Rashfield Manor. While I remember, I telegraphed Mrs Bremner to have a suitcase packed for you and sent to the town house.'

'Oh, Oliver, that was very thoughtful. I could have easily made do.'

'There's no need to, now.'

'It seems so extravagant.'

'I didn't think you'd be keen to borrow a nightdress from Mrs Murray, or, more importantly, wear the same gown two days in a row.'

Though she couldn't see his face properly, she could hear the teasing note in his voice. 'You think I'm a peacock.'

'I think you take pride in your appearance. You are always so perfectly turned out.'

'It's important in my line of work. Appearances matter. The theatre is a shallow business in that sense.'

'It's not a criticism, Lily. I like the effect. You dress with panache.'

'Thank you,' she said, appeased and flattered. 'It's a uniform all the same, though Monsieur Worth would have an apoplexy if he heard me say so. His gowns are much sought after and very expensive, but we have an arrangement. I may not be beautiful...'

'Lovely Lily, are you casting that up at me again?'

She laughed. 'I couldn't resist. I am not beautiful, but my figure shows Monsieur Worth's gowns off to advantage, so he dresses me for a significant discount, and in return I dress to be seen. It's a business arrangement. He also dresses some of my more famous clients.'

'Clever Lily.'

'As I said, it's a business arrangement, but I'm accustomed to dress for the city. In the country, I've been aware that my toilettes must seem very inappropriate.'

'I can't imagine you dressed more appropriately. I don't see why you should change, unless you want to.'

'I meant to ask. You said that you were free to spend Archie's money,' Lily prompted. 'The party at Rashfield, the party we are planning here—they *will* be at Archie's expense, won't they?'

'I prefer to invest his money in the estate.' Oliver shifted on the narrow seat. 'I have plenty of money of my own.'

'Are you very rich?'

He laughed. 'That's a very rude question.'

'Are you, though?'

'So my banker tells me. I have modest tastes, so there's plenty for me to spend on hiring ventriloquists and whistlers.'

'You know perfectly well we're hiring neither of them,' Lily said tartly. 'You're investing your own money in the estate, too, aren't you? The steam-threshing machine, for example—are you paying for that?'

'It needs to be a going concern. I'll do whatever it takes. I'm not really interested in talking about money at the moment. Did you enjoy yourself tonight?'

'Immensely,' she said, happy to change the subject, 'as you must know, for you were watching me more than the stage.'

'I didn't need to watch the stage. Your expressions told me all I needed to know.'

'I have missed it.'

'That was obvious. I had a glimpse of La Muguette for the first time. You know, don't you, Lily, how much I appreciate the sacrifice you're making to be here.'

'I know that I've told you countless times that it's a choice, not a sacrifice. What about you, did *you* enjoy yourself tonight?'

'I did. Very much, to my surprise.'

'What I will say, though, is that if we are to serve meat pies at our ball, I think we'll make them much smaller and with *proper beef* that really is proper beef.'

He slid his arm around her waist and pulled her close. 'Don't mention the pies. I think I may be developing a fever.'

All evening, it had been there between them. An awareness. A slow-burning desire that they had both encouraged. Caught up in the lax mood of the theatre, in the excitement of their plan, they had indulged their attraction and allowed themselves to be themselves. Not a marquess and marchioness. Simply Lily and Oliver. She put her hand on his forehead, pushing back his hat. 'Scalding hot,' she said, though she had her gloves on and his forehead was cool.

He put his hand on her forehead. 'Do you have it, too?'

'Yes,' she said, barely hesitating. For one night only. The word was barely out when his lips found hers. *At last*, Lily thought, pushing herself up against him as tightly as possible in the confined space of the cab. For this night only, she allowed herself to kiss him without restraint and he returned her kiss with equal passion. Tongues clashed…hands roamed feverishly over each other. Neither of them was aware that the cab had stopped until their driver rapped sharply on the roof.

Cursing, Oliver staggered out, clutching his hat in one hand, dragging Lily with the other. She was aware of the cabby staring at them, aware that it must be perfectly clear from their dishevelled appearance what they had been about, but she didn't care. All she wanted was to get inside and continue.

Oliver had the key to the glossy black door. Mrs Murray having been given strict instructions not to wait up for them. Two lamps stood, turned down low, on the marble hall table. Oliver locked the door and picked one up, turning up the wick. 'Are you sure, Lily?'

She nodded. 'For tonight,' she said, 'I'm sure. You understand me? If you don't wish…'

'I do wish. Tonight we'll be us. It will be our secret.'

'Yes.' She sighed happily. 'Yes.'

'I have the means— I have protection,' he said. 'I don't take chances.'

Nor did she, but he had spared her the need to bring the contentious subject up. 'Thank you,' she said instead. Following him up the broad staircase, she hoped that he knew where he was going. Mrs Murray had informed her she would be in the yellow room, but it meant nothing to her. Two flights up and, after opening two doors on bedrooms shrouded in covers, Oliver found one where the bed had been made up. He held the lamp high. The bedspread was gold.

'At last.' He set the lamp down on a chest of drawers and turned the key in the lock. 'I have been thinking about this all night.'

She put her arms around his neck. 'You were supposed to be concentrating on the acts.'

He nuzzled her ear. 'There's only one performance I'm interested in.'

She shivered. 'I hope nerves do not affect my performance.'

He kissed the pulse behind her ear. His hands stroked down her sides, pulling her closer. 'I have been convinced since the first time we kissed that *our* performance will be a triumph.'

'Yes,' Lily said, agreeing and responding to the touch of his lips on her neck. 'So have I.'

'There's only one problem.'

'Costumes,' she agreed. 'Inappropriate costumes. Take off your coat.'

She unbuttoned her own and put it down on a chair. As they turned round, their eyes met again. His eyes were dark with desire. A flutter of nerves assaulted her. Lily put one of her fingers in her mouth and began to ease off her glove. He exhaled sharply. Her nerves evaporated. She dropped the glove, gave him a deliberately sultry smile, and put the fingertip of her other hand in her mouth. Her glove had not quite hit the floor when he pulled her into his arms again.

Now their kisses had real intent. There had been enough flirting, enough teasing, enough dancing around at the fringes of passion. There could never be enough kisses, but these were kisses that demanded more.

She tugged at his waistcoat and he unbuttoned it, casting it on to the floor. She turned to reveal the fastenings of her gown and he made short work of them, smoothing the bodice down her arms. She cast it carelessly on to the chair. Her skirt was easier. Then the ties of her bustle, while he pulled off his shirt, and then she was in his arms again, and she could feel him at last, skin to skin, flesh to flesh.

'At last,' Oliver murmured, echoing her thoughts, kissing her neck, the swell of her breasts above her corset, smoothing his hands over her arms. 'I have waited so long.'

'So long,' Lily echoed, her hands on his back, feeling the ripple of his muscles, the tension in his shoulders, feeling him shudder under her touch. She pressed her face to his chest, breathing in the scent of his soap and his skin and his sweat, feeling the tickle of the sprinkling of hairs nuzzling her cheek. She tasted him, kissing, licking, kissing, enjoying the way her touch made his breath catch, made his chest heave.

'This now,' Oliver said purposely, indicating her corset.

She unlaced them quickly, letting them fall on to the floor and her petticoats, too, so that she was left in her chemise, her drawers and her stockings. Oliver ran his hand down her back, from the nape to the curve of her buttocks. 'Lovely, lovely Lily,' he said softly, picking her up and setting her on to the bed, quickly ridding himself of the rest of his clothes, leaving her in no doubt of how much he wanted her. Her own reaction was visceral. Her nipples ached.

'A moment,' he said, turning his back on her and fumbling for something in his pocket. Protection, she assumed, and, when he lay down beside her, saw she was right. They kissed again, slower this time because now they didn't want to rush, now was the time for relishing, enjoying every minute. She knew it. She instinctively knew he knew it, too. She had known from the moment she met him again that it would be like this.

His hand cupped her breast and began to circle her nipple. She could hear herself, little cries of *oh*, *oh*, *oh*, as he stroked, then his mouth fastened on her other nipple and he sucked. Her cries deepened. She reached for him, but he batted her hand away.

'Wait. Not yet.'

No man had ever told her to wait. No man had ever said, not yet. Lily waited, wondering if she could wait much longer as Oliver teased her nipples with his tongue and his hand, making her wriggle on the bed beneath him, slowly building the most exquisite tension inside her that she clung on to, willing it to last. He lifted his head, but only to find her lips again. A deep, deep kiss this time that made her feel as if she was turning inside out. Then his hand, feathering over her belly, finding the strings of her drawers, sliding between her legs and inside her.

Lily cried out. Oliver kissed her again, quieting kisses, but while he kissed her he stroked her, slowly, his finger sliding over her, inside her, over her, inside her, until she lost all restraint, crying out, tumbling over, pulling him urgently towards her, and just at exactly the right moment, finally he entered her. Filled her. Pushed high inside her as the waves of her climax shook her and shook her. She wrapped her legs around him, digging her heels into his buttocks, clutching his shoulders, biting the flesh there. 'Now,' she said, 'now.'

He thrust. She held him. He thrust. She held him tighter. He pushed harder. Higher. Faster. 'Lily,' he said harshly as he thrust. 'Oh, Lily, Lily, Lily.' The last was a deep groan as he came, pulling her tight against him, holding her so close she could scarcely breathe.

Her heart was racing, but her body was blissful. Still caught up in the aftermath of their lovemaking, she felt as if she was floating. She lay with her eyes closed, relishing the moments, acutely aware of Oliver beside her. When she finally opened her eyes, she noticed her chemise was torn. She had lost one of her stockings. Beside her, Oliver looked shockingly desirable, his smile lazily sated, his hair spread over the pillow, the marks of her teeth blossoming on his shoulder. She wanted to curl into him, let their sweat cool, let her head rest on his shoulder and drift off to sleep.

The thought brought her tumbling back down to earth. Lily sat up, pushing her tangle of hair back from her face. She had never had any such desire before in her life. 'It must be very late,' she forced herself to say.

He blinked, his smile fading. 'You're right, of course, we have a busy day ahead of us tomorrow.'

He sat up, pulling the sheet around him. She turned away to give him privacy to dress. For the first time that night, the silence felt awkward.

'It's simply that I prefer to sleep alone,' Lily said, because she always had until now.

'You don't need to explain. So do I.' She turned. He had pulled on his trousers and gathered up the rest of his clothes. He smiled at her, then bent to kiss her softly on the mouth. 'I have no regrets, if you don't?'

'None whatsoever.' She reached up to stroke his hair. '*Bonne nuit*, Oliver.'

'Goodnight, Lily.'

The door closed behind him. He didn't take the lamp. She wondered how he would find his way to his own room in the dark. Lily pulled the bedclothes up around her and buried deep down. The sheets were redolent of their lovemaking. A memorable performance. Their debut. And their finale. For one night only, she had specified to herself and to him, too, but already she regretted sending him away. It frightened her. She never, ever slept with any of her lovers. It was important to her, to call her bedroom her own, to go to sleep alone, to wake up alone. Important to Oliver, too. In this, as in so many things, they thought the same.

He would be asleep by now, she told herself. She ought to do the same. No regrets, she had said, but now she wondered if it was true. Tonight had been like nothing she had known before. She would be back in Paris by April. It was already the middle of February. Six weeks, possibly seven. More than enough time to ensure that Oliver's role in her life was over once and for all, without any regrets.

Though it was early afternoon, the London sky was iron-grey and dankly gloomy as Oliver and Lily descended from the hackney cab at the stage door of the Canterbury Theatre. The morning's fog had dispersed, but the air was still thick with a metallic tang that stung the back of the throat, tainted by the flakes of soot which floated down from the plumes of smoke puffing from the myriad of chimneys. The cobblestones were slimy and the gutters stank.

'It's a bit of a contrast from the gaudily lit front,' Oliver said, eyeing the blackened rear of the building dubiously. The few windows were blacked out. The door was firmly closed. There was no knocker.

Lily picked her way over the cobbles, holding her skirt high. 'The smoke makes the back of my throat itchy. Is it always like this in London?'

'I reckon. It's the same in Liverpool and Manchester. Surely it can't be much different in Paris?'

'The streets are as filthy in places like this, but the air, not so much.' She turned the handle on the door and yanked it open, smiling at his surprise. 'What they call variety in London is not so very different from what we call vaudeville in Paris and I make my living from vaudeville. At this time of day, the doorman will be most likely helping out on the stage. Now, all we have to do is find the manager.'

Lily stepped confidently inside and Oliver followed in her wake into a small vestibule stacked with cartons and crates. The air was damp and it felt colder inside than out. The gloom was lit by gas sconces at irregular intervals, revealing a long narrow corridor.

She had been determinedly businesslike this morning, producing a list at breakfast that proved to be the result of an earlier conversation with Mrs Murray. Before he'd even poured his coffee, she had begun to go through it, making it clear that there was to be no reference to last night. Did she regret it? Or was she making it plain there would be no repeat performance? The latter, he had concluded.

Lily was a woman who knew her own mind. When she had said she was sure last night, she meant it. When she had assured him she had no regrets, she meant that, too. To raise the subject again would be insulting. She was drawing a line in the sand. Business first. Exactly what he believed himself. Usually. Not that there was anything remotely normal about this situation. For example, he had never breakfasted with one of his lovers before.

'Watch your step.' Lily stopped in front of him, bringing him back to his surroundings. 'There's a trapdoor here. I wonder…'

'Oi!' A burly man in a long black coat and a muffler wrapped around his neck up to his nose came hurrying towards them. 'Have a care! What you doing here?'

'We are looking for the manager, or Mr Lovejoy, if he is available?'

'Lovejoy never comes in until five and Mr Soames is over at the Oxford with Mr Villiers, the owner. They're looking at signing up a new act, not that it's any of your business.' The man turned to Oliver. 'What does the likes of you want with them?'

'What about Mrs Adams, is she here?'

'What if she is?' The man continued to address Oliver. 'What's it to you?'

'I have a business proposition to make,' Lily said. 'If you could show us the way to Mrs Adams's dressing room?'

The man sighed heavily. 'Well, if you're happy to let her wear the trousers, mate.' He turned to Lily. 'I don't know if I can remember the way.'

She produced a coin. 'Will this jog your memory?'

He looked at it, but made no attempt to take it from her hand. 'It needs a bit more jogging than that.'

Lily put the coin back in her pocket. 'I wonder what Mrs Adams will say when she discovers you have deprived her of a lucrative engagement? I'll find out when I come back later.'

'Give it here, then! I'll take you, but I warn you, it ain't Annie you'll have to deal with. It's her husband and he will want a lot more than sixpence.'

He led them through a warren of corridors, up several flights of stairs and then down again until Oliver was convinced that they were going around in circles. Noises, banging, clanging and creaking could be heard which Lily said came from the stage, but he didn't see anything that looked remotely like the back of a stage. A rhythmic thump of feet he thought could be the ballet dancers rehearsing. Draughts blew from above and below. A long rope dangling from a rafter almost knocked off his top hat. At last, their guide stopped in front of a door behind which could be heard a distinctive trill.

'Annie don't like to be disturbed when she's warming up,' they were told, before he left them without knocking.

Lily, who seemed remarkably composed, knocked on the door. It was opened by a tall, thin man with a drooping moustache wearing a suit in a houndstooth check. 'She's busy.'

'Mr Adams?' Lily pasted on her professional smile. 'I would like to engage your wife for a private performance.'

He took a moment to study her, looking her up and down in a way that made Oliver's hackles rise. 'And you are?'

For the first time, Lily hesitated, slanting him a questioning look. They had not discussed this, but he could not see how their identity could be disguised. 'Lord and Lady Rashfield.' Oliver stepped forward, holding his hand out, realising with a start at the same time that this was the first time he had made the introduction in this way.

It had the required effect. 'My lord.' His hand was taken. 'A pleasure. Though my name is Whiting, Harry Whiting. My wife sings under her maiden name. And my lady.' A bow was sketched. 'It's a pleasure. Please do come in, welcome to our humble abode.'

'He's going to try to skin us, now he knows we're monied,' Oliver whispered as he stepped back to let Lily precede him.

'We'll see about that.'

'If you will forgive the state—the disarray, my lord, my lady. The dressing room is somewhat cramped.'

'Not enough room to swing a cat, as they say. Who's this, Harry?'

'Annie, my dear, may I present Lord and Lady Rashfield?'

In the confines of the dressing room, the singer looked a great deal larger than she had appeared on stage. She was clad in an eye-wateringly bright green dressing gown which gaped alarmingly to display a scarlet corset from which her mountainous bosom showed every sign of wishing to escape. Her hair was bound up in a scarf of peacock-blue, and her husband rushed to protect her modesty by draping another scarf, this one puce, around her shoulders.

She studied first Oliver, then Lily with the same appraising eye as her husband, before holding out her hand first to Lily. 'How do you do, my lady? I won't make a curtsy…there's no room. And my lord—how do you do? Harry, will you clear a seat for our distinguished visitors?'

'They have come to engage you for a private performance,' Mr Whiting said, scooping up a collection of clothes from one chair and indicating that Lily should take it. He threw the clothes behind a painted screen, then pulled the stool out from the dressing table. 'If you would take this, my lord?'

'I'll take that, Harry, I know how to balance on it. Lord Rashfield will have to stand. We can't offer you any refreshment, I'm afraid. As you see, we're a bit short in terms of facilities.' Annie chuckled. 'Unless you fancy a gin. I don't indulge myself, it's bad for the vocal chords, but there's always a bottle in Mr Soames's room. No? Well then, what I'd like to know is what kind of performance Lord and Lady Rashfield had in mind from the likes of me?'

'Don't undersell yourself, Annie,' her husband interjected. 'She's such a modest woman, my wife, but you'll not find another voice like hers in any other theatre in London.'

'Big voice, big personality, big physique,' Annie interjected with a rumbling laugh. 'That's what they say about me.'

'My wife likes her little jokes. What do you fancy having her sing? She can do Verdi, Donizetti, all the Italians.'

'We had the honour of hearing Mrs Adams sing here last night,' Lily said.

'Here?' husband and wife exclaimed in unison.

'Gawd,' Mr Whiting added, 'tell me you didn't touch the pies?'

Lily's mouth trembled. 'We were assured by the waitress that they contained proper beef. His Lordship enjoyed his very much.'

'Proper or not, I hope it didn't misbehave on you, my lord,' Mr Whiting said.

'No ill effects,' Oliver reassured him, trying not to look at Lily lest he laugh.

'Then you must have the constitution of an ox and are to be heartily congratulated, sir. My lord, I mean.'

'Harry, His Lordship isn't here to discuss his stomach.'

'We wish to engage you to sing at a—a social evening we are planning,' Lily intervened. 'It would be one night only, in just over two weeks' time. Perfectly respectable, I assure you,' she added. 'We are hoping that Mr Lovejoy will be our chairman and that we can persuade two or three of the other acts from last night's show to join us.'

'Have you asked them?'

'No, we wished to speak to you first,' Lily said blithely.

'No show without Punch?'

'My husband and I were very taken with your voice, Mrs Adams. Our ballroom has not the proportions of the Canterbury, but it will require excellent projection.'

'Well, I've certainly got that. You'll be wanting me to stick to opera, I'm assuming?'

'What else do you have in your repertoire?'

'I started out singing when I was a barmaid in me pa's pub. The glasses used to shake when I hit the high notes.' Annie laughed. 'I've been singing for my living since I was nineteen.'

'Same year you married me,' her husband interjected, 'and I'm sure these people aren't interested in those kinds of songs.'

'Oh, but we are,' Lily said. 'Do go on, Mrs Adams. Do you have any songs that are particular favourites with your audience?'

'Well now, "Johnny the Engine Driver" always gets the crowd going. Or "When the Band Begins to Play". It depends what you want.'

'*Lucia di Lammermoor*—that's quality for you,' Mr Whiting said.

'We could certainly begin with that. It will be familiar to our guests. And then something more popular. Nothing too risqué, mind you, but something that will encourage our guests to join in the chorus.'

'I could try, but as to joining in, I'm not so sure. These guests, where will you get them from?'

Lily blanched, though only Oliver noticed. Where indeed, he thought he could hear her say. 'We are sending out invitations for about one hundred and fifty of our—our acquaintances,' she said. 'Will you do it, Mrs Adams?'

'That very much depends on the fee.' Mr Whiting turned to Oliver. 'My wife has lately returned from a very popular tour of America. They loved her in New York. Couldn't get enough of her. When she got back to England, she could command any price.'

'How lately was that?' Oliver asked, earning himself a small smile from Lily.

'And what price do you command here, Mrs Adams?' she asked.

'I manage the finances for my wife.' Mr Whiting looked mulishly at Oliver. 'I was once Harry Wall, you know. A comic singer without compare, but I gave up my career to look after Annie.'

'We're not trying to cheat you,' Lily said. 'We'll pay above the going rate and we'll compensate you for your loss of earnings here.'

'That's a good point,' Annie said. 'What about Mr Soames, Harry? We wouldn't want to get on the wrong side of him, we need…'

'You leave Soames to me.' Mr Whiting coloured. 'He needs us more than we need him.'

This was said belligerently. His wife looked unconvinced, but remained silent. Oliver began to feel uncomfortable. 'We wouldn't want to jeopardise your longer-term prospects.'

'That won't be an issue for any of the acts we wish to hire, my love,' Lily said to him. 'Mr Soames will consider the press coverage more than compensates him for the loss of one night's revenue and there will be no shortage of acts willing to step in, I'm sure.'

'You've got that right and no mistake,' Mrs Adams said.

'What do you mean by press coverage?' her husband asked sharply.

'We have every expectation that our soirée will be reported with a great deal of positive speculation beforehand, and afterwards I anticipate it will be reported in detail.'

'Will they want to talk to us, the reporters?'

This question, they had discussed. 'They may,' Lily said. 'It will be the perfect opportunity for you to tell the readers where they can see the same performers for themselves. In the flesh, on the stage, so to speak.'

'So we'll fill the seats here and Mr Soames won't be out of pocket for losing us for one night. Quite the opposite. Will you tell him so?'

'Just as soon as I can be assured that we have secured Mrs Adams for the evening.'

'You try and stop me! We'll be there.' Mrs Adams surged to her feet, beaming. 'Who else were you thinking to have join us, apart from Lovejoy? Harry will be happy to speak to them if you have any trouble persuading them, though I can't see why you would. And Harry can rehearse us all, too.'

'For a small fee.'

'You'll need us to rehearse, won't you, my lady? And we'll need to see what the room's like, won't we, Harry? Will there be a place to change? I can't travel in my stage dresses, they're so heavy I can barely walk in them.'

'All of that will be arranged once I have spoken to Mr Soames and the other artistes.'

Mrs Adams grasped Lily's hand. 'You're a pair of queer hawks and no mistake, but I promise we won't let you down, will we, Harry?'

'A pair of queer hawks.' Lily sank on to a chair in front of the fire in the breakfast parlour some hours later. 'Do you think that the *Morning Post* will describe us thus?'

'I'd never heard the expression until this morning

but I reckon it's apposite.' Oliver sat down opposite her, stretching his legs towards the fire. 'What did she say to you afterwards? When we were on our way out and that husband of hers was listing out all the extra over-heads we'd be expected to pay for, I saw her whisper something to you.'

'She wanted to know who I was,' Lily said, studying her hands. 'Not that she suspected the truth, but she said to me, "You know what you're about, and I'd like to know how".' She forced herself to meet Oliver's eyes. 'I told her I didn't understand her meaning. "Have it your way," she said. "You don't have to worry I'll say anything to Harry, I know when I'm on to a good thing".'

'Do you trust her?' Oliver asked.

'Not to ask questions, or pass on her suspicions, such as they are? I think so. As she said, she's on to a good thing. She's a lot more up to snuff than her husband, I reckon, though she lets him think he's the one with the nous.'

'Harry Wall that was. I don't think he can have been very good, do you?'

Lily shrugged. 'Annie has an exceptional voice and comic singers such as Harry are ten a penny. Their arrangement makes sense, his managing her bookings and looking after her wardrobe. Those gowns weigh almost as much as she does, she told me. One of Harry's responsibilities is to walk behind her, holding them up from the ground when she goes on and off stage to make sure they don't get ruined.'

Oliver gave a snort of laughter. 'Like a page boy trailing behind the queen. There's no going back now, after today, Lily. Are you happy?'

'Are you?'

'We certainly achieved what we set out to do this morning. Or rather, you did. You left me nothing to do but watch and wonder.'

'It's what I do and have been doing for years and I very much appreciate the fact that you let me get on with doing it.'

'As you say, you've been doing it for years.'

'Yes, but most men—' She broke off, smiling. 'But then, you are a very unusual man.'

'Thank you.'

The fire crackled. The curtains were drawn. The room was warm and comfortable and it had been a long, tiring day. She had steadfastly refused to think about last night, determined to prove herself, and she had done so. No matter that what she had done was chicken feed to what she did back in Paris, she had done it well and Oliver was happy.

They had dined on the way back to the town house in a hotel. A dinner that was a triumph of ceremony over substance, with much flourishing of platters containing little worth eating. Restaurants in London left a lot to be desired compared to Paris, if this was an example, but she had refrained from saying so. They had valiantly eaten enough to stave off hunger, while discussing their plans for the coming days.

She slanted a look at Oliver, only to find that he was watching her. She could feel her cheeks flushing as she looked away. She was thirty-one years old, long past being coy, which she never had been, but nor had she ever been in this situation. Last night they had been lovers. Such lovers! But the man sitting opposite her was much more than a lover.

Today, they had presented themselves as yet another version of the Marquess and Marchioness of Rashfield. They were business partners of a sort. They were partners in crime, if it was a crime to put the estate he had inherited to good use in good shape.

In just over two weeks, they would play host to the cream of London society right here in this town house. Hosting the great and the good, the *ton*, who would have no idea that their hostess was also La Muguette, the esteemed Parisian agent and failed chorus girl, and that their performance as a newly-wed couple deeply in love was just that, a performance. Would Annie Adams cause trouble? Lily closed her eyes. She must not let doubts take hold now. There was no going back.

'Lily.' Her eyes flew open. Oliver was crouching by her chair. 'You're exhausted. It's been a long day, why don't you have an early night?'

He stood up, holding out his hand. She let him help her to her feet. She didn't want to go to bed, not alone, though that was what she knew she ought to do. One night only, that was the pact she had made with herself. But one night simply wasn't enough. All that one night had done was make her crave more. If she didn't satisfy the craving, then it would always be there, she reasoned, a doubt. She would miss him. She didn't want to miss him, so the obvious recourse was to sate herself.

Was she fooling herself? And Oliver? Lily eyed him doubtfully. He had been as businesslike as she all day, for there had been no need for them to play the newly-weds. She wasn't sure how to cross from one role to the other now. She wasn't even sure that Oliver wished to. Though he was still holding her hand. Was he waiting for her to give him a sign? She was behaving like a simpering virgin, for goodness sake!

'Oliver!'

'Lily?' He quirked a brow, smiling at her.

'Oliver.' She smiled up at him. 'Should we— Would you— Will we…?'

'Oh, God, yes.' He sighed deeply, wrapping his arm around her waist.

'It doesn't mean— I mean I don't wish you to think that—or feel obliged.'

He laughed softly. 'I promise I will tell you if that happens.'

She wrapped her arms around his neck. Warmth was flooding her veins. 'So will I,' she said.

They kissed, slow, languorous kisses in the firelight, kisses that warmed and teased, and which would have gone on and on were it not for their clothes. Oliver cupped her breast through her gown and her corset. Her nipple was hard, desperate for his touch. One more long, slow kiss and they left the morning room, hurrying up the stairs, pausing to kiss on the first landing, and then at the top of the second flight.

The lamp was turned low on her dressing table. The fire burned behind a screen. They kissed again and the kisses became urgent as they hurried out of their clothes, anxious to touch, to taste. Naked from the waist up, Lily pressed herself against him, feeling the hard length of his erection pressing against her drawers, her nipples hard against his flesh.

He steered her over to the bed, casting off the rest

of his own clothes, kissing her again as he eased her on to her back. More kisses, over her breasts, tracing their shape with his tongue, then his mouth on her nipple making her cry out, arch up, reach for him. More kisses, down the dip of her belly, his hands untying her drawers, pulling them down, and then more kisses, the inside of her thighs, and then between. No one had kissed her like this, kneeling between her legs and bringing her to a frenzy of desire with his mouth, his tongue. It was too much. Her climax caught hold, making her cry out, reach wildly for him as it pulsed through her.

'Oliver! Oliver!'

'Coming,' he said with a laugh in his voice. 'Give me a moment to look after...'

The bed creaked. He was beside her, reaching for her, kissing her. Then pulling her over, on top of him. 'Yes?' he asked.

Lily leaned over to kiss him. 'Yes,' she sighed as he lifted her, as he began to slide inside her. 'Oh, Oliver, yes,' she said, as she sank back to take all of him in. She tried to take it slowly, but her body didn't want to be patient and nor did he, pushing harder as she moved up, sank down on him, his hands on her bottom, his eyes fixed on her, mouthing *yes, yes, yes*, with every thrust. She was lost in the second wave of her own climax when he came, shuddering, high inside her, his back arching, his mouth feverish on hers as she fell forward to kiss him, their bodies locked together, slick with sweat.

She didn't want to move, not even after their breathing had eased back to normal, but she forced herself to, at last. Oliver smiled, pulling her against his side, and she let her head rest on his chest, feeling the tickle of his hair on her cheek. His hand settled on her thigh, stroking up and down, rousing and at the same time making her eyes flutter closed. She felt her bones had melted. She curled in closer to the warmth of his body. He pulled the sheet over them. He settled her head more comfortably on his shoulder.

Oliver lay awake. He had a cramp in his arm, but he didn't want to move lest he wake her. He didn't want to do that, because then he'd have to go to his own bed and he didn't want to go to his own bed. He wanted to stay here, with Lily. To fall asleep with her and to wake up in the morning with her, and to make love to her again. This was what kept him awake.

It wasn't like him. It was very, very unlike him. He had never met a woman like Lily. He had never imagined there could be a woman like Lily. And he was married to her! Not really married. Soon to be unmarried, in fact. April was not so far away and he'd promised that their marriage would be over by April, that she could return to Paris, to her own world. A world that she loved and that today had demonstrated she was eminently suited to.

Lily sighed in her sleep. Her leg was draped over his, one of her hands rested on his belly. He was wide awake and now he was aroused, and April was not so far away at all. He didn't want to lose her.

Oliver pushed back the sheet and began to detach himself, inch by inch. In April, he would be able to return to his own life, in New Kilmun. By April, he'd be freeing himself from the manacles of this inheritance. He ought to be looking forward to April. Lily was going, there was no avoiding that, and by the time she left, he'd probably be glad.

Morning Post,
21st February 1877

Entente Cordiale

A week today, the Fifth Marquess of R. will introduce his bride to society when the newly-weds host a ball at their town house in Mayfair.

Readers will recall the concerns expressed in this illustrious journal by country neighbours of the couple's Berkshire estate, regarding their fitness for the roles they had so recently stepped into, Lord R. being an industrialist with no experience of managing the grand estates he inherited.

We were reliably informed that the local gentry felt a more English helpmeet would have safely embedded him into the rural idyll. The new Lady R. was too French in her ways and too sophisticated in her style to suit these good people, we were told. Reading between the lines, it is not too difficult to see that the young ladies of Berkshire, the daughters of these good people, felt they had been snubbed.

You and I, Dear Reader, are more open to the winds of change blowing through the stagnant waters of the Establishment. This is the nineteenth century, the age of progress and industrial revolution—a time for fresh faces and fresh ideas to infiltrate the hidebound and outmoded customs and conventions that society's Luddites cling to.

Lord and Lady R. are undoubtedly an unconventional match. Little is known of the lineage and history of the new Marchioness, who has her own unique style. A slender figure, impeccably gowned by Monsieur Worth of Paris, Lady R. is not an English Rose, but has that certain je ne sais quoi…*a Parisian elegance that we venture to suggest will set a new trend.*

Those who have questioned the legitimacy of this union have clearly not set eyes on Lady R.— Lord R., we must discreetly add, understandably cannot take his eyes off his new bride!

The invitations have gone out. For the lucky recipients, we are reliably informed, a most unusual entertainment will be proffered. A refreshing change for jaded palates which, now the Season is underway, are already bored to tears by the latest crush!

Have we whetted your tastebuds? Has the little bird we spoke to given us a hint of what will transpire at a certain town house in Mayfair next Wednesday?

A scintillating symposium of celebrated showmen, Dear Reader. That is what Lord and Lady R. plan. Their guests, we will happily wager, might be many things, but they will not be bored.

Chapter Ten

Mayfair, London—28th February 1877

With the assistance of Mrs Bremner and Riddell, who had become regular travellers on the train between Rashfield and London, and aided and abetted by a small army of hired staff, the Mayfair town house was ready. For this momentous occasion Lily had chosen to wear a Worth evening gown made of burnished red silk embroidered with flowers and leaves of autumnal gold. The bodice was in the shape of a corset, with a deep vee at the front and a daringly low décolleté, made modest with a corsage of antique lace. Lace insets were set into the side panels of the skirt, which had a bustle and a sweeping train, but which was otherwise unadorned, relying on the fabric and the figure for effect.

Until now, Lily had never had occasion to wear it, for it was much more revealing than her usual taste and, despite its lack of ostentation, far too sumptuous. A pair of long kid evening gloves and a gold fan were her only accessories, in keeping with his radical politics, she had told Oliver, when he suggested she inspect the family jewels for something appropriate.

'You were absolutely right,' he said, joining her as she made a final tour of the ballroom, 'you need no adornment. Lily, you look utterly divine.'

She made a sweeping curtsy. 'Thank you, my lord. And you, may I say, look deliciously, devastatingly, dashing.'

'Deliciously? You've been spending too much time listening to Mr Lovejoy rehearse.'

'No, those words were all my own, *mon amour.*' She opened her fan, eyeing him provocatively as she fluttered it. Oliver was dressed in a black-tailed evening coat with a silk collar which emphasised the breadth of his shoulders, white satin waistcoat and white shirt with a pleated front. His trousers were cut narrow with black braid seam on the outside of the leg. 'Too French, do you think?' Lily closed the fan. 'Should my gaze be more doe-eyed?' she asked, assuming a suitable expression.

'Good God, no, you look as if you're begging for scraps from the table.'

Lily chuckled. 'You see now why I never made it as a leading lady.'

'You're nervous.'

'With cause,' she said, becoming serious, 'but I won't let you down.'

'I'm more concerned that I'll let you down.'

Lily cast a quick look over her shoulder to make sure none of the staff was about. 'We are in this together, remember?' she said, taking his hand and lifting it to her cheek. 'These last two weeks, you have been tireless. Back and forward, back and forward to Rashfield

Manor, and in between dealing with all the correspondence your man in New Kilmun sends you.'

'You've been the same, Lily.'

'Accept a compliment, just this once.' She kissed his knuckles, then let his hand go. 'Tonight is going to be the performance of your life. I was never a leading lady, but I have been on the stage countless times. From now on, don't forget that there will be people watching us. Our every move, everything we say, will be noted. It's not only the reporter who will be keen to take notes. There are our guests, all the agency staff, and the cast—don't forget, Oliver, that they are going to be watching us, too.'

'If I wasn't nervous before, I am now.'

'Bon!' Lily said, 'so now you are ready to go on stage. Shall we make one last tour of the set?'

'In a moment.' Oliver took her by surprise, pulling her into his arms. 'I want to say something.'

'You don't need to thank me again.'

'Oh, but I do. I have a speech ready and rehearsed, and I'm determined to deliver it. When Archie died,' he said, in a more serious tone, 'it turned my world upside down. When you came up with this madcap plan for me to regain control of my life back, I confess I was very sceptical at first. I didn't want to think about failing, but you were right. The court case is still dragging on and on and likely to continue for months yet. If it wasn't for you, I'd still be kicking my heels, or more likely I'd have gone back to New Kilmun and left Archie's tenants in the hands of the trustees. They have a very different future ahead of them and you've played a big part in securing that.'

'Trivial, compared to what you are doing.'

'Lily, I wouldn't have been able to achieve anything if we were not married.'

'It has hardly been a hardship. The truth is I've enjoyed it.'

'You've stolen my line,' Oliver said, smiling ruefully. 'Every step we've taken since has been risky and what we're about to do tonight is the riskiest step of all, but I'm enjoying every minute of it, because of you.'

There was a look in his eye she hadn't seen before. Earnest? More than mere sincerity. Her instinct was to pull herself free and run, because he was saying what she hadn't allowed herself to think. 'Oliver,' she cautioned.

He shook his head, putting a finger to her mouth to silence her. 'There's no need to panic. This isn't leading up to anything profound, save to say thank you from the bottom of my heart.'

Now, contrarily she felt deflated. 'As I said, there's no need.'

'These last couple of weeks, watching you with Annie and all the others, it's been a reminder of how much you're sacrificing. And being with you, making love with you—Lily, I want you to know that that's been like nothing else I've known before, too.'

'I do know,' she said in a whisper, 'because it's been the same for me, but...'

'But all good things must come to an end. This speech and our time together,' Oliver continued. 'If we make a success of tonight...'

'I know we will.'

'Well, if we do, then I think—I believe that we won't

hear any more from Hale and his merry men. I know you must be very anxious to get back to Paris.'

'I said I'd stay here until April. It would look bad if I left straight after our ball tonight.'

'I don't want you to go. Not yet, I mean,' Oliver said, 'but by April…' He stopped, winced, shook his head. 'By April we'll be yesterday's news. There will be nothing to keep you here.'

'Good,' Lily said, nodding, because of course it was good. 'Excellent,' she added. 'But in the meantime…'

'In the meantime.' Oliver sighed. Nodded. Smiled. 'In the meantime, we have another four weeks together. I'd like us to make the most of it.'

'What do you mean?'

'No idea. Enjoy it. Have fun. Not—I don't mean that we'll stop progress in Berkshire, but there's no harm in letting other people get on with what we've set in motion. What do you think?'

'Yes, I would like to—to make the most of the time we have left. Four weeks.' *Only four weeks!* 'A sort of holiday?'

'In a manner of speaking.'

'I will be very busy when I go back to Paris.' *In four weeks.* 'And you, when I leave…'

'I'll have more than enough to occupy me.'

She nodded firmly. 'It will be the same for me. So, yes, what you suggest—why not?'

A soft harrumph made them both turn to find Riddell standing in the doorway. 'The first of the carriages have drawn up, my lady,' he said.

'Thank you,' Lily said. Then, turning to Oliver, 'Ready to step into the limelight, *mon amour*?'

'My love.' He bent his head to kiss her lightly, careful of her lip rouge, then held out his arm. 'Once more into the breach, as they say.'

'It is "unto",' Lily said, smiling up at him. 'Don't fluff your lines.'

Oliver stood with Lily at the top of the staircase to receive their guests. They both, it transpired, had a facility for remembering names and putting them to faces. The prompt cards which Oliver had requested Sinclair make up, with a very few salient facts for each guest, had served him in good stead. It was an old trick of his, which had helped him through many meetings in the past with investors, competitors and committees.

Who would have thought it would serve to help him through an ordeal like this? But it did and, within ten minutes of Riddell's booming introductions, the shaking of hands, introducing his darling wife, Oliver's nerves had given way to a steely determination to get the job done and get it done well.

Curiosity had triumphed. The artful piece in the *Morning Post* had done its work. By eleven o'clock, when the entertainment was due to begin, Riddell informed them that all of their guests had arrived, though how the man kept track was a mystery.

'My jaw aches with smiling,' Oliver whispered to Lily when the last of their guests had entered the ballroom.

'We have a respite now.' Through the open double doors, hired footmen hurried to dim the gas sconces, while others turned up the oil lamps which lined the makeshift stage. 'Everyone's eyes will be on the stage, but remember...'

'There are eyes everywhere,' Oliver said, catching Lily unawares, and snatching a kiss. 'And this is just in case that reporter chap is watching,' he said, pulling her closer. This time, he kissed her more slowly. She made that tiny little sigh that never failed to set his blood racing. Something he could not afford to happen, in these blasted tight evening trousers, he recalled, releasing her just a fraction too late. Fortunately, a drumroll distracted her.

'That's Mr Lovejoy's cue,' Lily said, tugging at his hand. 'Come on, I want to see...'

'You've seen it a hundred times.'

'I want to see what everyone else thinks.' She took his hand, leading the way round the edge of their guests to the back of the ballroom.

'Ladies and gentlemen.' Lovejoy bounded on to the stage with the backdrop that Lily had commissioned from the scenery painters at the Canterbury. 'Welcome to this most illustrious, inimitable and impressive of evenings. Allow me to introduce myself. I am Leopold Lovejoy and I shall be your chairman for this evening of elemental excess. An education, I hope, and an exorbitant entertainment for your delight and delectation.'

Lovejoy paused, but the audience, having no idea they were expected to applaud, were silent. He twirled his moustache and rolled his eyes. Oliver glanced down at Lily, but her eyes were fixed on their guests, her professional smile fixed on her mouth.

'Our first act,' continued Lovejoy, 'is an adoringly delicious diva. Ladies and gentlemen, show your ap-

preciation with a joyous germination of spontaneity.'
Lovejoy paused again, looking around his audience with
a mischievous smile. 'That means put your hands together,' he said in a mock aside. 'I give you the peerless
Miss Annie Adams.'

No one clapped, so Oliver took the initiative, calling out, 'Bravo!' Lily joined him as the orchestra struck
up, but only a smattering of others did. Annie appeared
on stage and Oliver had to bite back a laugh. She had
dressed for the occasion in a gown that seemed to be
entirely constructed of pearls and crystals, with a tiara
on top of her hair and a monstrous necklace that could
only be paste covering most of her bosom.

'Good evening, ladies and gentlemen. It is a pleasure and an honour to be performing here for Lord and
Lady Rashfield.' Annie nodded at the lead violin of the
small orchestra and they struck up.

Whatever their guests were expecting, it was not the
sheer power and beauty of Annie's voice, as she opened
with one of the most popular pieces from *La Traviata*.
The applause at the end of the song was politely enthusiastic. Oliver began to relax as Annie continued, taking on the Queen of the Night's aria from *The Magic
Flute* with gusto which was received with equally enthusiastic applause. Her final song, a heart-wrenching
aria from *Lucia di Lammermoor* received the ultimate
accolade of a full ten seconds of silence followed by
several calls of *encore!*

'I think this is going well,' Oliver whispered as Lovejoy reappeared and raised a few claps.

'The next act will be the test,' Lily said, linking her
arm into his and lifting her face for a kiss. 'Mr Brown

from the *Morning Post* is standing stage left,' she whispered in his ear.

The next act was The Great Mephisto, the conjuror. He began tamely enough with a few card tricks, but cleverly engaged some of the gentlemen in the audience to act as his assistant—and, unwittingly, his dupe. His next trick, however, required him to mingle with the audience and to retrieve items from their persons, beginning with cards and coins, but his *pièce de résistance* was to remove an object from one person and retrieve it from another. Oliver had witnessed the trick several times now and never failed to be fascinated. Even Lily didn't have the key to how he did it.

The conjuror jumped down from the stage and began to work his way through the audience. He chose gentlemen again at first, but after three coins and a card, he stopped beside one of the ladies. As he tried to put his hand on her ear, she shrank back in horror. Oliver heard Lily's breath hitch, felt her body bracing, and then the Great Mephisto waved a large sparkling stone in the air.

'A diamond,' he declared, pocketing it. 'I hope I get invited back here, usually it's a bit of coal.'

The sally received a laugh. Lily relaxed. When he was finished, producing three doves from a seemingly empty top hat, the Great Mephisto received a spontaneous round of applause and a couple of bravos. And so it went on, with Mr Lovejoy becoming ever more exuberant, until the final act of the night and Annie's reappearance.

'This is a song called "Riding in a Railway Train",' she announced. 'It's about a gentleman snatching a kiss from a fair unsuspecting maid in a train carriage while it goes through a tunnel. Sound familiar to anyone? Gentlemen? Ladies?'

Annie came to the edge of the stage, leaning over precariously. 'Now then, ladies and gentlemen, there's a tradition in the music halls, where the audience joins in with the chorus, for the last song. Do you think you can manage that?'

There were a few murmurs. Annie cupped her hand over her ear. 'I said, do you think you can manage that? That's better. It's a simple refrain, it goes like this.'

A nod to the orchestra and Annie sang the chorus, then began to rehearse her audience. They were bemused, but she cajoled, she heckled and finally she won them over.

She'd never been kissed on a train before,
but he snatched it, as bold as brass.
She'd never been kissed on a train before,
but like his ticket, it was first class.

Lily beamed up at Oliver, as their guests, conducted by Annie, sang the refrain one more time, then burst into a storm of applause. He smiled down at her, shaking his head. 'I can't quite believe what we've seen. We aren't paying Annie nearly enough.'

'I think they all deserve a bonus.'

'Lovely Lily.' He kissed her, his hand resting fleetingly on her shoulder. 'That one was for Mr Brown. This one is for me.'

'Rashfield! Unhand that lovely wife of yours or you'll set a new trend for kissing in public and that won't do

at all. Let me congratulate you both on a most unusual evening. Most unusual.'

'A most original evening. We must send you an invitation for...'

'Really very refreshingly different. What a voice that woman has. Will we see you at...?'

'Eel pie! Never had that before, never wish to try it again, but other than that, really a most entertaining evening. I wonder if we'll see you at the club on Thursday?'

'My dear Lady Rashfield, I fear that sherry cobbler has quite gone to my head. You must give me the recipe.'

'I must compliment you on your gown, Lady Rashfield. Worth, I presume? I have not the figure for it myself...'

'A night at the music hall, in Mayfair! My mother will never credit it. Are you thinking of taking up your seat in the House, Rashfield?'

'Never danced a polka quite like that. Thought I was going to have an apoplexy.'

'Congratulations. My wife here was shaking her head when we read the announcement in The Times *last month. "Never heard of her," she said—yes, my dear, you did. After tonight, there won't be anyone in the* ton *who hasn't heard of you. Excellent night. Excellent. A lovely change from the run of the mill.'*

At last, long after two in the morning, the final guest was waved off. Almost everyone had stayed to take supper in the dining room, which had been transformed into an eel pie shop, and then to dance. The reappearance of the Great Mephisto's doves during a quadrille had caused much consternation, but the conjuror, summoned from his dinner in the kitchen and, bereft of his black velvet robes, looking more like an accounts clerk, had quickly coaxed them on to his shoulders.

'Is it too late for a glass of champagne?' Oliver asked. 'You haven't had anything to drink all evening and I've asked them to put a bottle on ice in the breakfast parlour.'

'I never drink when I'm working, but it's never too late or too early for champagne,' Lily said, following in his wake.

The fire was burning and the gas sconces were turned down low. Oliver opened the bottle and Lily sank on to the wing-back chair at the fireside with a sigh. 'Thank you.' She touched her glass to his. 'I think that went as well as we could possibly have hoped.'

'That's what I'd call damning with faint praise. Brown assured me he would submit a positive piece—though he was hardly likely to say otherwise, mind you. But Annie had our guests singing along with a song of dubious content. And you heard everyone when they were leaving, Lily, they were effusive.'

'People always are, to your face. For me, I think actions speak louder than words.'

'That's true.' Oliver dropped into the chair facing her, taking off his necktie and unfastening the top button of his shirt. 'It's one of the reasons I leave managing sales to someone else. Why can't people simply say that they have no plans to buy something, instead of humming and hawing or, worse still, saying they'll be in touch and immediately becoming unavailable.'

'Look, Mr Whatever, our salt is the best and you

won't get a better price,' Lily said in a pompous tone. 'So just buy it and let me get on with more interesting things such as—such as adjusting my steam-powered grain counter.'

'You know me pretty well. What does a steam-powered grain counter do?'

'Counts salt grains, of course, to ensure that every package contains the exact same amount, I imagine. Don't you have one? They are the very latest thing, I'm told.'

Oliver laughed. 'That's what happens when you're away from the business too long. You lose touch with the latest developments.'

Lily took a sip of her champagne. It was excellent and perfectly cold. 'Do you? Lose touch, I mean?'

'I try to keep up, but things move so fast in industry and the people with the best ideas are often the ones doing the job.'

'And you've not had the time to spend with them?'

'I've realised I'm not indispensable when it comes to the day-to-day running of things, but it's not enough to keep doing what you're doing in the same way. Progress.' He looked over, grinning sheepishly. 'There's no stopping it.'

'So the sooner you get back to New Kilmun, the better. Oliver, don't you think, then, that it would be better for us to spend the next four weeks trying to get Rashfield Manor on a more stable footing? You won't want to waste time with me.'

'I don't consider it a waste.' Oliver finished his champagne. 'I've acquired a taste for this. Would you like some more?' He got up to take her glass. 'You don't look very comfortable there—wouldn't you like to get out of that dress?'

'Is that a proposition?'

'Yes.' He held out his hand. 'We can take the champagne with us, if you like?'

Lily allowed herself to be helped to her feet. 'I like,' she said, wrapping her arms around him and lifting her face for his kiss. 'I like, very, very much.'

Chapter Eleven

'The reviews are in,' Lily said, handing the *Morning Post* to Oliver. '*A* review, I should say.'

'I need my coffee first,' he said, pouring himself a cup and topping up Lily's. 'You're up early.'

'I couldn't sleep.' She concentrated on buttering her roll. Once, she had allowed herself to fall asleep in his arms, a mistake she had determined never to repeat. She had woken up alone and her first feeling had been one of disappointment. Why hadn't he stayed? What would it be like to make sleepy, barely awake love? She had never wished to before. Now she would never know.

Since then, no matter how tempting it was to curl into Oliver's sated body, to have his arms around her, Lily had forced herself to remain wide awake, refusing to relax when they lay together in the aftermath of lovemaking, refusing to give in to the temptation to break her own self-imposed and long-standing rule. A lover was for lovemaking. Making love with Oliver was like nothing else, no one else. But sleeping with him smacked of intimacy, of familiarity, of something far more permanent than she wanted. Did Oliver feel as she did? No, she wouldn't allow herself to speculate about that either, for it was pointless.

It was ironic that they were so frank with each other during the day, but at night, at their most intimate, they were increasingly more guarded. They never spoke afterwards. There was no pillow talk. Lily had never mixed business with pleasure and she had no intentions of doing so now, even if the source of both were this man sitting opposite her, frowning over Mr Brown's piece in the newspaper.

'Fine,' he said, casting it aside and catching her staring at him. 'It does exactly what we needed it to do. I'll happily dispense with having to read that rag again.'

'So we're dropping Mr Brown?'

'He was never going to become my best friend. Do you have other ideas?'

Was she imagining his brusqueness? He hadn't finished his coffee yet, perhaps that was it? When he was sitting across the table from her in his suit, she found it difficult to reconcile him with the man who had made such passionate and unrestrained love to her a few hours before. Did he have the same difficulty with her?

'Lily! Whatever is on your mind, why don't you just ask me?'

'Mr Brown,' she said, picking up the newspaper. 'If we drop him now, isn't there a risk he'll go back to digging up dirt?'

'And retract all the effusive praise he's heaped on us this morning. "Refreshingly egalitarian".'

'"Unfashionably tactile".'

'"Deeply attached",' Oliver quoted sardonically.

'He has form for changing his tune when it suits him.'

'True. Have we made a rod for our own back, cultivating him? I can't see the point in cultivating him any further, when we have what we wanted from him. Look at those.' He picked up a stack of letters and cards addressed to Lord and Lady Rashfield and pushed them across the table to her. 'Actions speak louder than words, you said last night. I think those speak for themselves. I don't think we need concern ourselves with Brown.'

Lily flicked through the mail. 'What are we going to do about these? If we snub everyone...'

'I don't know!' Oliver pushed his coffee cup to one side with an exasperated sigh. 'Victims of our own success, that's what we are. I've had a letter from Hale, too, asking me if I plan to take up my seat in the House.'

'Is that a positive endorsement? Has Sir Everard finally accepted you as a worthy successor?'

'If he has, he'll change his tune pretty quickly when he discovers what we're planning, which I am thinking we should tell him, and the rest of them, sooner rather than later.'

'But why does he want you to take up your seat? That man, what was his name—Fisher? He asked you the same question last night. Was Archie involved in politics?'

'Ha! Archie in the Lords? That I'd have liked to see. I wonder what cause he'd have supported?'

'The adoption of a Moorish style of architecture in a renovation of Windsor Castle?' Lily quipped.

'I can imagine that he'd have thought that an excellent idea, but making the effort to do something about it—no, not Archie.'

'What would you speak up for, Oliver? Supposing that you did take your seat, there must be a great number of things you'd like to change?'

'The Factories Acts never go far enough, as far as I'm concerned, in protecting workers' rights, but I'd be in a small minority, trying to force everyone to comply with my own standards. I'd be wasting time better used to making sure my own people are looked after, my own factories are safe. What would you speak up for?'

'They wouldn't let me in,' Lily said. 'I'm a woman, remember.'

'I never forget that. What, you think I do?' Oliver pushed his coffee cup aside. 'I try to stick to the rules. I don't mix business with pleasure, but that doesn't mean I find it easy.'

'You don't?'

'If you must know, when you're sitting across from me at breakfast, all laced up in your uniform, as you call it, all I can think of is unlacing you. I want to kiss you, not bid you a polite good morning, but unless we're going to invite guests to breakfast, there's no need to put on a show, and in any case, I don't want to kiss you to put on a show. I want to kiss you because I want to kiss you.' Oliver made a helpless gesture. 'And that would be mixing business with pleasure.'

One of her questions answered and she almost wished it had not been. Should she tell him it was the same for her? Her instinct was to protect herself. 'I am sorry to be a distraction. It's as well that I am not going to be here for much longer, *n'est-ce pas*?'

'So you don't want me to kiss you good morning?'

He was circling her palm with his thumb. It was making her arm tingle all the way up to her shoulder and then down. It was making it difficult for her to breathe. Lily withdrew her hand on the pretext of picking up her coffee cup. 'A minimum fee,' she said. 'For the chorus and all performers, not just the headline acts. That's what I'd speak about.'

'Now that is a truly radical idea,' he said, accepting the rebuff.

It was contrary of her to feel disappointed. 'Very, and very unlikely ever to happen, too. Imagine having to pay every chorus girl a rate that will keep them from having to earn more in whatever way they can, whatever their age or experience. Especially when for every chorus girl you employ, there's a hundred others waiting in the wings who would be happy to take on the role for less.'

'That sounds familiar,' Oliver said drily. 'Who'd have thought that your world and mine had so much in common?'

'I've been discussing the situation with Annie over the last couple of weeks. There's no one like me working in London—not that she knows who I am, you needn't worry. She's lucky, she's got a talent that really makes her stand out and, after last night, she's going to be able to charge a premium, as will all of them.'

'Mr Soames isn't going to be very pleased about that.'

'Mr Soames,' Lily said, 'is going to have full houses for weeks. He'll not carp about a few bonuses. But it won't last, Oliver. It's a tough life for people like Annie, respectably married, trying to put a bit by for her retirement, which will come sooner than she wants.'

'And compared to most, Annie's a star?'

'Precisely.'

'You don't have plans to expand your business to London, I take it?'

'It was tough enough breaking into the theatre world in Paris. I'm making a real difference there.'

'So London and Manchester and Liverpool and Glasgow and all the rest of the cities with theatres will have to wait for another Lily to come along? You'll eschew changing the big wide world and concentrate on changing your own little bit of it? That's not a criticism incidentally, it's what I do, too.'

'We both focus our energies where we can be sure we can make a difference.' Lily picked up a packet from Mr Sinclair. 'More news from Hélène. I heard from her only yesterday. Would you mind if I read this now?'

'Of course not.'

Oliver opened *The Times*. Lily slit open the parcel from Mr Sinclair. Inside was a letter and a newspaper clipping from Hélène. She read both quickly, then scanned the clipping again. 'Oliver?'

'You'll never believe this.' He shook the newspaper. 'A whole article about New Kilmun and a very positive one, too. Our methods, safety measures, and a commendation on the town itself.'

'That's wonderful.'

'It's not all wonderful. There's speculation about what the future of the Rashfield estate will be, if I'm to continue with my success in the north. I wonder if Hale was behind it. I'm thinking that— What's wrong? Have you had bad news?'

'I'm not sure.' Lily held up the clipping. 'This is from *Le Petit Parisien*. "Where is La Muguette?" is the headline. It's the usual combination of speculation and ridiculous supposition that they deploy when there's no other news. I've been absent from Paris for some weeks now. Could I be taking a nine-month respite, to recoup my health?' Lily's lip curled. 'If I'd had a child every time *Le Petit Parisien* asked that question, I could probably staff one of your factories.'

'What!' Oliver stared at her in horror. 'You mean this is not the first time they've published such vile, vicious venom?'

'Now who's been spending too much time in Mr Lovejoy's company?'

'That was a very poor joke. Let me see that.'

'It's in French.'

'Then read it to me.'

'I've already told you…'

'Read it to me, if you please.'

He had never spoken to her in such a curt manner. She considered rebuking him, but one look at his face and she decided not to. Lily translated the piece, mortified, for it sounded so much worse when she read it out. 'As I said,' she concluded, 'it's nothing new.'

'Are you honestly telling me— How can you bear to read this—this—?' Oliver broke off, taking a deep breath. 'It's utterly vile.'

'And totally groundless.'

'You told me you'd never done anything you were ashamed of. I don't need reassurance on that count.'

Her lip trembled. 'Thank you.'

Oliver got up to sit beside her. 'It's perfectly natural to be upset. If it was me, I'd be round at the newspaper office, demanding blood.'

'It wouldn't be you, though, would it? You're a man.'

He swore again. 'I never thought— It never occurred to me. I've no experience of this kind of thing. How do they get away with it?'

'What point would there be in my challenging what they imply? They'd manage to turn it against me. A respectable woman would ignore such allegations as beneath her. A woman trying to protect her reputation by denial implies that she has no reputation to protect. And as to my army of unborn children—oh, I've given them all away, of course. It's not as if I can prove that I've never given birth.'

'So you remain silent, and they publish whatever lies they think will sell?'

'It's not all bad. It gets my name in the newspapers and look, it also says what I do.'

'Don't try to pull that one on me, Lily. You're on the verge of tears and it takes a lot to make you cry.'

'How ungentlemanly of you to point that out.'

'I've never claimed to be a gentleman. I'd offer to give you a hug, but you'd probably slap me.'

'Poor little Lily?'

'You're about as far from that as it's possible to be. I think I'm going to have to take the risk.' Oliver wrapped his arms around her. 'For my own benefit, because I reckon you're going to tell me there's nothing else I can do.'

She let herself be held. She didn't need it, she told herself, but in spite of that, it made her feel better. She closed her eyes, resting her cheek on his shoulder, breathing in the familiar smell of his soap. Then she forced herself to sit up.

'This kind of mud-slinging sells newspapers. My regular disappearance from Paris to visit my home in Roscoff is usually the trigger for this story—I take great care, you see, not to let anyone know that I have a house there.'

'Is it likely that man is behind it? The theatre manager who fathered a child with your friend?'

'It's possible. Certainly, he will know I'm not in Paris, because he's had dealings with Hélène, but there's no need to worry that she will have anything to do with this. Like your Mr Sinclair, she's the soul of discretion. It's probably nothing. Muck-raking simply because there's no other news.'

'But it might be something more sinister, is that what's troubling you?'

'Oh, I don't know. Do *you* think I'm making too much of it?' She sounded needy. She sounded uncertain. She had felt both before, but she'd refrained from expressing them. Lily made an effort to sound more confident. 'It's most likely a coincidence, that's all. There's nothing to link La Muguette's disappearance from Paris with Lady Rashfield's appearance in London.'

'But when Lady Rashfield disappears and La Muguette reappears...' Oliver began to shuffle the invitations, as if they were a pack of cards. 'It was my idea to come to town and make a splash. I was the one determined to take the *Morning Post* on. Now I'm wondering if it was a mistake, despite the success of last night.' He pushed the invitations to one side. 'It might have been safer to let it blow over, get on with what we set out to do, keep out of the spotlight. I've got us into a damned mess.'

'You wanted to stand up for yourself and for me.'

'So I've been an ass, but a well-intentioned one.'

'Oliver. I agreed with the plan and we had fun last night, didn't we, bringing the music hall to Mayfair? We gave Annie and Mr Lovejoy and all the other acts, and Mr Soames, too, an audience that they can capitalise on. And as for our audience, I reckon we gave them an evening they'll never forget.'

'Nor will I,' Oliver said. 'Not a single moment of it.'

She gave in to the need to touch him, linking her fingers through his. 'I won't either.'

'I've learned a lot about your world in the process, too, though I suspect the Canterbury and the acts there are small fry to what you are accustomed to dealing with, only you are too modest to say so.'

'Vaudeville, variety, music hall—in a way it's the same thing, only a question of scale. In Paris, such theatres are more egalitarian—high and low society, you know.'

'I do now. It's fascinating, a whole different world I had no idea existed.'

'Like your New Kilmun. I know it exists, but I know nothing of it.'

'I never dreamed all this would still be dragging on nearly—good Lord, nearly ten months after Archie died. Of course, I've not been away the whole time, but since November I've only paid the most fleeting of visits.'

'You miss it.' Lily grimaced. 'That's a stupid thing to say, you miss it dreadfully, just as I miss Paris.'

'It's not that I'm thinking of it all the time and it's not that I haven't relished the challenge of what we've had to do since we married in Bordeaux. You know that I enjoy every moment in your company.' Oliver slanted her a wicked smile. 'Day and night. But, yes, I miss it. Reading that piece in *The Times* reminded me of where my heart lies. That sounds mawkish.'

Lily squeezed his hand. 'New Kilmun is your dream. You've devoted your life to making it what it is. All this, it's temporary, a challenge as you said, but it's not where your heart is or mine. I enjoyed last night because it was an act, but the very idea of continuing in that role, going to any of those parties or balls—Oliver, it's simply not me.'

'Nor I. We need to hatch an escape plan.'

'Why don't you go north for a few days, a week, and leave Rashfield Manor to me?' It was a sensible proposition, but her heart sank as she made it. A whole week, when they only had four left.

Oliver, to her relief, quickly shook his head. 'I thought we agreed last night that we wanted to make the most of the next four weeks?'

'Business before pleasure?'

Oliver pursed his lips. 'What if we could find a way to have our cake and eat it?' As Lily shook her head, he smiled. 'A trip to New Kilmun. Together. What do you say to that?'

'Oh, Oliver, I would love that, but...'

'I think—yes, I really think that might be the answer to our problem.' He pushed back his chair and picked up *The Times*. 'Listen, Lily, this could work to our advantage. I'm a "conscientious industrialist" who "cares about the quality of his product as well as his staff". I've been away far too long and, what's more, I'm married now. Surely such a man would wish to introduce his wife to his life's work?

'Think about it. It's the perfect opportunity for us to escape the tangle we've got ourselves into. I can claim some sort of minor crisis. Everyone knows that I'm an industrialist before I'm a marquess, thanks to the press, so we won't be snubbing all these people,' he said, tapping the invitations.

'What about Rashfield Manor?'

'We can do what I suggested last night, have some other people take up the reins for a while. I haven't had a chance to tell you, but Iain Sinclair has asked me if there might be a permanent position for him there. He'd be the perfect manager, with our trusty miller at his side, don't you think?'

'Yes, that would be wonderful. I would love to go, but—but as your wife, Oliver? Wouldn't you feel it was wrong?'

'It was wrong of us not to go in the first place! If anything could be held up to challenge our marriage, now I come to think of it, it's the fact that we've not yet gone to New Kilmun. A visit there would have put all those questions to bed, without having to go to the trouble of our performance last night. Not that I regret that,' Oliver added. 'Look, I know it's a radical solution, but we need to put some distance between ourselves and this world, and you know, there's a few problems stacking up in the north that I really could be doing with sorting out myself.'

'I don't know, because you never mentioned them.'

'I didn't see the point, because I didn't think—but now I see it's the perfect solution. We'll need to go to

Rashfield for a day or so first, bring Sinclair with us and leave him in charge, but—oh, Lily, just think, in three, four days, I could be back where I belong.'

He was already looking different. She recalled how she'd felt walking into the Canterbury two weeks ago. The excitement of it, the thrill of being back in the world she had made her own. Oliver had been away from his world for much longer than she and, what's more, she really did wish to see it. To be able to imagine him there, when she was back in Paris, would make it so much easier to leave. Not that it would be difficult. *Oh, but it would.*

Lily thrust this alarming thought to the back of her mind. 'If you're sure it's what you want?'

'You know how it is, you say something on the spur of the moment and, as soon as you've said it, you know it's exactly the right thing? I think it's what we both need Lily, I—I *feel* it.'

She couldn't resist, for his sake and for hers. He was right, too, she told her conscience, it would certainly put to bed any final doubts about their marriage. 'Then we'll go.'

He beamed at her, throwing the newspaper back down on the table. 'This time, I *know* we're doing the right thing.'

'But what shall we do about all these invitations? And Mrs Murray, will we be asking her to close the house up again?'

'Fortunately, we didn't engage any permanent staff. Tell her it's a temporary measure while we take stock. That's not a lie. As to those—could we put a notice in the press? The Marquess and Marchioness of Rashfield send their apologies, but urgent business unfortunately takes them—that kind of thing?'

'That's an excellent idea. I'll draw something up, shall I?'

'Thank you.' Oliver was already on his feet. 'I have a thousand other things to do.'

She pushed back her chair. 'Then we'd better get on.'

'Oh, Lily.' He swept her into his arms. 'Lovely, lovely Lily. I'm going to break all the rules now and kiss you for no other reason than that I cannot resist you.'

'That sounds like the perfect reason to me.' She twined her fingers into his hair, pulling him towards her. 'Please do.'

Chapter Twelve

One week later

They travelled from Euston on the London and North Western Railway, changing to a local line at Crewe. Oliver's salt works were on the Cheshire plain, at the confluence of two rivers, and within easy reach of the commercial and population hubs of Manchester, Warrington and Chester and the port of Liverpool. In other words, the perfect location for such an enterprise.

A small, private railway line connected the factory complex to the nearby town of New Kilmun, Oliver told Lily, but his own house lay to the west. A carriage met them at the rural station for the short drive, past a little village. 'Alan Masterton, my deputy, lives here and few of the workers who prefer not to live in New Kilmun.'

'Why not?' Lily asked, turning her gaze away from the window. 'Aren't your rents cheaper?'

'And the houses are much better quality, but some people prefer their independence and I don't blame them for that. You could say that I'm the same, moving out of New Kilmun so people can't keep an eye on me.'

'Because you live such a decadent life?' she teased.

'Yes, there's a constant stream of painted women walking up the path and the brewery is never away from the place, dropping off barrels at least three times a week. Then there's the deliveries from Fortnum & Mason—because I dine off—off…'

'Caviar and quails in aspic?'

'That sounds as vile a combination as eel pie and that gravy they call liquor,' Oliver said with a mock shudder. 'The truth is that I have no desire to be held up as an example, good or bad. It's the main reason I chose to move out of New Kilmun. Our town isn't the first of its type, you know. I first got the idea years ago, following a visit to a place called Saltaire in Yorkshire, a purpose-built town housing the workers of Sir Titus Salt's mills. They have very strict rules there—there's no pub, for example, and anyone who lives there has to sign a pledge to abstain from alcohol. They are also obliged to attend church services weekly.

'Good, clean living is what Sir Titus aspired to and I can't disagree with that, but I don't see it as my job to dictate what men and women who work bloody—dashed hard—all week do with their time off. I'm rambling. The long and the short of it is, I like my own space, just as you do, remote from my place of work. And when it comes to judging whether any of the people in New Kilmun are setting a bad example, I prefer to let the people who live there decide.'

'How do they do that?'

'There's an elected Association. They decide if something or someone needs to be addressed and how.'

'Is that how you see the collective at Rashfield Manor working? Basically self-governing?'

'Exactly like that. It sounds radical, but it's an idea that goes back to the ancient Greeks. You see, the fancy education I got at school with your brother has some uses.' The carriage began to slow. 'We're here.'

Lily wiped the condensation from the window to look out. The carriage turned in through a wide gateway, where a short gravel path led to a substantial red-brick house with a steep slate roof. There were bow windows on either side of the front door, and plain sash windows on the two storeys above, and the whole was surrounded by a neat set of wrought-iron railings painted black.

'It's not huge,' Oliver said, handing her out the carriage. 'Compared to Rashfield Manor and that great big town house in Mayfair it's a cottage, but it's more than sufficient for my needs and I can guarantee it's warm and draught free.'

'Then as far as I'm concerned,' Lily said, tucking her hand into his arm, 'it's perfect. I'm looking forward to seeing inside.'

Oliver produced a key from his pocket and opened the door before helping their driver unload the luggage and paying the man off. 'Mrs McNair, my housekeeper, will have left us dinner to heat up and we'll sort our own breakfast—I'm capable of that much. There are outbuildings at the back, and a small walled kitchen garden with a glasshouse that Mrs McNair's son, Peter, looks after when he's not at school.

'And this,' he added, as a small tabby cat that looked like a miniature tiger with white paws leapt out from a bush to brush against his leg, 'is the inventively named Stripey, who keeps the house free from mice. She's not the friendliest of felines,' he added, as the cat, tail held high, stalked through the open door, 'but she's very good at her job. Shall we?'

He held out his arm, allowing her to precede him, shutting the door behind him and turning the gas sconces up to reveal a long, narrow hallway, the pan-elled walls painted pale green rather than stained, the oak floor polished, scattered with rugs. 'The main rooms are all on this floor,' Oliver said.

'There's a book room here,' he said, opening the first door. 'Then this is the drawing room, which I only use when I have guests. Down there is the dining room and on the other side is the sitting room, which is the room I use the most. The kitchen is downstairs through that door. And upstairs, there are two bedrooms on the first floor with the bathroom in between and on the top floor there's another two rooms that I don't currently use. Why don't you take a look around and I'll take your luggage up and have a look to see what Mrs Mc-Nair has left us to eat? You must be hungry…it's been hours since we ate.'

'Oliver.' Lily put a hand on his arm. 'The house is perfect. It's such a relief to be away from Rashfield Manor, away from London, and not to be surrounded by staff, but you don't have to run after me. Let's freshen up, wash the soot and grime of the journey away and then eat.'

'I'll show you how the water system works.' He

smiled at her puzzlement. 'All being well, it will come out of the tap in the bathroom.'

Although Mrs McNair had set the table in the dining room, when Oliver confessed that he usually ate in the kitchen when he was alone, Lily insisted that they do the same. The room was warm from the stove and he was pleased to see she approved of Mrs McNair's excellent if plain fare, which they ate at the pine table in the middle of the room. He was on edge, but he couldn't understand why. There was no need for them to adopt their public personas, there weren't even any staff in the house to disturb them. Which, it suddenly dawned on him, was precisely why he was on edge!

'I've just realised,' he said. 'This is the first time we've ever been properly alone together. *And* it's the first time I have ever been alone in my own house with a woman. Other than Mrs McNair, that is, and the only thing I've ever desired from her is my dinner.' He cursed under his breath. 'That came out all wrong, sorry.'

Lily, who had been toying with a slice of apple pie and cream, set her spoon down, colouring faintly. 'It is odd that we've never actually been perfectly alone in all the time we've been married. Both times.'

'Would you like a cup of tea? The cure for all ills, according to Mrs McNair.'

'After my dinner?' Lily pretended to look appalled. 'No, thank you. I thought you didn't like tea.'

'Not in the morning, but sometimes, after dinner when I'm alone.' He got up to set the kettle on to boil. 'It's my guilty secret.'

'Sometimes, when I'm alone in my apartment, I have

a dish of carrots cooked in butter and orange for my dinner. Nothing else. And I eat it in my dressing gown by the fire with a glass of burgundy.' Lily smiled across the table at him. 'That's my guilty secret. You have your tea and I will have your wine, since you only poured it to keep me company.'

He got up to do as she bid, conscious of her eyes on him, making him feel awkward carrying out the mundane task.

'To think that only this morning we were taking coffee from a solid silver pot that is probably about a hundred years old, served in hand-painted Royal Crown Derby china cups that belong to a service made specially for the Third Marquess,' Lily said as he put the brown earthenware teapot with the chipped spout down beside a plain white teacup and saucer.

'I happen to think it tastes better this way.'

'I asked Riddell what the creature on the Rashfield china was. I thought it might be a turkey.'

Oliver spluttered. 'It's an owl, from the Rashfield coat of arms.'

'So Riddell informed me.' Lily took a sip of her wine. 'Have you ever been in love, Oliver? I know that's a strange question to ask one's husband, but it's also strange, isn't it, that we've never talked about it?'

'I don't think so. What I may or may not have felt for the women in my past isn't the least bit relevant to my feelings for you.'

'And what about what I may or may not have felt for the men in my past? You've never asked me about them.'

'They are none of my business.' Oliver took another sip of his tea, wondering at this strange turn in her mood. 'I know you've had lovers. I don't wish to know any more than that.'

'Most men do want to know, though,' she persisted. 'They want to know how many and for how long, and, of course, they want to be assured that they are the most important, the only, the best.'

He was surprised into a crack of laughter, which he immediately regretted. 'You're serious.'

She smiled bitterly. 'I always know that it's the end, when those questions begin. Not that it's happened often. In my whole life, I've had three lovers, before you.'

No! His gut clenched, a reaction so visceral he thought he'd spoken aloud. He didn't give a damn about the other three men. What he didn't like, not a bit, were those last two words. *Before you.* Because there would be an *after you* and he wanted to be the last, the only.

Where the hell had that come from?

Oliver picked up the teapot, spilling some tea on to the table as he poured. Lily didn't belong to him. There was always going to be an after, their arrangement had always been intended to have a natural end point. In as little as three weeks their marriage would be over, the clock would start ticking down to their divorce and that *after* would begin. He didn't want to think about it.

'I shouldn't have said anything.' Lily misinterpreted his silence. 'I don't know why I did.'

She never said anything without a reason. 'I'm not interested in those other men, Lily. If you've done nothing that you're ashamed of…'

'I have not.'

He pushed his unfinished tea to one side and reached for her hand. 'The press, is that it?'

'It's what they do, it's what sells papers. That will never cease, unless I give up my work and settle down to domesticity.'

'I can't see you doing that.'

'No, I will maintain my independence. You are very unusual, in my experience. Most men struggle with that concept.' She turned her hand over to lace her fingers in his. 'You don't want to take over my business because you assume your sex alone would make you better at it, as some have. You don't want to tell me where to bank my money, or advise me on inappropriate friendships, or move into my apartment or *take care* of me, as others have attempted to do. Because that's what men do, isn't it, they take care of us frail females?'

'You're as frail as the foundations of this house.'

'A great many of us pretend. Even I did, when it was only Anthony and I. He was terribly bad with money and embarrassed about it, too, but any time I suggested that I take over his financial affairs, he took it as an affront. If he had let me, he might not have died in debt.'

'But you loved your brother.'

'Yes.'

'Lily, what is this really about? I'm sorry to be so stupid, but I don't understand what it is you're trying to tell me or ask me.'

A very good question. Lily unclasped her hand to take a sip of from Oliver's wine glass. Being here, in Oliver's house, had overset her. This was his home, his sanctuary, a citadel that no other woman had been permitted to breach. She had been feeling jumpy enough, without that admission. Why had she raised the topic of her other lovers? To prove that he was different? She already knew that. To prove that he didn't care? Why didn't he care?

She took another sip of Oliver's wine. He was waiting patiently, giving her time to assemble her thoughts. Not many people did that. Most men jumped in and told her what she was thinking. Why did Oliver have to be so—so perfect! No, he wasn't perfect, far from it, but he was...

Perfect for her? She finished the wine. He topped it up. He knew she wouldn't drink it, she rarely allowed herself more than two glasses unless it was champagne, but he also knew she liked to nurse a full glass. *You see, perfect!*

But not for her. This was the point of the conversation. 'I've never been in love and if being in love means handing one's hard-earned life on a plate to a man, then I'm very happy that I never have.'

'I can totally sympathise with that.'

An excellent response, she told herself, refusing to allow herself to be hurt. But if he meant that, why was she here? Over the last week, she had questioned the sense of this visit, the blurring of the lines between real life and the life they had been acting. Each time, Oliver himself or Oliver's arguments prevailed. It was a shortcut to his future and hers, a guarantee that their marriage would not be questioned and that would subsequently allow their marriage to end. *And yet you want to be here, Lily.* True. She wanted to see his world for herself, to be able to imagine him here when she was

back in Paris, when this odd collision, this coming together of northern industrialist and Parisian theatrical
representative, was over.

'Our managing to work together then, it is an aberration for both of us.'

'An aberration that has been very successful, and
enjoyable, too, hasn't it?'

'Because we know it's only temporary,' Lily persisted. 'And we haven't quite succeeded yet so we
shouldn't get too smug or complacent.'

'After tomorrow, no one will question our marriage,
and if all goes well, in two weeks' time when we make
the formal announcement about setting up the tenant
collective, there will be no turning back. There's a lot
of work ahead, that's true, but I think the combination
of Iain Sinclair and our enthusiastic miller will do the
trick, don't you?' Oliver said. And then, when she nodded, 'So what is it you're really worried about?'

'You don't regret my being here? You don't think
I'm intruding? You don't think it's storing up problems? You're going to flaunt me as your wife in front
of all these people who mean so much to you and then,
in three weeks' time, I'll be gone. How will you explain
that? You seem awfully sanguine about everything.'

His face fell and he looked as if he was going to say
something before changing his mind. 'I am very far
from sanguine, Lily, trust me!' He leaned over to take
both of her hands in his. 'I'm just trying to concentrate
on the task in hand. But there's something else both-
ering you.'

Was that true? Was he actually in as much emotional
turmoil as she was, but doing a better job of concealing

it? 'We haven't even talked about how I am to extricate myself from this situation of our own making. It's not as if we can ask the Great Mephisto to make me vanish in a puff of smoke.'

'We agreed the story we'd put about, way back. I mistook my feelings in the throes of grief. We acted prematurely.' Oliver winced. 'It still makes sense, but you're right, we'll have to sow the seeds of it for it to be believable.'

'We've only got three weeks.'

'I know.'

Could they wait another week? Another month? Give themselves time to manage their finale? The question hung in the air between them.

'I promised that you'd be back in Paris by the start of April,' Oliver said. 'You've sacrificed more than enough. We'll manage.'

There, Lily, now you have your final answer and it was the right one!

Oliver was perfect for her, because he understood perfectly that they had no future.

'We could stage something,' Lily said, summoning her stage smile. 'A grand falling out.'

'And our leading lady exits dramatically, stage left, then turns up in Paris a few days later?'

'No, that wouldn't do. I shall slink off the stage like a thief in the night. So quietly that no one will notice.'

'Save me,' Oliver said, lifting one of her hands to his mouth, turning it over to press a kiss on her palm. 'I'll miss you terribly. I don't mind admitting that.'

I'll miss you, too, more than I dare say.

'We still have three weeks,' Lily said. 'Our plan was to make the most of them. I suggest we do just that.'

Oliver let go of her hand. 'To answer your question from ages ago: I've never been in love either and I have never wanted a wife. I'm not in love with you, Lily, if that's what's scared you. I've never met a woman like you. It's because you're you—and because I'm me— that's why it's so good between us, isn't it? We're two peas, but we live in different pods. Sorry, that was a stupid thing to say.'

'No, I couldn't have put it better.' He didn't love her. He wasn't in love with her. She knew that. The last thing she wanted was a declaration of love, so it shouldn't hurt when no such declaration was made. But it did. Even though they were two peas destined to live in different pods, exactly as he said, it hurt that he didn't love her, because...

She had the distinct feeling of standing on the edge of a cliff and wanting to jump. Lily pushed back her chair. 'Shall we talk about my exit some other day? Since we only have three weeks...'

Oliver pushed his chair back, taking her hand. 'Shall we spend the next hour reminding ourselves how good it is between us?'

'You think you can do that in only an hour?'

'Now that is a challenge I can't fail to rise to.'

The tension between them evaporated as she stepped into his arms. He didn't love her, but he desired her and that was what she wanted. 'I think,' Lily said, breaking the kiss for air, 'you already have.'

'It's your fault,' he said, smiling wolfishly. 'Lovely Lily, I can't resist you.'

'Then don't,' she said, happily abandoning all her

worries and reservations because they only had a precious three weeks left, after all. 'I don't want you to.'

They kissed again and Lily let some of her desperation show in the way she clung to him, dragging kisses from him, not wanting to stop kissing him, still kissing him as they made their way from the kitchen to the hallway, still kissing as they climbed the stairs and fell into her bedchamber, and still kissing as they struggled out of their clothes. Mouths and hands claiming each inch of exposed skin, wanting to mark every inch of each other's bodies, saying nothing, their feverish, passionate kisses saying everything.

When he entered her, their mouths still clung, their tongues matching each thrust, her heels digging into his buttocks, her hands clinging to him, her body arching against him as he thrust and they kissed, thrust and kissed, until she cried out, her climax ripping through her, sending him hurtling over the edge with a harsh groan before calling out her name.

Afterwards, they lay for a long time, still intimately entwined. And after that, when he should have left her, she held out her hand to him and he came back to bed. Wordless still, they lay wrapped in one another's arms, listening to one another breathe, wordless, wide awake. Then his hands stroked her flank and her hands smoothed over his buttocks, desire reawakening inside her as they kissed, slowly now, but with intent. He pulled her on top of him, sliding into her, and this time they rocked, slowly, achingly, delightfully slowly, to the end. And this time, when it was over, she rolled on to her side, pulling his arm around her waist, and when he nestled into her, she whispered, 'Don't go.'

Chapter Thirteen

'How do I look?' Lily asked, unable to prevent herself, though she had already asked the same question twice this morning.

'You look perfect as always,' Oliver answered, just as he had the previous two times. 'Just the right mixture of elegance and practicality,' he added, before she could ask him to clarify.

'If you think so.' She turned away to peer out of the carriage window, still unconvinced, but it was too late to do anything about it now. This morning, while the sky showing through the gap in the curtains was still dark grey, she had woken to find herself still wrapped in Oliver's arms. When she tried to ease herself away, his arm had tightened around her waist. She could feel his arousal against her bottom.

When she wriggled, not to get away but to get closer, she felt the sharp intake of his breath and then his mouth on the nape of her neck and his hand sliding up to cup her breast. The next time she looked, the gap between the curtains had shown daylight. Oliver got out of bed, but he pulled her with him, holding out her wrapper, taking her through to the very intimidating bathroom, where he had shown her how to work the complicated shower contraption.

Then he would have left her, but last night had freed her from restraint, so she untied her wrapper and stepped under the shower, completely naked in front of him. Then, picking up the sponge, she had soaped it, all the while watching him, daring him to leave, or to join her. To her delight, he had chosen to join her. Hot water jets, soap, slippery skin and Oliver had made for a unique experience. A never-to-be-forgotten experience. She had three weeks to collect and store up more of them.

Starting today. 'Tell me again,' Lily said, turning towards Oliver, 'what we are to expect.'

'I'm not exactly sure. I asked Alan Masterton to keep it informal. We'll take a walk around the town together, so that you can see it for yourself. I'll introduce you to the people we come across and then we'll head to the Green, where there will be refreshments for whoever chooses to attend, served in the Hall. We'll take tea, chat and then, when you've had enough, we'll leave.'

'Do you have any idea how many people will be there?'

'It's Saturday so the factories are closed. New Kilmun has about five hundred houses, a population of about two thousand.'

'Two thousand!'

'Men, women and a large number of children. You must have played to theatre audiences almost as large.

Anyway, they won't all come, they've their own lives to get on with on their day off.'

She stared at him, but he didn't look as if he was joking. 'I had no idea there would be so many.'

'There will be a good deal more, once we get our canning factories up and running. We've already got plans to build at least another hundred houses.'

'Good grief. I had no idea you were so— That New Kilmun was so— That you were responsible for so many lives! The Rashfield estate by comparison is— Goodness, I would never say insignificant, but you must have thought it so. And to think that Sir Everard Hale had the *nerve* to suggest that you needed his helping hand.'

'I don't know anything about farming or land management—at least I didn't.'

'All the same, though, Oliver, I had no idea of how insulting those trustees were to you. I had no idea that you were so powerful. To be responsible for two thousand people and you are looking to take on more! I feel such an idiot.'

'You're talking yourself into a panic for no reason.' Oliver took her hand. 'I'm not "responsible" for two thousand people. I provide employment, I pay them a good wage and I offer them a decent place to live. It's up to them, every individual, every family, to make what they want of it, whether they send their children to school or attend the evening classes themselves, join the various institutes, whether they want to work their way up the ladder in the factory, or if they prefer to stick with what they know.

'If they want to go to church they can—if they don't

then it's no skin off my nose. And if they choose to come to congratulate us today that's fine, but if they don't—I'm no Sir Everard Hale, or Archie, come to that, expecting people to tug their forelocks at me and looking for my nod before they cut their toenails.'

'Have you asked Mr Sinclair to pass that philosophy on to your soon-to-be former tenants? The winds of change will blow through Rashfield Manor, with the approval, I'm sure, of most of the tenants and to the disgust of most of the landed gentry.'

'That's their problem. You've won over those tenants, Lily, just as you won over Soames and Annie and Lovejoy, and all the lords and ladies of the land who came to our Mayfair variety show. You'll win over the people here at New Kilmun, too—all you have to do is be yourself.'

'But that's precisely what I'm not! If I was myself, these people would be scandalised by our marriage.'

'You have never not been yourself and as yourself you can charm anyone you set out to charm.'

'But none of them mattered as these people do, to you. They were an audience in a play that's about to close. New Kilmun isn't a play. These people are the permanent cast in your life. If they don't like me, then it will reflect badly on you and if they do like me, when I disappear, then it will reflect badly on you.'

She stopped, biting her lip, aware that she sounded hysterical. 'I'm sorry. I am making far too much of this. I must trust your judgement. If the boot was on the other foot, and I was introducing you to the Paris vaudeville—' She broke off, for that was something she found utterly impossible to imagine. She clasped her hands tightly together, staring down at her gloves. 'Forget I spoke. I will compose myself. We must be nearly there.'

'I'm flattered,' Oliver said quietly. 'That this matters to you. I'm flattered and grateful, but there's no reason for you to worry. Do you honestly think I'd have brought you here otherwise? This is my life's work, Lily, and I'm not even half-done. Have a little faith in yourself.'

She bristled immediately. 'I have every faith in myself.'

'Rightly so. You simply needed reminding of it.'

'Oh! You said that deliberately.'

'It worked.'

She was obliged to smile. 'It did. I won't let you down.'

'That was never in doubt. Now, if you'll look out the window, you'll see the railway station. We're going to walk from there. Are you ready?'

'Oliver, there's a crowd of people waiting.'

He craned over her shoulder and gave a laugh that was partly a groan. 'A welcoming committee. At least we've rehearsed this scene at Rashfield, back in January.' He pulled on his gloves and straightened his hat. 'Ready, my love?'

Her heart was beating furiously and her mouth was dry. Lily nodded and fixed her smile to her face. 'Ready.'

A band struck up 'For He's a Jolly Good Fellow' as Oliver jumped down from the carriage and turned to help her out. She heard him mutter something under his breath as she stepped down.

A personable man in a brown suit who looked to be about the same age as Oliver came hurrying over.

'This wasn't my idea, my lord, I know you don't like a fuss being made. It was the Association, they insisted.'

'Never mind,' Oliver said, slapping on his back. 'It's good to see you, Alan, but I really wish you'd stop addressing me as "my lord". Let me introduce you to my wife. Lily, this is Alan Masterton.'

'Lady Rashfield.' He made a deep bow. 'It is a long-overdue pleasure. I've been telling my lord— Oliver that the townsfolk have been anxious to meet you ever since the announcement in *The Times* back in January. Though of course I understand,' he added, glancing at Oliver, 'that you have had other pressing matters to deal with.'

'Mr Masterton, I am delighted to be here now. How do you do? Oliver speaks extremely highly of you.' Lily held out her hand and, after a brief moment of surprised hesitation, he shook it.

'Thank you, my lady. Welcome to New Kilmun. As you can see, we are all looking forward to making your acquaintance. I should warn you, my lord— Oliver— I should warn you that the factory board have turned out in full with their wives at the Hall and we've had to put up a marquee on the Green for the children because pretty much everyone in the town is planning on attending the tea later. Oh, yes, and the band—they want to play a couple of dances, so if you and Her Ladyship would prepare yourself to lead everyone out. I really am sorry, my— Oliver.'

'You shouldn't apologise, Mr Masterton,' Lily said, pinching Oliver's arm. 'It is a huge compliment to my husband.'

'Indeed, my lady, only your husband isn't very keen on compliments, as you doubtless know.'

'I do, very well,' Lily said. *Her husband.* When had it ceased to sound odd? 'The merest hint of praise has him turning the subject.'

'My wife,' Oliver retorted, 'has an equal horror of accolades. Three times this morning, I complimented her appearance, yet she insisted she was ill dressed.'

'I did not say I was ill dressed! What I said was— Oh! That is the second time today that you have managed to take a rise from me and I— We are embarrassing Mr Masterton.'

'Not at all, my lady. Domestic bliss in all its glory! Myself and my good lady also enjoy affectionately teasing each other. And at the risk of earning a rebuke, may I say that I think you look extremely elegant.'

'Merci, Monsieur,' Lily said, dropping him a small curtsy.

'And may I offer my sincere congratulations on your marriage, which it's clear to me, is going to be a long and happy one.' Lily slanted Oliver a glance, but his expression was impassive. 'Now, Oliver,' Mr Masterton continued, 'if you would say a few words to these fine people, then we'll leave you to show Her Ladyship round the town and I'll go ahead to the Hall, to make sure all is ready.'

Oliver tucked his arm firmly into Lily's as they arrived in front of the crowd. 'Ladies and gentlemen, boys and girls, thank you for taking the time to come to meet us. Though I think we all know it's not really me you're

interested in, is it? So without further ado, it is my pleasure to introduce to you my wife.'

A cheer went up. The sea of faces in front of him
were all familiar and all smiling. He was surprised at
how emotional he felt as the band struck up again and
this time everyone sang along. 'For She's a Jolly Good
Fellow' was lustily sung. His wife dabbed at her eyes.
His wife. The song came to an end with three cheers,
bringing a lump to Oliver's throat, making his thanks
and hopes that he would see everyone later at tea sound
hoarse.

As they dispersed, Lily managed a watery smile.
'You have seriously underestimated what people feel
for you, my lord.'

'I'm a good employer, they appreciate that.'

'Oliver, this is me, Lily, talking, not Lady Rashfield.
Whatever you do here, you obviously do very, very well.
These people came here of their own accord to welcome you. You heard Mr Masterton, he made it clear it
wasn't what you wanted, but it was what *they* wanted.'

'What they wanted was to see you.'

'Oh, you really are impossible! Come here, my lord.'
She reached up to kiss his cheek. 'If I was you, I would
be as pleased as punch.'

He opened his mouth to make some denigratory remark, then changed his mind. 'Well then, I am, if you
tell me to be. Now, shall we take a walk around the town
and you can make my head swell by complimenting me
on what a wonderful paradise I've created.'

'I suspect I'm going to find that very easy to do.'

The train station was a few minutes' walk from the
main body of the town, which was built on a grid sys-

tem, with the residential streets on one side of the main thoroughfare and the civic buildings and park on the other. Most of the residents were at the Hall, but they were waylaid several times from doorsteps and gardens, men who worked in the factories, their wives, the occasional grandparent. Lily, her earlier misgivings seemingly forgotten, was in no hurry to move on from any of them, her interest in each family, how long they had lived at New Kilmun, what each of them did, so obviously genuine.

She wanted to know everything, asking question after question of him as they proceeded, and all of them so practical that he was hard put not to laugh at times. Did every house have a pump in the scullery? And what about the privies, were they shared? Oliver was extremely happy to reassure her on this point. What shops were there? What markets? Did everyone have a garden big enough to grow vegetables? And if people were ill? He led her away from the rows of housing to the street where the cottage hospital stood and then on to the school.

'All children, boys and girls, stay in school until they're at least thirteen, which is longer than they're obliged. If they show promise and they want to continue to learn, we make sure they can.'

'Even the girls?' Lily asked.

'I don't think the case has arisen.'

'Perhaps because it is not expected to arise,' Lily said. 'You haven't thought of that, have you?'

'I don't need telling twice, though, as Alan would say. Did you go to school?'

'Day school, for a few years, where I learned to sew

and to speak French and, though I didn't think so at the time, both have proved extremely useful.'

'Did you resent Anthony's having a decent education?'

'I don't think so. It never occurred to me then that I was missing out. My father died when I was twelve or thirteen, leaving my mother more or less dependent upon Anthony. If the school you both attended had taught him how to make a pound stretch, then that, I reckon, would have been a more worthwhile education. Do they teach that sort of thing in your school?'

'Domestic Accounts, at evening classes. Did your mother have to take you out of school then, when your father died?'

She shrugged, that particularly Gallic, dismissive shrug that meant she wished the subject to be dropped. 'My mother did not keep in the best of health. My father's death sent her into a decline. There was no money for me to go to school and no money to pay for a nurse for my mother.'

'So you nursed her and then you nursed Anthony.'

'And all the while dreamed of becoming an actress.' Lily smiled wryly. 'I think if I'd told my mother *that* it would have sent her much earlier to her grave.'

'And then when she died, you were reliant on Anthony for your bed and board and Anthony relied on you to be his nurse.'

'You know this, Oliver, it's ancient history. Then you came along and gave me the chance at last that I'd been looking for, though it took me three years to work up the courage to take it.'

'Most women would never have found the courage.'

He put a finger over her mouth, before she could retort. 'I know, better than most, that you are decidedly *not* most women. You are a phenomenon. I'll make enquiries. If any of our female pupils show promise in the future, they'll be encouraged to carry on with their learning.'

'*Merci*. Mr Masterton is right. You don't need telling twice.' They had come to the crossroads near the station. Lily stopped to look back at the rows of little terraced houses, the church and the cottage hospital, the school. 'It is not a beautiful town, but it is very practical.'

'I'll settle for that. It's what people need,' Oliver said, aware that he sounded defensive.

'I meant that in a positive way. Everything close at hand that you need to live—the shops, the market in the little square, the hospital and the school, all close to where people live. I would imagine that having all this makes it easy for you to recruit the best workers and to keep them?'

'I told you from the start, I'm a businessman, not a philanthropist. Do you approve, then?'

'You don't need me to approve. I am fascinated. To have all this in your mind for so long, and then to have built it and seen it flourish. You must be so proud.'

'It's not finished.'

She gave his arm a shake. 'Then be proud of what you have achieved *so far*.'

'I am and glad you've seen it. Now, if we cross the main road here, we can take a walk through what they call the Wilderness, the bit of the park that's been left as it was before we started building. It leads up to the main park and that's where the Hall is.'

'That sounds perfect.'

She was silent as they meandered through the woodland glade. What was she thinking? He remembered how he'd felt, watching her at the Canterbury, the concentration on her face as she studied each act, the sheer joy she took in being in the theatre, and the next day, a very different Lily negotiating terms, cajoling Soames into giving her what she wanted, and getting all of them, their Mayfair music hall, to throw their hearts into their performance. She was in her element and he'd loved every moment of being there with her, but he'd never really felt part of it. She didn't need him and he'd never have been there if it wasn't for her.

Was that what she was feeling now? That she was a visitor to another world? She could act her part as his consort, but he didn't need her and she had no other role. Lily had worked so hard to make a niche for herself. He shied away from imagining what she'd gone through. To try to realise a lifelong dream of being on the stage for any female was a bold venture, but for one like the Lilian he recalled, gently brought up, with no experience save as nursemaid to her brother—no, he didn't want to imagine it.

But as they made their way to the gathering at the Hall and she once again stepped into her role as loving wife, adapting seamlessly to her audience of children and grandmothers, his Board and their wives, his factory workers and their families, Oliver began to see that there must always have been more to her than the gauche young woman he had married the first time. Why had he not spotted that?

Anthony's illness had been a long and painful one. She'd had no support, no family to turn to. She'd resented having to marry him, though she'd kept that well hidden from him at the time. She'd hated being dependent and she had had a plan to free herself, too—even when she was living in Sandgate, she'd been working towards that. And he was oblivious to all of it, thinking only that he had discharged his debt of honour. What a blind, pompous prig!

'I didn't see any sign of a theatre, though I did spot a public house,' Lily said, interrupting his regretful musings. 'One little oversight, my love, that I really felt I must bring to your attention.'

'Consider it built,' he said. 'It shall be my wedding present. We shall name it after you.'

He spoke without thinking, half-serious, but Lily flinched. 'The last thing the townspeople will want is a theatre named after the woman who divorced their beloved founder.'

'Lily, I didn't mean…'

'Listen, the band are striking up and we are expected to take the lead.'

Chapter Fourteen

New Kilmun—one week later

It was early, judging by the grey light outside, not much after six. Lily carefully moved Oliver's arm from her waist and inched to the edge of her bed. Grabbing her wrapper, she tiptoed out of the bedroom and closed the door behind her with a sigh. In the kitchen, she raked the coals, stoked the stove and set the kettle to boil.

A soft thud preceded Stripey's appearance from the scullery where the window was always left slightly ajar for her. The cat twined herself around her legs, purring loudly. Lily stooped to scratch the damp fur of her forehead. Stripey tolerated it for precisely ten seconds before she padded over to her empty bowl, looking up expectantly.

'You certainly know what you want and how to get it, young lady,' Lily said, pouring the required milk. The cat lapped with dedicated concentration until the bowl was empty, before sitting herself down in front of the stove to wash her face. She would swat away any further attempt to pet her. 'Oliver was right,' Lily told her, setting about making the coffee, 'you are the least affectionate cat I have ever encountered.'

Stripey turned her back to finish her toilette, before curling up into a ball. The cat had a hard night's hunting to sleep off. Lily put the coffee-pot down on the table, collected a cup and saucer from the dresser and sat down. She had woken with mildly fluttering butterflies in her belly for two days in a row.

Yesterday, Oliver had woken up when she had tried to sneak out of bed and they had made love. When they made love, Lily forgot everything save the increasingly desperate need to lose herself in him, to see him lose himself in her. Their lovemaking was not only a deep pleasure, it was an escape into a world that was only theirs, a world where there was only Lily and Oliver, seeking to please and to tease.

In this world they eked out every moment of each journey to their climax, holding on to those moments afterwards for longer and longer, so that one act of love often segued into another, so that they were joined all night together one way or another, making love, entwined even when they were sleeping. She had never imagined lovemaking could be so deeply satisfying, nor that such pleasure could be gained from giving pleasure. She had never wanted anything from lovemaking save mutual satisfaction. Now she couldn't imagine making love with any other man.

The butterflies fluttered in her belly. Lily poured herself a cup of coffee and took a sip. She knew what they were trying to tell her. She was on very dangerous ground.

The coffee was strong and very hot. It scalded her throat and burned her stomach. Stripey stretched, arched her back and stalked scullery-wards without a backward glance. The cat had had what she wanted, milk, a heat, a nap, and now she was off to survey her own domain. Lily took another sip of coffee. New Kilmun was not her domain. She knew that. She'd never imagined it would be, but so many people here thought otherwise.

She had visited the factory with Oliver. She now knew enough about the process of open-pan salt making to last her a lifetime. She didn't pretend to share his enthusiasm for industrial methods, for the apparently endless innovations that steam engines allowed, or even for the plans he had reverently shown her laid out on the long, polished boardroom table, for the new canning factory.

She was, however, fascinated by his fervour, by his focused determination to do even the smallest of tasks to the best of his ability, because those were traits she shared. His ethos, his tactics, his ambition and his determination to have everyone involved in his endeavours share in the success, all of this she empathised with—all of these aims, on a much, much smaller scale in a very different business, were her own. But there ended their common ground.

No, Lily reminded herself, there was one more, very significant thing they shared: a fierce and determined independence. Everything they had in common, everything that had made their unlikely alliance so successful, was destined not to bring them together, but to keep them apart.

As she poured herself a second cup of coffee, the butterflies settled down, to be replaced by a horrible sinking in the pit of her stomach. There was no place for her here, and even if there was, she didn't want it. She didn't fit. Even her clothes, which were the perfect uniform in Paris, were completely wrong here in New Kilmun. If she really was Oliver's wife, what would she do with herself? She'd be a helpmeet.

Lily laughed drily at the term. A helpmeet! A prop for the master. The angel of the house! Lord, but the idea was too ridiculous to contemplate. She'd be bored senseless and, more importantly, she'd have no income. No money, no power. She'd go back to being a dependent. She had come far too far to be dependent on anyone ever again.

It was time for them to discuss her leaving. She wrapped her arms around herself. *Time for some home truths, too, Lily.* She would miss him. Of course she would miss him. She would miss their lovemaking. They were, in his own words, 'good' together, physically well matched and mature enough to recognise that, and to enjoy it.

There was also the fact that, from the outset, there had been a time limit on their relationship. She nodded sagely to herself. The craving she had for him, it was like any other craving—as soon as you tell yourself you can't have something, that's all you want. It had been when they had set an end date on their marriage that their desire to make love had increased, hadn't it?

Was that all she felt then, a craving? Lily was too honest to let this settle. In the last week here, playing husband and wife in his house, their lovemaking meant more than sating desire. They slept in the same bed every night. They showered together every morning. Look at her, sitting here in her wrapper, in the kitchen, her hair down, her feet bare, waiting on her husband to join her for breakfast!

She was enjoying it because she knew it wasn't real then, that was it. This was an aberration. A new role she was playing and playing it so well that, like so many other leading ladies, she was under the illusion that she was in love with her leading man.

Lily jumped to her feet. She was absolutely *not* in love. Love was something very different. Love meant sacrifice and submission. If she was in love, she'd be doing everything she could to persuade herself that she could live here in Oliver's world, that she'd be delighted to be his helpmeet if she could be by his side, on any terms. The notion was repugnant, so she wasn't in love.

She would miss him. She cared for him, because she respected him. She *liked* him. He understood her. She understood him, but that wasn't love. It was empathy and one didn't build a life together on empathy. In fact, it was their empathy that made it impossible for them to build any sort of life together. Why she was tying herself in knots, when Oliver himself had given her no sign of even wishing to discuss the matter, she had no idea!

Lily picked up the coffee-pot to empty out the grounds and refilled the kettle. She got the beans from the larder and put them in the grinder. It was time to put an end to this little pretence of domestic bliss. The butterflies were a reminder of that. Time to put an end to these cosy breakfasts and falling in with whatever Oliver proposed for the day. Time to focus on the reason they had married, complete the handover of Rashfield estate and then put an end to their alliance. It was time, Lily decided, to discuss just how they would do that.

'Good morning.'

On cue, Oliver appeared in the kitchen. His hair was damp. He was already dressed in trousers and shirt. There would be no sharing of the shower today. An excellent sign, Lily told herself, that they were both of the same mind. 'I'm making fresh coffee.'

'Let me make it.' He wrapped his arms around her waist, pulling her to him. He smelled of soap. 'You were up early.'

'I couldn't sleep. I didn't want to wake you.'

'I was awake, but you were at such pains not to disturb me, I assumed you wanted some time alone?'

She tried to shrug, she tried to smile, she tried to make some inconsequential remark, but the butterflies had been a warning she couldn't ignore. 'I really think we need to talk about my leaving,' Lily said. 'We can't keep ignoring it.'

Oliver sighed. 'May I have my coffee first?'

The bell on the wall shook. 'That's the front door,' Lily. 'I'll make the coffee. You go and answer it.'

Oliver tipped the messenger boy and closed the front door, going into his book room with the intention of adding the telegram to the stack of outstanding correspondence he planned to deal with this morning. He sat down at his desk and picked up the letter opener, but then set it down again. He had had a premonition this morning, when Lily crept out of bed, that her 'exit' was what she wished to discuss. She was right, too, they needed to address it. The question he had first to address himself however was, must it inevitably be an exit?

But there was no question of any other outcome. That's what he'd been telling himself when he lay awake in the night with Lily in his arms, counting the days left to them. She had to leave for the very simple and straightforward reason that her life was elsewhere. She was a theatrical agent. There were theatres in London. There were theatres even closer at hand, in Liverpool and Manchester. He had promised to build a theatre here in New Kilmun. Oliver shuddered, recalling Lily's scornful reaction to his flippant suggestion of naming it after her. He tapped the letter opener impatiently on the blotter. The point wasn't the existence of theatres anywhere other than Paris. The point was that Lily was adamant she didn't want to share her life with anyone. Her independence was too hard fought and too precious to her.

He should understand that—he was the same himself. *Had* been the same himself. Until he met Lily. *My wife.* Twice over, they had married, but she wasn't his wife and she didn't want to be his wife. Not his real wife. Even though it was more obvious to both of them every night they spent together that this was more than a love affair.

They never spoke of their feelings, but there was more there in their kisses than desire, more there in the way they lay after making love, wrapped in each other's arms, breathing in unison, pressed together, skin to skin, as if they wanted to melt into each other.

Was he in love with Lily? The letter opener fell from

his hand. It was one of those questions he hadn't asked himself because he didn't want to know the answer. Was he in love with Lily? Of course he bloody well was!

Was Lily in love with him?

If being in love means handing one's hard-earned life on a plate to a man, she'd said, and then, *No, thank you very much*, or words to that effect. He didn't want her to hand her life on a plate to him, any more than he wished to hand his life on a plate to her, but he was in love with her all the same.

Oliver groaned. *What a mess!* How could he be so sure he was in love when he'd never been in love before? He didn't want to lose Lily, but how long would that feeling last? She had cautioned him more than once about the dangers of falling in love with a role. Was that what he'd done? If so, then it would be easy enough for him to rein his feelings in, wouldn't it?

He was a practical man above all else. It was utterly impractical to imagine a life with Lily. She didn't belong here. She wouldn't want to belong here. He didn't belong anywhere else. He didn't want to harness her by his side, or to take the very thing she valued most from her, her independence. Lily's independence was what defined her. And him.

He groaned again, dropping his head into his hands. *What a damned mess!* Lily was waiting for him in the kitchen, wanting to talk about her departure. Was he planning on going down there and declaring his undying love? To what purpose? Suggest they remained married? Marriage implied a shared life, a shared roof, a couple, not two individuals who lived in two different countries.

Why raise the subject when there was no solution?
He wasn't even sure that love was what he was feeling.
And as for Lily—he had no idea what she felt, but he
was pretty certain that if he spoke up, forced her to ar-
ticulate whatever it was, then he'd be putting an end to
what they had. Better to leave it and make the most of
these last two weeks. Safer.

Oliver got up. He didn't like playing safe, it went
against the grain. Still musing on this, he picked up the
telegram and slit it open. What he needed was coffee.
The telegram was from Sinclair. He scanned it quickly.
Swore. And headed to the kitchen.

'Lily!'

'I wondered what had happened to you? Your coffee's getting cold. What is it?'

He handed her the telegram. 'We'll need to get back
to Rashfield Manor as soon as possible. I'll need to get
hold of Alan. How long do you need to pack?'

'Sit down a minute. Drink your coffee. Let me think.'

'There's nothing to think about. Sinclair says that
the piece will be in today's *Times*.'

'Which will be delivered here any minute now,
with the first post. "Warned to expect our plans will
be leaked." Who warned him?' Lily asked.

'No idea. He's obviously dashed that off in a panic.'
Oliver drank his coffee standing up. 'I'm going to finish
getting dressed. I'd recommend you do the same. Whatever is in *The Times*, we need to get to Rashfield as soon
as possible, see what we can do to limit the damage.'

Lily nodded. 'Oliver…'

'I know, we need to talk. We will, I promise, but let's

make sure our plans haven't been scuppered, before we embark on scuppering our marriage.'

The Times and the first post had arrived just before Mrs McNair and Lily and Oliver departed for Rashfield not long after, arriving at the Manor in the late afternoon. The article leaked almost every detail of the planned Rashfield collective, even going as far as to name Mr Sinclair as the future manager. Despite the earlier positive piece in the same newspaper, this article condemned the move as revolutionary and its architect as a short-sighted radical.

'What the hell is going on?' Oliver demanded of that man, who was waiting for them in the study. 'Who has been talking to the press?'

'I don't know. It's not Jamie Edgehill, I'm sure of that. He's completely behind us, as are most of the tenants, and besides, I can't see any of them speaking to *The Times*, can you?'

'A piece like this has to have come from someone with an axe to grind.' Oliver threw himself down on the chair behind his desk. 'One of our neighbours? Could they have been speaking to Hale? He's been determined from the first to deprive me of control of this estate.'

'But Sir Everard is an old-fashioned gentleman,' Lily interjected. 'Men like him would see it as bad form to speak to the press.'

'The antiquated views in that piece sound exactly as they've come from his archaic head.'

'Oliver,' Mr Sinclair said, 'I did warn you that what you're doing…'

'Is dragging this estate into the nineteenth century. Can't they see that?'

'The Rashfield estate has been in your family for centuries,' Mr Sinclair said patiently. 'There's nothing wrong with you wanting to modernise, but as far as the Establishment is concerned, you're handing a large piece of England's heritage into the hands of the hoi polloi. Heresy! And where might it lead? The overthrow of the accepted order?'

'Poppycock!'

'I know, but vested interests are very powerful. Peers of the realm simply don't give up their heritage voluntarily.'

'Well, this one is going to do just that and hand it over to a group of people who will make a much better job of farming it, with some investment, some education and a vested interest.'

'Oliver, you know that and I know that, and in fact whoever wrote this piece in *The Times* acknowledges that. If you were keeping your stake in the lands, it would be a different matter, but you're not.'

'The Marquess of Rashfield is devolving power to the people,' Lily interjected wryly. 'Is that it?'

'Exactly it,' Mr Sinclair agreed. 'What if you set a trend? Where would that lead?'

'To more efficient farming, better crops, more food—I don't see the problem.'

'Oliver, don't be obtuse, it doesn't suit you.' Lily gave him a wry smile. 'You knew perfectly well how radical a solution this was. I remember, for you told me so yourself when you first told me about it.'

'I did, you're right. What I'd like to know is how the

devil word got out about this? Are you sure it wasn't Hale?'

Mr Sinclair picked up the newspaper. '"In these troubled times for farming",' he read, '"a fresh approach from an outsider, a man with a head for business, could be precisely what such neglected lands need, if that same man retained control." I can't imagine that Sir Everard Hale would agree with that, do you?'

'If it's not Hale behind this, who do you think it might be?'

'The most likely source *is* one of your neighbours trying to scaremonger, I'm afraid.'

'That's precisely the conclusion *we* reached on the way here.'

'You might have tried to charm them with a party, but your views will never endear you to the county set.'

'Something else that you pointed out to me as a risk some time ago,' Oliver said, grimacing at Lily. 'Well, there's nothing for it, we're going to have to bring forward our official announcement to tomorrow. Can that be done, Iain?'

'If that is what you want. But is there nothing to be said for making one last attempt to convince some of your neighbours that it's a good idea and no threat to them? Garner some goodwill. And I mean by that the wives every bit as much as the husbands, which is where you, Lady Rashfield, come in.'

Mr Sinclair looked at her expectantly. 'How?' Lily asked.

'Your brief stay in London was reported very positively in the *Morning Post*. It set you both up as being in the vanguard of—what did they call it?—something about the winds of change. But the same piece suggested that the local gentry here were too old-fashioned to appreciate you. Stagnant waters, I think was the phrase used. That, as you can imagine, did not go down well.'

'Even though it's true?' Oliver said sardonically.

'It's not true of all of them,' Mr Sinclair said. 'There's still time to win some of them over. Have them to dinner. Talk to them about the benefits of what you're planning. Let them see that they could benefit, too. Let them prove that they're open to change.'

'You know that's not my style, Iain.'

'Lady Rashfield has a way with people.' Mr Sinclair smiled warmly at her. 'The local gentry might not have appreciated your attempt at inclusion when you held your ball here, but everyone else did. I hear nothing but praise for the time you've taken to find out about what would make life easier for the women on this estate, too. If you can do the same with the wives of the gentry, find out what we could do that would make our collective more acceptable, then we'd have a much better chance of success.'

'And without that?' Oliver asked, frowning.

'As I said, why make things more difficult? Take a few weeks to cultivate these people. We won't win them all over, I'm not so naive, but with just a few allies our work will be so much easier and ultimately more profitable, too. You know how difficult it is to implement change from your own experience at New Kilmun. There will always be those who resist it, but most people simply need to be coached, jollied along, feel that they're part of it. To be honest, Oliver, I'm surprised that you've not done that here.'

'Because I've no time. I want rid of the place. It has no part in my future.'

'Yes, but it all seems so rushed. What's wrong with taking a few weeks to do as I suggest? And while we're on the subject, I think it would help greatly if we discussed the future of the Manor, or there will be wild speculation about it turning into a workhouse or lying-in home.'

Mr Sinclair looked expectantly at Oliver. Oliver tapped his finger on the blotter, looking over at Lily. What did he wish her to say? What Mr Sinclair said made sense, but it would require her to remain here for at least another month. Her head told her that would be a huge mistake. Travelling south in the train with Oliver earlier, her head had been urging her to say that she had to go now, not in two weeks but straight away, because the butterflies were back and every moment she spent in his company was dangerous.

Ought she to broker a new deal, grant Mr Sinclair the weeks he required, but put an end to any intimacy with Oliver? Then she'd be managing the risk of becoming too attached to him. In fact, she'd be detaching herself from him slowly, weaning herself from him, so that when she did finally leave it would be a great deal easier. But her head told her that would be a mistake, dragging things out with no end date. And there was her business. And the letter from Hélène that she hadn't told him about yet.

'Oliver!'

'Lily, I…'

'Oh, you first. Please,' she added, 'I can wait.'

'Lily, I think we need to come clean with Iain. We

know we can trust him and it's only fair that he understands why what he asks is impossible.'

Impossible. He was right. She should be flattered that he thought it so, it showed that he respected her and was determined to honour their agreement. She nodded, guiltily relieved that it was he and not she who was going to explain. He got up and poured a glass of cognac, but instead of drinking it, handed it to an astonished Mr Sinclair. 'You might need this.'

Then he pulled a chair over to sit beside Lily, taking her hand. 'Despite the fact that you've twice witnessed us promise to love, honour and obey until death do us part, Iain, it has always been our intention to divorce. Yes, I thought you might need the brandy,' he added, as Mr Sinclair spluttered.

Lily listened as Oliver succinctly described their reasons for marrying. Listening to him, she couldn't help thinking that it sounded cold and very calculated, for he laid out only the facts, as if theirs had been a business proposition and not the payment of a debt of honour. She had almost forgotten that was how it had begun.

It had so quickly become a joint crusade, the pair of them united in their determination to win and on their own terms. Lily leaned closer, so that their shoulders touched. Mr Sinclair was looking utterly confounded, but he had said not a word. He was an excellent listener. He took his time to assimilate all the facts. He rarely spoke without carefully constructing his response.

'So that's why we went to New Kilmun,' Oliver was saying now. 'And that's why we went to all the trouble to host the party in London and to make sure that it was reported in the press.'

Mr Sinclair shook his head and took a large gulp of the cognac. 'Are you saying that— I'm sorry, I'm still not sure what it is you're actually saying? I knew that the wedding ceremony in Bordeaux was to allow you to claim the estate, you were plain enough with me on that, but I thought—I assumed that it was a permanent arrangement, that you'd decided to make good on the first ceremony, so to speak.

'And anyone seeing you together as I have— I mean it's plain to everyone that you are—that you are— Curse it, Oliver, it's clear as day that the pair of you are dashed fond of each other.' Colouring furiously, Mr Sinclair finished his brandy. 'Anyone can see that.'

Lily waited for Oliver to dispute this. He said nothing. 'I'm very sorry,' Lily said, getting up to refill his glass. 'It never occurred to us that you would be misled by our performance.'

'I can't believe it *is* a performance.'

It didn't feel like it to her either, but it *was*. And Oliver? Why was he looking at her so oddly? 'I was an actress,' Lily said.

'An actress?' Mr Sinclair took the glass back and took another sip. 'On the stage?'

'That is usually where actresses are to be found. I'm curious, Mr Sinclair—all those years you have been paying my allowance, did you never try to find out anything about me?'

'I promised I wouldn't. That was the arrangement. I thought that you lived in the countryside somewhere. In a cottage. In a village.' He eyed the glass of cognac longingly, but set it down. 'But, Oliver, you are not an actor.'

'I've had Lily to coach me.'

'I see,' Mr Sinclair said, looking unconvinced. 'Well, whether your marriage is an act or not, it is my considered opinion that the best thing you can do is to carry on with it and cultivate your neighbours. There's no point in rushing into a big announcement about our plans before we're ready.'

'No, Iain, I don't think so. If that piece is a taste of things to come, we're not going to win hearts and minds with just a few dinner parties. It's results that will matter. We'll show them that our methods work, we'll lend them our machines and we'll even share our new practices. That will shake them up and those with the nous will see that we're blazing a trail that it would benefit them to follow. We won't be stealing their business, there's more than enough to be getting on with.'

'I don't know, Oliver, I still think that...'

'No, Iain. I'm sorry, but on this we are not going to agree. Besides, Lily has her own life to be getting on with. I've promised that she will be back in Paris by the beginning of April.'

'But that's less than three weeks away.'

'More like two. I can't ask her to stay. She's done more than enough for me already.'

'But another two weeks, call it a month, and...'

'Forget it!'

'Oliver,' Lily found herself saying against her better judgement, 'perhaps I could reconsider...'

'No. We'll discuss this later,' Oliver said.

'I'll take my leave and let you talk now.' Mr Sinclair got rather unsteadily to his feet. 'I hope, for all our sakes, not least your own, that you manage to persuade Lady Rashfield to stay. I know I'm speaking out of turn. You can blame it on the cognac, but our chances of success are improved by her being here. Now, if you'll excuse me.'

The door closed behind him. 'Oliver, if it really is a matter of such importance, I could consider...'

'I don't want you to make any more sacrifices on my behalf.' He got up, going over to his desk to pick up *The Times* again. 'I need to think this through. We've been too quick to react in the past.'

I need to think this through. What happened to *we*? 'There's something I forgot to tell you, with everything else that has been going on. I had a letter from Hélène this morning. Monsieur Worth has been asking about my whereabouts. The description of the gown I wore to our London debut, the red and gold one, he recognised it as one he had made for me. He wanted to know if I had lent it to the Marchioness of Rashfield.'

'Because it would be good business for him, if she wore his gowns, most likely. Monsieur Worth's dominance of the world of fashion is the least of our worries, Lily. If you don't mind, I'd like to be alone.'

She tried and failed not to feel rebuffed. 'What about dinner?'

'I'm not hungry. I think I'll take myself out for a walk, clear my head.'

Chapter Fifteen

Oliver did not appear for dinner and Mr Sinclair made his excuses, saying he had too much work to do and would take a tray of cold meat in his room. Lily, sitting alone in the dining room pretending to eat a very delicious fricassee of chicken, was glad to be spared the need to make conversation.

Rashfield Manor felt colder than ever after the warmth of the steam heating in Oliver's house at New Kilmun. The rooms seemed huge and overly ornate. Though Riddell was as discreet as he always was, she was aware of him lurking while she tried to eat, waiting to be of service. The drawing room was empty, but the fire was burning in the grate, evidence of the presence of more servants.

Lily couldn't settle. Where was Oliver? What was he taking so long to think about? Why didn't he wish to discuss it with her? Why had he been so vehement in his rejection of her suggestion that she remain here for another month? Why had she offered, when she knew perfectly well from Hélène's letter that her presence was needed in Paris? And why hadn't she told Oliver this?

Yet another in what seemed like an endless series of unanswered questions. It wasn't the first time that her deputy had asked her when she would return. She hadn't wished to worry him. No, that was a lie. She didn't want to return early. There were nearly two weeks left. She didn't want to give him a reason to suggest she leave.

She got up to peer out of the window into the dark. As if she would see him, if he was still out there. It had been hours. What was he doing? What was he thinking? *Why* was he so adamant that he didn't want her to stay? She turned away from the window. More to the point, why had she offered?

She knew exactly why she had offered. She had put what she wanted before what was best for her business. She wanted to stay and yet it could not possibly be in her best interests to do so. What was she doing, pacing about in this freezing cold room waiting on a man who had clearly decided to make his own decisions without involving her? A man who had once again refused to discuss the crucial matter of their parting. Which could be taken to mean that he didn't want her to go.

Only now, just this afternoon, he had made it very clear that he didn't want her to stay. A man who had also given the impression that he felt nothing profound for her beyond physical attraction and empathy. In other words, he didn't love her. He had even told her so. Everything had been an act that had fooled Mr Sinclair because she had been such a good coach.

Lily put a screen in front of the fire and stalked up to her room. The bed was turned down. There was a warming pan in the sheets. A gust of longing for her own apartment, her own bed, her own locked door that no one could breach, shook her. She undressed hurriedly, pulling on her nightdress and her wrapper, and wriggled under the covers. Oliver didn't want her to stay. He had obviously decided that he didn't need to talk to her about what happened next regarding Rashfield. She was needed in Paris. Well then, the most sensible use of her time now would be to make her own exit plan.

A tear leaked from her eye. She swiped it away. She would miss him, that was perfectly natural, after all they had been through, but once she was back in Paris, she would throw herself into the life she had left behind and there would be no time to miss him. In Paris, her life was her own. She made her own decisions. She didn't have to wait for someone else to come back from their walk to tell her what he had decided!

She didn't have to wait to discuss how she would leave either, she was perfectly capable of deciding that for herself and the sooner the better. In Paris, she was in control. If she made mistakes, they were her mistakes. In Paris, she had been perfectly *happy* with her life.

Fired up, Lily began to plan, becoming so embroiled in the process that she was astonished to hear the clock chime midnight. Oliver must have gone to bed. There would be no lovemaking tonight. She would sleep alone. Fine. *His choice!* She plumped her pillow and told herself that even if he had come to her room she would have turned him away. *Her choice.* Tears welled in her eyes. She threw herself down on the pillow and pulled the sheet up to her neck, willing sleep to come.

* * *

'Lily?'

She started awake, sitting up in bed. 'What time is it?'

'I don't know. Four? Lily…'

'Oliver!' He was standing by her bed, holding a lamp. He was still dressed, though he wasn't wearing a coat. *Where have you been?* She bit back the question. 'What are you doing here?'

'I need to talk to you.'

'I was sleeping.' She glared at him. *You see, not lying awake wondering where you were!*

'I'm sorry. I've been trying to decide—should I wait until the morning?'

'You're here now, you might as well tell me what you've decided.' She had fallen asleep in her wrapper. She hadn't unpinned her hair, but half of it had come undone. She must look a fright. 'I've made a few decisions of my own.'

Oliver turned up the lamp on the bedside table. His hair was all on end. He looked exhausted. She had to clench her fists to stop herself reaching for him. 'I've been planning my exit in your absence,' Lily said, watching him carefully.

'That's what I'd like to talk to you about.'

'I see.'

Oliver smiled oddly at her, sitting down on the edge of the bed. 'I doubt it. I love you, Lily.'

She felt as if all her breath left her at once in a rush. She opened her mouth to speak, but nothing came out. She must have misheard.

'I know it's come as a shock,' he said. 'It was a shock to me, when I realised it this morning. That's why I needed time to think. I had to be certain.' He leaned closer, taking one of her hands. It was still curled into a fist. 'I am sure. Absolutely sure. I love you.'

Oliver loved her. Oliver *loved* her.

She unfurled her fingers, twining them with his. 'How do you know?'

He laughed softly. 'I knew you'd ask that. I've been asking myself the same question on and off all day. How do I know? How can I be certain?'

'All day?' *Oliver had been in love with her all day!* 'You never said a word, gave no indication.'

'I was overtaken by events.' He thought for a moment, then shook his head. 'I decided not to say anything. I was afraid that if I said anything, it would ruin what we had left to us, so I decided not to speak up. And then I read the telegram, and then—as I said, events overtook me.'

The events of the day. The mists of sleep cleared. She had cried herself to sleep. Lily unclasped her hand from his under the pretext of tidying her hair. 'So, you've decided that Mr Sinclair is right, that we should play Lord and Lady of the manor for a while longer.'

She meant to rile him. He made no answer for a moment, studying her face in a way that disconcerted her because she always had the feeling he could read her mind. She defiantly held his gaze. 'I offered to stay, Oliver, remember?'

'I don't want you to make any more sacrifices for me.' He caught her hand as she tried to jab a pin into her hair. 'I don't want you to stay with me because you feel obliged. I've been thinking a lot about what Iain Sinclair said—not about us playing Lord and Lady of the manor, but about us, Lily. "It's as clear as day that we are dashed fond of each other" were his words, I believe.'

'We are acting. You told him so.'

'I told him that you'd coached me. I didn't say I was acting.'

'But we were. You are.'

'Am I? Do you think I've not asked myself that question? I've asked myself that and a hundred other questions. Am I in thrall, infatuated, in lust? Is it the situation? Is it our living in each other's pockets? Do I feel safe to let myself care for you because I know you're leaving? From the very start, there's been something between us, Lily, you must have felt it?'

Yes! 'We are suited,' she said, desperate to prove him wrong because she so desperately, terrifyingly desperately wanted him to be right. 'Physically suited. We're "good together".'

'We're bloody fantastic together and lately...' He took her hand again. 'Lily, I know you've felt it, too, though neither of us dared put it into words. We don't need to. When we make love, it's as if we're creating a single one out of ourselves.' He swore under his breath. 'Those things sound fine in your head, but when you say them out loud you sound like a fool. When we make love—when I make love with you, that's what I've been doing. Showing that I love you, even though I didn't even know it.'

Tears were welling in her eyes again. Why did he have to speak so eloquently? She willed the tears not to fall.

'It's not been an act,' Oliver continued, his voice

soft but firm. 'Not for me, not for a long time. Weeks? That's why it's been so easy, but it's also why I never questioned it until this morning. When you sneaked out of bed, I lay there thinking, Lily's down there in the kitchen, trying to work herself up to making me talk about her leaving, and it was like hitting my head against a wall. Lily leaving. It's not like me to procrastinate. I should have known there was a reason.'

Must the reason be love?

The thought made her panic. She wasn't in love. She couldn't be in love. When she returned to Paris, she would gradually forget him. Well, no, she wouldn't forget him, but her memories would be pleasant. If she loved him, she wouldn't want to go to Paris. So she couldn't be in love. And Oliver—no, she wouldn't allow him to be in love either, because if he was and she left she'd break his heart and—no, no, no, that was ridiculous. He was mistaken.

'I love you, Lily. I know you don't believe me, I know you'll take some convincing, because you have this notion of love entailing sacrifice...'

'It does! How can you expect me to love you when it would mean I would have to give up everything?'

'It's because I don't want you to give up everything that I know I love you. You know I don't want to take over your life, you know that I've no interest in dictating what you do and how you do it. I love you as you are, Lily, I don't want you to change.'

'But I'd have to change.' She was gripping his hand tightly now. She wanted to be persuaded. She knew it was impossible. 'I'd have to stay here and do what you wanted me to. I'd have no money of my own. Even if

I did love you, Oliver, I'd come to resent all of those things so quickly. I'd feel suffocated. I'd think to myself, what was it all for, Lily, all those years of fighting to survive, having to accept that I wasn't good enough, having my dream torn to shreds by critics and theatre managers! Then trying again, making a new dream, a whole new dream of my own! Not like yours, but it's mine, and it makes me happy.'

'Oh, Lily, I love you so much.' His voice was rough with emotion. He gently smoothed away the tears that were streaming down her cheeks with his free hand. 'When I think of what you must have suffered, I'm humbled. I swear, I don't want to change you. You were wrong about love. It's not about handing your life over on a plate. It's about sharing the plate. Ultimately, it's about wanting to make someone happy.'

'But you can't make me happy.'

Her words made them both flinch. 'You make me happy,' Oliver said, after a moment's fraught silence. 'I've never wanted to share my life with anyone, but that's because I hadn't met you. I don't know how we'll do it, but if there's a way to mould our lives together, then I want to try because I know if we do, whatever compromises and sacrifices we make—and we'd both have to make them—then I know I'd be happier, Lily, with you rather than without you. That's how I know I love you.'

He was waiting for her to speak. She wanted to believe him, but she couldn't. Did Oliver make her happy? More than anyone else. If Oliver was her only source of happiness, would she be happy? 'I can't,' she said wretchedly. 'I'm sorry, but I can't.'

'Can't what? I'm not suggesting we make any decisions right now. There's so much—too much—believe me, I've tried. But we'll find a way.'

'I'm sorry.' She longed to tell him the one thing he wanted to hear, but she couldn't. 'I know you believe what you're saying, but it's simply not how the world works. You and I might reach an accommodation, but there would be powerful pressures and expectations that would be impossible to resist. I can't see how we could possibly find any way to be together that would protect what we've both worked so hard for, and sacrificed so much for, which is to be ourselves.'

'If you wanted to, we could find a way. If you loved me?'

She watched him, her heart aching. It was the most difficult thing she had ever done, not to speak, but she kept silent as he battled, wanting to persuade her, seeing from her face that it was useless.

Carefully, he untwined his fingers from hers. 'Then you don't love me.' He stood up. 'I won't try to persuade you. Another reason I know I love you,' he said with a grim little smile. 'I don't want half-measures. There's too much at stake for half-measures. Compromise, sacrifice—you're right, they are precisely the things you would resent.'

'I'm sorry.'

'I want you to be happy, Lily, not sorry. I think…' His voice broke. She watched on miserably as he struggled to control himself, knowing that if she gave in they would both eventually be miserable.

'I think it's best if you go,' Oliver said.

'What?'

'Tomorrow or the next day. I think it's best for both of us if you leave. However we manage it, it's going to be messy.'

'But Mr Sinclair's plan…'

'Pointless, Lily, and you must know that. We'd make it much worse, cultivating those people for a few weeks and then dropping them. I've decided to go ahead and announce our plans as soon as possible here. I'll write to Hale and his merry men as a matter of courtesy.'

'You've decided— Do you need me to— Ought I to be here for the announcement?'

'No. I don't think I could bear it.'

'Oh, Oliver.' She scrambled out of bed and threw herself into his arms.

'Oh, Lily.' He pulled her close, nuzzling his face into her neck. 'Oh, Lily, I love you so much.'

She stilled, realising her mistake too late. He dropped his arms and took a step back. 'There, you see. That's precisely why you have to go.'

She nodded, feeling sick. 'We'll put out some story about my being ill, or visiting relatives, someone dying. Something that takes me away for a few months. That will give you and Mr Sinclair time to tie things up here without anyone asking awkward questions about me and when I return to Paris, no one will make the connection.'

Oliver's attempt at a smile crumbled. 'If you ever change your mind, you know where to find me. Goodnight, Lily.'

The door closed behind him before she could respond. She stood, unable to move for a long time, but the door remained closed. Stunned and frozen, Lily turned up the oil lamp and threw some coal on to the fire. She might as well start packing. There would be time enough for her to cry when she was back in Paris.

Chapter Sixteen

Morning Post,
11th May 1877

Will His Runaway Marchioness Return?

When the Fifth Marquess of R. and his bride cel-
ebrated their marriage by recreating a Music Hall
in their Mayfair town house, we were pleased to
share with our readers the hope that this uncon-
ventional couple would be a much-needed breath
of fresh air in society.

Alas, Lord R.'s industrial roots forced him
north to attend to his machines, depriving Lon-
don and the ton *of what would without doubt have*
been the brightest stars of the Season.

Six weeks ago, Lord R. confounded the local
gentry of Berkshire when he announced that he
would be bringing his industrial nous to the es-
tate he inherited. An intense and comprehensive
programme of modernisation which included the

introduction of a number of steam-powered machines is already underway, which is anticipated to make the land highly profitable. The profit, however, will not go into His Lordship's well-lined pockets, but will be 'ploughed back', to use the Marquess's own words, into the land.

A 'collective' has been formed of the farmers and other interested parties, to which the Marquess has made over all of his property. Lord R., in effect, has made himself estate-less. And though he retains ownership of the manor house, has made it known that it will be transformed into holiday accommodation for his industrial workers and their families.

This revolutionary approach to land ownership has not been universally lauded. Sir E. H., who served as trustee and curator of the lands in the interim of the death of the Fourth Marquess and the marriage of the Fifth, has made his reservations about this merging of industry and aristocracy clear on several occasions. Unsurprisingly, those same reservations are shared with some of Lord R.'s closest neighbours.

But, Readers, we ask you, in this modern age, when our great country is the Workshop of the World, is it not right that we should innovate on our lands as well as our factories? Permitting the farmers who till the soil to profit from it must surely encourage them to produce more. We heartily endorse this ethos and pour scorn on those who have claimed—as some have, Dear

Reader—that it will end with votes being given to the farmers' wives.

When Lord R. announced his marriage, you will recall that we queried his motives. Was his bride acquired for profit, rather than passion? Recent events on the R. estate having proved conclusively that profit was not a consideration. What, then, of passion? Those who have witnessed the couple together are in no doubt that a warm, some say fervent, attachment exists— demonstrably exists—as we saw for ourselves at the aforementioned Mayfair extravaganza.

It is with some puzzlement that we now report the apparent disappearance of the chic, elegant Lady R. Her presence did not grace the gathering His Lordship addressed to announce his fledgling farming collective. A little bird tells us that her person has not been seen at all at R. Manor for at least six weeks. It was with growing concern that we further discovered Lady R. was not resident in her husband's home in Cheshire either.

It has been more than three months since the nuptials were celebrated. Lord R. has returned to the industrial North. Word has it that Lady R. has retired to some unspecified location in the country—perhaps to recoup her health, perhaps to anticipate a happy event.

We confess to concern at the Marchioness's disappearance. Have this couple colluded to fool us all? Could it be that Lord R., having divested himself of his estate, has now divested himself of a wife he no longer needs to serve his purpose?

*We would remind Readers that Lady R. was of
obscure origins and without kith or kin. A ruthless
industrialist with a revolutionary streak would
have no compunction in using such a female to
his own dastardly purposes.*

*Will Lady R. return and prove us wrong? Or
has the Marchioness of R. disappeared for good?*

Paris—the end of May 1877

The article in the *Morning Post* was a week old when
Lily received it, care of her bank, from Mr Sinclair. Outraged, disgusted and sick at heart, she had telegraphed
Oliver immediately, offering to do whatever was necessary to exonerate him from the vile insinuations. He
had not replied to her telegram, nor had he answered
the letter she had written the same day. Mr Sinclair's
compliment slip had said nothing at all. She was forced
to conclude that Oliver didn't want her help. Or that he
simply didn't want to hear from her?

The message of silence was clear enough, Lily told
herself as she wandered through the Jardin de Tuileries.
She had always loved Paris in the springtime, when
the trees came into leaf and the children played in the
parks, sailing their boats on the ponds. Now, it wasn't
the children she noticed, it was the young lovers, walking arm in arm, seated together on benches, their heads
bent towards each other as they whispered, oblivious
of the passers-by.

Paris loved lovers. Kisses were greeted with indulgent smiles, not jeers. The city seemed to be made for
kisses, the arbours and shady nooks in the many parks,

the narrow streets of the Isles, the little squares formed where the grand boulevards met, every table outside every café, all seemed to be populated by lovers.

She had not permitted herself to read the English papers. She had imagined, so naively, that being able to picture Oliver at home in New Kilmun would accustom her to his absence, that it would be a comfort, just as she had so foolishly imagined that all the memories of their time together would be mementoes.

The reality was that picturing Oliver going about his business without her was painful. Recalling any of their nights together was an agony. Missing him was visceral, as if she was missing part of herself. It would ease in time, she kept telling herself.

When had she ceased to believe that? When had she finally admitted to herself that she was in love with Oliver? She passed the Comédie Française, where she and Hélène had been discussing terms for three acts yesterday, and into the gardens of the Palais Royal and her favourite spot at the fountain. It was quiet, most people were at lunch. She took a seat and tried to turn her mind to business, and the possibility of persuading Annie to fill a vacancy at the nearby theatre, but even this interesting prospect failed to capture her attention.

She was in love with Oliver. How did she know, given she had so vehemently denied it to herself? It was perfectly straightforward. She simply knew in her heart of hearts. She was in love with him and there was nothing she could do now to fall out of love with him. She was going to have to find a way to live with that. The prospect was extremely daunting.

Had she made a mistake in refusing to consider the

possibility of a life as Oliver's wife? She still couldn't see how it would work, but she couldn't deny her heart's desire that it was possible. He wouldn't expect her to hand her life over on a plate. Her own words brought a wry smile to her face. Compromise and sacrifice would be required, he'd said, but she didn't want to compromise or sacrifice. Wasn't that precisely what she had done, though, in rejecting him?

Love, Oliver had said, meant that they would be happier together than apart, but it also meant putting a lover's happiness first. He couldn't make her happy. Cold fingers of regret clutched at her heart as she recalled saying those words, making her shiver in the spring sunshine. He couldn't make her happy. Was that true?

She got up to circle the fountain, taking off her glove to reach into the cool waters in the stone basin. Oliver couldn't make her happy, but being with Oliver would make her happy. Being without him—oh, being without him was becoming more painful every day. If she could imagine him happy, then it would be easier, but his silence—it wasn't a rejection, she now saw clearly, it was pain. She had broken his heart.

Lily dropped on to the stone edge of the fountain, heedless of her gown. No half-measures, he had said. All or nothing, he had said, and she had opted for nothing. She had what she'd always had, success and financial security, independence, a role that she was good at. Was she truly happy? No, she wanted more. She wanted Oliver. Not at any cost, but there must be a price they could agree that they would both be willing to pay. How? She had no idea. Did she want to try?

Lily got to her feet. There was a telegraph office on

Rue de Rivoli. If she hurried, there was a chance she could catch the evening train and be in Folkestone by the morning. As early as tomorrow, she could be with Oliver.

An hour later, she pushed open the huge ornamental iron doors that gave on to the courtyard of her apartment on the Boulevard de Sebastopol. As she hurried towards the staircase, a figure came towards her out of the shadows. Her heart leapt, though she knew she must be mistaken. A similar height. A similar breadth. Dark clothing.

'Lily.'

She stopped in her tracks. 'Oliver?'

'Surprise,' he said with a feeble laugh.

She stood rooted to the spot, absurdly shy, overwhelmed by the rush of emotions that sent her heart racing and made her mouth dry.

'I got your letter.'

'I saw the piece in the *Morning Post*.'

'So I gathered.'

'They said— They hinted— They implied that you had— That we had— As if you would have…'

'Used you for my own dastardly purposes? They weren't too wrong.'

'Don't say that! Don't ever say that! You did not— Never— It was my idea in any case.' Lily shaded her eyes with her hand. 'How long have you been waiting here?'

'A couple of hours.'

'You must be thirsty. Hungry?'

'I don't want anything other than the opportunity to talk to you.'

'Yes. Of course. Come up, what am I thinking of.' She hurried towards the staircase, letting him follow in her wake. This was her chance, but dare she take it? What if Oliver had come to tell her he had discovered he was mistaken? He didn't love her. He hadn't missed her. His feelings had been precisely what she had suggested, an effect of the role they had been playing, the time they had spent together.

She put the key in the door and ushered him into her apartment. 'Down the hall, the salon is at the front. Would you like a cup of coffee? A glass of wine?'

'Nothing.' He opened the door to the salon, taking off his hat and gloves. 'This is quite lovely. Exactly as I imagined.'

'*Merci.*'

Lily unpinned her hat and dropped it with her gloves on one of the chairs. She had never allowed herself to imagine him here. It felt—right. She recalled the night he had come to her bedroom to confess his love. She had made it very difficult for him. She had refused to listen. It hadn't occurred to her until now how brave he had been, knowing that she was almost certain to reject him.

'Lily, I came here because…'

'Oliver, before you say another word, I have realised, too late, probably, that I love you.' Relief poured through her. He was gazing at her, as if he couldn't understand what she'd said. Yes, she recalled showing him precisely that face. 'I love you,' Lily said firmly, standing her ground. 'I don't know when or how it happened, but I know that it has happened.'

He made no move. 'How do you know?'

Her own question. No answer had ever meant more. Her life did not depend on it, but her happiness did. 'I have everything I have ever wanted here. You are the one thing I never thought I'd want. When I left you, I realised you were the one thing I wanted more than anything.'

Still he remained where he was. 'At any price?'

She shook her head slowly. 'If you love me...'

'You know I do, Lily, that's one thing you can't doubt.'

'I don't, but when you told me so, that's one of the things I didn't understand. You said that you loved me as I am, that you didn't want to change me, but I couldn't see, Oliver, how it was possible for us to be together unless I changed.' She took a tentative step towards him. 'But I love you, just as you are, and I don't want you to change either.'

She dared to touch him, placing her palm over his heart. 'I love the essence of you, but the how and the why we make that love work— I don't know.'

He caught her hand, but still he made no other move towards her. 'Do you want to make it work?'

'I want to try. We would have to tell people who I am, Oliver. I couldn't bear to live in fear of my past being used against you.'

'Then we'll tell them, our way, just as we've done before.'

'It will cause a huge scandal.'

'We'll tell it our way. I'd be lying if I said that I don't

care what anyone thinks, but those I do care about, I've faith that we'll prove to them they're wrong, Lily. I love you and I'm proud of you, too. Why should I be ashamed of your past if you're not?'

His words almost overset her. 'Thank you,' she managed to say, her throat clogged with tears.

'It won't be easy. We'll have to compromise, make sacrifices, significant changes to our lives. Both of us, Lily?'

'I know.'

'You'd be my wife. My *real* wife. I'd expect to be consulted. Not to have more of a say in your decisions, but to have a say.'

'I'd expect the same from you.'

He smiled faintly. 'I'd tell you that goes without saying, but it doesn't, does it? I should have been clearer before.'

'I wasn't ready to listen. I needed to miss you. Properly.'

'And have you?'

'Desperately.' She lifted her hand to his face, feeling the familiar combination of smooth cheek, rough beard. 'I want to find a way for us to be together. I still don't know how or if it can be done, but I know you were right in wanting to try. I love you so much. If we can find a way, we'll make it work. You were right about that, too.'

She waited. He made her wait for a long moment and she held his gaze as he did, but she already knew what he was going to say, because although she could give him any number of explanations, there was only one that her heart cared about. They were better together.

'I love you, Lily.'

'I know.'

He laughed then, softly, and cupped her face in his hand. 'Show me.'

She felt as if she was smiling inside. Warmth seeped through her, as if the Paris spring had finally arrived inside her apartment. She took him by the hand and led him through the bedroom, drawing the shutters against the sunlight. Then she began to undress for him, slowly unbuttoning her jacket, her eyes fixed on his face, as she slid the sleeves down her arms and let it fall, quite deliberately, at her feet. Her skirt was next, and with it her bustle.

Oliver's breathing was ragged as he watched her, rooted to the spot. She had never felt so powerful, so utterly sure of herself and so utterly sure that what she was doing was right. This was for him. A laying bare of herself, for him only. She took her time with the buttons of her blouse. He groaned as she dropped it to the floor, as she smoothed her hands over her body, the swell of her breasts, down to the indent of her waist, unfastening her petticoats.

'Lily. Dear lord, Lily.'

He took a step towards her. She twined her arms around his neck, pressing herself against him. 'I love you so much,' she whispered as their mouths met in a long, lingering kiss. She could feel his arousal hard against her. Her nipples tingled, aching for his touch, but she wanted this to be different. She broke the kiss and began to undress him, letting her hands smooth and tease as she unbuttoned his clothing, relishing the heaving of his chest, pausing as each item of clothing was discarded to kiss, to stoke the fire of her own arousal to melting point, and then to stop.

When he was naked, she curled her hand around his erection, sliding it up and down, watching his face, the burning heat of his eyes on her, the clenching of his muscles as he struggled for control. She nudged him backwards on to the bed and stroked him with her tongue. He groaned. Writhed beneath her. His hands clutched at her sheets.

'Lily!'

She lifted her head.

'Together,' he said. 'This time. First time. Together?'

'Yes.' Their lips met. 'Yes,' Lily sighed, as their bodies met. 'Oh, Oliver, yes.'

The sun was sinking. Oliver, wrapped in a bedsheet, gazed at the view out over the Paris rooftops, through the windows of the salon. Lily, dressed only in a wrapper, came into the room carrying a bottle of champagne and two glasses. Her hair was a delightful tangle. Her lips were smudged with their kisses. They had made love twice, but as she smiled saucily at him, he felt himself stir again. She opened the bottle with an expertise he secretly found arousing and poured two glasses.

'This seems appropriate for the occasion, although in fact you still haven't told me precisely why you are here,' she said.

He sat down beside her on the *chaise longue*. 'I'm here because of your letter.'

'When you didn't reply I thought you were ignoring me.'

'Never. Barely an hour went by since you left when I haven't thought of you, wondered what you were doing, whether you missed me.'

'I missed you so much!'

'I believe you,' he said, adding with a wicked smile, 'though I'm very happy for you to show me again, in a moment.'

'Oliver!'

'Lily.' He kissed her again, softly. 'I got your letter and I thought, surely you wouldn't have written if you didn't want to see me again.' He kissed her. 'And I thought, what was the point in my clinging to the notion that it would be wrong for me to try to persuade you to take a chance.' Another kiss. 'Because even though you hadn't told me you loved me, in fact you were at great pains not to tell me, you didn't actually tell me you didn't.'

He kissed her again. 'I came here with hope and nothing else. No plans. Those are for us to make together. Because we're in this together now.' Another slow, deep kiss. 'And always.' He touched his glass to hers. 'To the future, together. Whatever that may be.'

'To us,' Lily said, taking a sip. 'So, in essence, you came to tell me that you love me?'

'Well, I can't exactly propose since we've already been married twice!'

'That's true,' she said, laughing. She took another sip of her champagne, then set it down on the table. She lay back on the *chaise longue* and untied the sash of her wrapper. 'There are other ways to show me.'

* * *

The Times,
3rd June 1878

Artistes Required

La Muguette Theatrical Agency would like to extend an open invitation for artistes and thespians to enlist in an exciting venture, new to the British theatrical world, but well established in Paris.

While the permanent premises of the business will be in Manchester, offices will be established in London, Glasgow and other major cities as required.

Applications in person are invited at nominated theatres to be confirmed later, where personal testimonies from those already successfully represented will be available to view, including that of renowned international soprano Annie Adams.

Join our growing band of talented performers and share the benefits of professional representation.

* * * * *

Historical Note

As ever, there's a ton of research embedded in this book—and, as always, any mistakes or errors are entirely my own.

Oliver's model town of New Kilmun is based on Sir Titus Salt's town of Saltaire, though minus the many 'worthy' lifestyle restrictions imposed on those residents. I got the idea for his salt works when watching an episode of the BBC programme *Bargain Hunt*, in which the presenters visited the Lion Salt Works in Cheshire.

Lily's house in Sandgate was inspired by one of my visits to my friend Peter in Hythe—a lovely old-fashioned seaside town where he and I have completed the same walk Lily undertakes, from Radnor Cliff to Folkestone, countless times. Occasionally you really can actually see France! The pier where the boat train to France came in has now been converted into a bit of a foodie heaven, with lots of pop-up restaurants and bars that I'm sure Lily would heartily have approved of.

In England, marriage certificates were introduced in 1837 for the registration of all marriages. In France, then as now, it was the civil ceremony which made a marriage legal and not the religious one. It's unlikely that the French authorities would have checked whether a couple were already married to each other, but I cannot say with hand on heart that Lily and Oliver would have been able to marry a second time, as I have them do—please forgive this little bit of artistic licence!

The 1857 Matrimonial Causes Act made divorce in England considerably easier and cheaper. Lily and Oliver would have been granted a divorce on the grounds of her desertion of the marital home, had they stayed separated. In 1792, after the French Revolution, it was relatively easy to get divorced in France, but divorce was abolished altogether in 1816 and not reinstated until 1884.

I have relied heavily on Lee Jackson's excellent book *Palaces of Pleasure* for all things theatrical, but Stephen Clarke's *Dirty Bertie, An English King Made in France* was another colourful source—I only wish I'd had the page space to use more of it.

As far as I'm aware, there was no such thing as a theatrical agent in Lily's time, though by the time *Variety* magazine was launched in 1905 it did seem to be an established role. Well done to my heroine for being so avant-garde!

The Canterbury was indeed one of the more respectable music halls and was frequented by the Prince of Wales around about Lily's time. The acts described are true to what was on offer, including ballet dancers in pink tights. Annie Adams was a real singer, as was Hortense—La Snédèr—though I've taken a few liberties with her career.

Leopold Lovejoy is my own invention and a tribute to Leonard Sachs, chairman on the BBC programme *The Good Old Days*, which older readers might remember. I was forced to watch with my mother back in the days when there were only three television channels to choose from. You can judge for yourself what an ordeal that was by checking out the clips on YouTube. The song 'The Rat Catcher's Daughter', which Annie sings, was actually made popular by another singer—Sam Cowell.

For those of you who like insider information, Oliver and Anthony's friendship was inspired by the song 'Two Little Boys'—the Splodgenessabounds version. I can't tell you the kick I get, putting the name of that band into a historical note! And Anthony's rescue of Oliver from the ice is my tribute to the film *It's A Wonderful Life*.

And, last but not least, names—I have such fun with names. In this book various housekeepers and servants are named for my sisters and my friend Peter. Stripey was a cat I adopted when I lived in Cyprus. Rashfield, Abbey Hill and New Kilmun, like so many places and titles in my books, are local to me. Hélène is a small tribute to my French neighbour, who is always delighted to help me out with language and culture queries. And Oliver? A challenge to myself to make a hero out of a name that's not classically heroic.

What next? Dare I try Kenneth? Perhaps a bridge too far!

COMING NEXT MONTH FROM

HARLEQUIN
HISTORICAL

All available in print and ebook via Reader Service and online

THE NIGHT SHE MET THE DUKE (Regency)
by Sarah Mallory

After hearing herself described as "dull," Prudence escapes London to Bath, where her new life is anything but dull when one night she finds an uninvited, devastatingly handsome duke in her kitchen!

THE HOUSEKEEPER'S FORBIDDEN EARL (Regency)
by Laura Martin

Kate's finally found peace working in a grand house, until her new employer, Lord Henderson, returns. Soon, it's not just the allure of the home that Kate's falling for...but its owner, too!

FALLING FOR HIS PRETEND COUNTESS (Victorian)
Southern Belles in London • by Lauri Robinson

Henry, Earl of Beaufort and London's most eligible bachelor, is being framed for murder! When his neighbor Suzanne offers to help prove his innocence, a fake engagement provides the perfect cover...

THE VISCOUNT'S DARING MISS (1830s)
by Lotte R. James

When groom Roberta "Bobby" Kinsley comes face-to-face with her horse racing opponent—infuriatingly charismatic Viscount Hayes—it's clear that it won't just be the competition that has her heart racing!

A KNIGHT FOR THE DEFIANT LADY (Medieval)
Convent Brides • by Carol Townend

Attraction sparks when Sir Leon retrieves brave, beautiful Lady Allis from a convent and they journey back to her castle. Only for Allis's father to demand she marry a nobleman!

ALLIANCE WITH HIS STOLEN HEIRESS (1900s)
by Lydia San Andres

Rebellious Julián doesn't mind masquerading as a bandit to help Amalia claim her inheritance—he's enjoying spending time with the bold heiress. But how can he reveal the truth of his identity?

YOU CAN FIND MORE INFORMATION ON UPCOMING HARLEQUIN TITLES, FREE EXCERPTS AND MORE AT HARLEQUIN.COM.

Get 4 FREE REWARDS!

We'll send you 2 FREE Books plus 2 FREE Mystery Gifts.

FREE Value Over $20

Both the **Harlequin® Historical** and **Harlequin® Romance** series feature compelling novels filled with emotion and simmering romance.

YES! Please send me 2 FREE novels from the Harlequin Historical or Harlequin Romance series and my 2 FREE gifts (gifts are worth about $10 retail). After receiving them, if I don't wish to receive any more books, I can return the shipping statement marked "cancel." If I don't cancel, I will receive 6 brand-new Harlequin Historical books every month and be billed just $6.19 each in the U.S. or $6.74 each in Canada, a savings of at least 11% off the cover price, or 4 brand-new Harlequin Romance Larger-Print books every month and be billed just $6.09 each in the U.S. or $6.24 each in Canada, a savings of at least 13% off the cover price. It's quite a bargain! Shipping and handling is just 50¢ per book in the U.S. and $1.25 per book in Canada.* I understand that accepting the 2 free books and gifts places me under no obligation to buy anything. I can always return a shipment and cancel at any time by calling the number below. The free books and gifts are mine to keep no matter what I decide.

Choose one: ☐ **Harlequin Historical** (246/349 HDN GRH7)   ☐ **Harlequin Romance Larger-Print** (119/319 HDN GRH7)

Name (please print)

Address   Apt. #

City   State/Province   Zip/Postal Code

Email: Please check this box ☐ if you would like to receive newsletters and promotional emails from Harlequin Enterprises ULC and its affiliates. You can unsubscribe anytime.

Mail to the **Harlequin Reader Service:**
IN U.S.A.: P.O. Box 1341, Buffalo, NY 14240-8531
IN CANADA: P.O. Box 603, Fort Erie, Ontario L2A 5X3

Want to try 2 free books from another series? Call 1-800-873-8635 or visit www.ReaderService.com.

HARLEQUIN
PLUS

Try the best multimedia subscription service for romance readers like you!

Read, Watch and Play.

Experience the easiest way to get the romance content you crave.

Start your **FREE TRIAL** at
www.harlequinplus.com/freetrial.